GET RICH

SLOW

4TH EDITION

GET RICH
SLOW

4TH EDITION

BUILD A FIRM FINANCIAL
FOUNDATION...
A DOLLAR AT A TIME

Tama McAleese, CFP

CAREER
PRESS

Franklin Lakes, NJ

GET RICH SLOW, 4TH EDITION
Cover design by Cheryl Cohan Finbow
Printed in the U.S.A. by Book-mart Press

To order this title, please call toll-free 1-800-CAREER-1 (NJ and Canada: 201-848-0310) to order using VISA or MasterCard, or for further information on books from Career Press.

The Career Press, Inc., 3 Tice Road, PO Box 687,
Franklin Lakes, NJ 07417
www.careerpress.com

Library of Congress Cataloging-in-Publication Data

McAleese, Tama.
    Get rich slow : build a firm financial foundation— a dollar at a time / by Tama
McAleese.— 4th ed.
        p. cm.
    Includes index.
    ISBN 1-56414-706-1 (pbk.)
        1. Finance, Personal. 2. Investments. 3. Portfolio management. I. Title.

HG179.M3736 2004
332.024'01—dc21   2003054648

DISCLAIMER

This book is designed to provide accurate and authoritative information of a general and current nature only. It is published under the express understanding that neither the author nor the publisher has the specific background to, or is engaged in rendering legal, accounting, or other professional services through this format. Any information, therefore, should be evaluated in the context of each individual's particular and unique financial circumstances, and the knowledge that the benefits of various financial strategies may change or may not be applicable in every case. The services of competent legal and accounting professionals should be sought and consulted before implementing any strategy outlined here.

It is also assumed that tax taws and economic dynamics change on a constant basis, and other uncontrollable factors including editing or space limitations may limit or even prohibit the use of certain investment options or financial planning strategies.

Because a basic financial education is desirable and helpful to begin self-reliance and personal empowerment toward financial independence, this book was developed as a helpful tool and basic building block upon which to develop additional personal money management, financial planning, and investing skills.

CONTENTS

Preface

A man found an eagle's egg and put it in the nest of a backyard hen. The eagle hatched with the brood of chicks and grew up with them. All his life the eagle did what the backyard chickens did, thinking he was a backyard chicken. He scratched the earth for worms and insects. He clucked and cackled. And he would thrash his wings and fly a few feet into the air.

Years passed and the eagle grew very old. One day he saw a magnificent graceful majesty among the powerful wind currents, gliding with scarcely a beat of its strong wings. The old eagle looked up in awe.

"Who's that?" he asked.

"That's the eagle, the king of the birds," said his neighbor. "He belongs to the sky. We belong to the earth. We're chickens."

So the eagle lived and died a chicken, for that's what he thought he was.

—Author unknown

Introduction

If you stripped the wealthy of their riches and literally gave all their money to the middle class and to the poor, who would have it in 15 years? The answer is easy: The rich would have most of their wealth back—with interest, not because they are smarter or more deserved, but because they know how to recover it. Americans love to transfer their wealth to the affluent. To most, it's called spending; to the rich, it's gross sales and revenues. The rich also tend to do a better job of managing what they accumulate. Learn to think and invest like the rich, then let time provide the transportation to deliver you to your wealthier future.

The number-one retirement plan in America today is to win the lottery. Homeowners are using their mortgaged-to-the-hilt real estate "boxes" as virtual ATMs, putting their homes at risk by borrowing from the equity to satisfy ravenous appetites for material goods. Keeping up with the Joneses while the Joneses are trying to keep up with the Rockefellers will make everyone in town rich—except you.

The average worker doesn't need a raise as much as he or she needs to better manage and invest the hard-earned paychecks they currently receive. But many consumers spend more time packing underwear for weekend getaways and summer vacations than they do planning their financial futures.

Most of what middle-income consumers learn about their money comes from financial advisors with vested interests and, perhaps even more dangerous because of their lack of formal financial education but built-in credibility, well-meaning friends, neighbors, companions, and fellow workers. Between these groups, a lot of financial misinformation gets dispensed. Folks are taught that, though smart enough to earn their paychecks, they are not savvy enough to manage them.

Nothing could be further from the truth. Financial "experts" have purchased vacation homes and yachts at the expense of their customers, while their customers are nursing bottom lines that have shrunk significantly in the last few years. Many 401(k)s look more like 201(k)s! Other people gladly will watch over your money for you at their profit— perhaps at your expense. You can become the CEO of your personal financial corporation. You can take control and manage your investments as well as the pros. Look at their track records over the last few years! Make the commitment to take back the power over your financial destiny. You will become wealthier over time if you make time your friend, not your enemy.

It's not the money, honey, nor the talent that makes the rich wealthy. It's the way they think about financial matters that makes their capital grow. Do you feel like you are racing toward retirement faster than your retirement savings are growing? As a retiree, are you worrying that your company will reduce your benefits or that the victories of medical science will allow you to outlive your shrinking retirement nest egg? Then it's time to become fiscally fit.

Plan fr the Worst, Then Hope for the Best

Your ancestors gave up everything to come to America: their families, their friends, their homes, and their way of life. Some arrived only with the clothes on their backs, vulnerable, and scared, but brimming with hope and determination that a better life was within their grasp. Today's investors don't have to take that much risk to become wealthier. But you have to understand the hidden agenda of capitalism to win your money game.

Did you ever notice that when you put the two words *The* and *IRS* together, it spells *theirs*? Sit tightly on your wallets and pocketbooks. The only money Uncle Sam has to manage and redistribute to those less fortunate than you is yours.

In this book you will learn some controversial personal finance strategies: Why retirement plans, such as 401(k)s may *not* be in your best interest, how your home could be your *worst* investment instead of your best; and why your guaranteed pension may not be so "*guaranteed*" in the future. Instead of envying the rich, learn to think more like them.

Why read this book? Because *learning* about your money is every bit as important as *earning* it.

CHAPTER 1

Winning the
Money Game

Two men on a hunting trip encountered an angry bear with little tolerance for intruders in her territory. While one hunter ran for his life toward the nearest tree, the second man sat down on a rock and began tightly tying his shoelaces.

"What are you doing?" called the first man over his shoulder, panting heavily. "You can't outrun that bear."

"I don't have to outrun the bear," answered the second man. "All I have to do is outrun you."

Like our intrepid hunters, you are involved in a serious race—winning your money game. Inflation may be outpacing you, while the financial industry is outthinking and outmaneuvering you. Banks and insurance companies are outsmarting you, and your government is outvoting you. Everyone else, it seems, has their own agenda for your money.

Capitalism was not crafted as an entitlement for the middle class. Our forefathers were quite affluent for their day, and they planned this country's basic rights and tenets so that the wealthy could stay rich. Capitalism is a business system, designed by the rich who use their influence with policy-makers to make themselves even richer. Capitalism offers a simple agenda to follow: a winning formula for wealth—if you understand how the system works to create it.

Buying a big home with a big mortgage makes you *poorer*, not *richer*. Earning a large income but spending most of it makes you *poorer*, not *richer*. Leasing cars because you lack the down payment makes you an indentured servant to the owners of the companies you lease from. Being wealthy means you have wealth, not mortgages, home equity loans, car payments, and credit card balances. If you want to become wealthier, stop spending so much and start your wealth-building plan.

You are *not* entitled to a job for life; *not* entitled to company-paid healthcare; *not* entitled to a pension for your golden years; *not* entitled to be cancer free or to be treated with the best medical science that money can buy; or to be safe in your homes without fear of terrorism or acts of war. You are *not* entitled to have your children leave home forever and marry happily (and stay married). You are *not* even entitled to keep your money (as you have witnessed during the last three miserable stock-market years). Capitalism *does* entitle you to choose that road you travel, to make wise choices that will create wealth over time.

In the story about the bear that began this chapter, the main character knew he was in serious danger. He used his wits to survive. Real-life financial victims work hard for their money. Being middle-income is, hopefully, a temporary condition. Middle-class mentality, however, is to follow the crowd.

In America, you choose whom you want to be like. People generally fall into one or more of the following categories: worker, borrower, savvy consumer, or greedy shareholder. *Workers* will earn incomes as long as they do not interfere with the profits of the owners. *Borrowers* are particularly vulnerable because without a job, they cannot pay their bills for the material things they have already bought. Then it's off to the bankruptcy court. *Savvy consumers* buy cheaper foreign products over those produced by their American colleagues because they are balancing their own budgets. *Greedy shareholders* win, hands down. These owners of American corporations offer jobs to workers, send bills owed to it with interest to other workers in debt, and live beneath their financial means.

The basic rules of the money game are simple. The goal of this timed event: to grab as many dollars as possible before you are downsized, your health goes bad, or you get tired of fighting traffic gridlock to work every day. When the clock winds down, the players with the most dollars win.

Take Back the Power

In the musical *Camelot*, King Arthur makes a series of weather edicts: the snow may never slush upon the hillside; by 9 o'clock, the moonlight must appear each evening; flowers must be in bloom by early spring; and so on. Based upon the belief that he is supreme ruler of both heaven and earth, he concludes that "in short, there simply is not a more congenial spot for happily ever after than here in Camelot."

Unfortunately, by the end of the story, King Arthur's queen has run off with Sir Lancelot, his country is at war, and even his personal safety is at risk. The moral? Anticipate opportunities and risks that you can plan for or prevent, and adapt to those things over which you have no control. Think your wallet is the secret to your financial future? It's just the opposite: *You are the answer to your pocketbook's future.*

The rules to financial success are in the fine print, and most Americans don't take the time to notice, let alone read, the fine print—not on their monthly credit card bills, not on their mortgage statements, not on their investment reports, not in their pension plan documents, or the thousands of contracts they eagerly sign. They believe what they are told. Consumers believe that someone somewhere must somehow be protecting them. After all, Americans are entitled. We are entitled to a lot less than we think.

Don't be fooled by S.O.S.: Signs of Success and Signs of Status can become Signs of Stress, Signs of Silliness, Signs of Sadness, and ultimately Signs of Surrender. Folks don't buy a house today; they charge it! They don't buy cars, they lease (that is, rent) them!

The average financial consumer gets financial promises and products instead of real-life solutions. They believe they are well-diversified, but the pieces (products) of their financial picture aren't designed to work together like a finished puzzle. Savers throw money toward financial goals, picking blindly among financial products that may benefit the salesperson more than the customer. They listen to the sales pitch and ignore the actual contract limitations and exclusions. They believe they're buying from experts with psychic hotlines to tomorrow's financial headlines. This is not an effective method of ensuring financial security.

When investors lose money, some panic and pull out of all their growth investments, missing the next market upturn. They console themselves with the thought that they did the right thing and saved what was left.

Many Americans are surviving from paycheck to paycheck, figuring they'll keep their jobs and their lifestyles. When they do get a windfall such as a large tax refund or an inheritance, they're back to the mall to spend it as fast as they can. If your primary breadwinner were out of a job for three months, would your family lose its good credit rating? If he or she remained jobless for six months, would the family car be repossessed? After a year without work, I'd bet the mortgaged home would be in jeopardy. Too many families have more month left at the end of the money.

You will probably never win the lottery. But in your lifetime, you *will* earn a small fortune. How much have you managed to squirrel away so far? Americans have higher incomes than ever before, but are making the rich richer, not themselves. If you are a member of "high" society—high mortgage balance, high credit card debt balances—you are running with the wrong crowd. It's not what you make that counts, but what you keep after spending, taxes, inflation, and redistribution of your income by your government and financial middlemen.

Maybe you believe Papa Government will give you a handout if you fail. Where will it get enough money to subsidize everyone's needs? When Social Security began, 42 workers supported each recipient. Currently, fewer than three employees contribute for every recipient, retiree, disabled worker, or dependent receiving benefits. Company pensions struggle to support growing lists of retirees. Uncontrollable healthcare costs may be the biggest expense of this century. Even Medicare will pay less to those with higher incomes. Americans expect access to the greatest healthcare system in the world. But who will pay?

You are saving and investing for two: you and some stranger poorer than you. Because *you* are the government, it is *your* pocketbook that will be redistributed by taxes, government-mandated social or entitlement programs, subsidies, or pork barrel projects. Unless you learn how the wealthy keep their money, your government will eventually manage your money for you. Leave your wealth unprotected and others will redistribute it back to those less fortunate than you (minus administrative costs). You can prevent this fate.

Monthly money magazines and newsletters want to be your personal financial guru. However, they are in the publishing business, not the investing business. Their profits come from full-page advertisers and your $29.95 annual check. Publishing companies hire journalists with upbeat writing styles, whether they have a background in the subjects they are reporting about or whether their last article came from a monthly issue of *Wine & Dine*. Recall their recent track records?

Your broker wants to manage your money and share in your retirement returns. By selling wrap accounts, specially managed accounts with annual fees, you could be shelling out even more in total charges per year than in comparable mutual funds, yet not improve investment performance. Between notorious stock brokers, infamous analysts, and unethical accountants, your money may be safer under your mattress.

I won't insult your intelligence by promising to send your children to college for free, to cut 80 percent off your current insurance premiums, to show you how to buy real estate with no money down, or threaten your wealth with a psychic stock market meltdown prediction. What I will do is show you how to hold onto and grow your money.

The rich can better afford sloppy money management. They can also afford to lose money if they (or their advisors) are wrong. Bill Gates can lose a lot of "moola" before he worries whether he can pay his medical insurance premium in old age. You cannot! *The less money you have to work with, the harder that money must work for you.*

When in a Swamp, Dress Like a Frog

Good money management has changed little in the past 50 years. By using the KISS (Keep It Simple, Stupid) theory of money management and learning how to diversify, you can keep your money healthy and growing. Though the recent "tech wreck" (the stock market meltdown of 2000) highlighted how important it is to *diversify* (not to put all your eggs into just one investment basket), the public has no idea how to use real diversification principles. They still think that buying a bunch of different financial products does the job.

Insurance companies, banking institutions, and brokerages use marketing to sell products, no matter how risky to your investment principal, how illogical the basic concept, how expensive the product, or how inferior the underlying investment concept. Glittery ad campaigns use greed and fear devices to encourage emotional buying, eliminating common sense from the sales presentation. Customers are whipsawed from product to product, and a commission goes to the salesperson right off the top of your money.

If you became seriously ill, you would probably visit a competent physician for an initial diagnosis. If, however, your doctor advised that one of your body parts be removed in a hospital at once, would you quietly comply? You would certainly seek a second opinion, perhaps even a third.

Smart buyers can easily get reeled in by an award-winning sales presentation. *Learn enough to trust yourself!*

You don't need to be a rocket scientist to master basic money management and simple investing options. Learn to translate the fine print, eliminate the "sizzle" of the sales pitch, and develop a schedule to work your wealth plan.

Get Rich Slow can't make you a one-minute manager, help you search for excellence, thrive on chaos, or develop the habits of highly effective people. It can, however, help you become the millionaire next door.

Women and Investing

Women have been labeled as mattress stuffers, procrastinators who rarely get in on the hottest deals, and unwilling to take the kind of risks that make big money in the investing arena. In my opinion, these very attributes create successful and prudent investors!

Women can't tear a phone book in half with their bare hands, but any woman who can manage today's tight budgets or live successfully on a fixed income may be more capable than some CEOs to manage a major corporation. Women come with money managing genes, which means that they think first, act later, and they are careful. Women are information-diggers, yet they often lack confidence in their own ability. As caregivers for much of their lives, they can be less assertive about their convictions and more apt to allow spouses or other family members to handle their financial matters or influence their decisions.

As a mom, you have a lot on your mind. How much should the tooth fairy bring? How should you schedule dancing, Scouting, T-ball, Little League, swimming, and other enrichment classes? Who's driving next week's carpool? What's for dinner? Where will you get the money for Amy's braces?

Wait a minute! Who is watching your money? If your financial life is on autopilot because being a mom is more than a full-time job, take a breath and ask: Are you working for your family at your own financial detriment? You can do both. Look at your chore list again. Make space and implement your own wealth plan.

CHAPTER 2

It's a Jungle
Out There

Every morning in Africa, a timid and frightened gazelle wakes. She knows she must run fast that day or she will be eaten. At the same time, a powerful lion also awakens. He, too, must run fast—faster than the gazelle—or he will eat nothing and ultimately starve to death.

Whether you picture yourself as a courageous lion in control of your financial destiny, or as a gazelle carefully picking your trail over the rocky financial terrain, when that sun comes up, you had better be running. The financial industry wants to seduce you with its large buildings (for which you pay) and mega advertising blitzes (for which you pay), and sell you the sizzle instead of the steak (for which you may pay dearly).

Herman had barely escaped with his life from a pleasure sailboat that overturned during a nasty storm at sea. He clung for hours to a rubber raft that automatically inflated when it hit the water. Now he sat in the middle of his temporary rubber home waiting for a rescue ship to appear on the distant horizon.

As shark fins cut the surface of the water and circled around his bobbing rubber cage, nudging the sides of the rubber raft, he closed his aching eyes for a moment and relaxed. Perhaps he could even take a short nap—if only that annoying, mysterious hissing sound would stop. What was making that noise anyway? His ignorance or denial of the facts didn't alter their seriousness.

Too many people assume the bills will somehow get paid, their child will receive financial aid for college, or the government and their employers will foot the bill for a comfortable retirement. They pass on middle-class traditions that don't work in today's changing world, and they trust the financial industry. The mistakes described in this chapter are examples of the most destructive and sinister.

1. Spend Now, Plan Later

If you became stranded under an avalanche of snow during a winter ski vacation, what's the first thing you would do? According to survival experts, you should dig a small hole around your face and spit. Why? The saliva should fall downward, giving you an idea of which way is up. Then dig upward as fast as possible.

Which way is up? Let's spit for a moment. In which direction are you heading? Are you standing on solid ground or are you trapped under a mountain of debt from obsessive spending?

Americans love to spend. In fact, our national motto should be "Shop till you drop." Capitalism and the Material Girl Effect have encouraged consumers to spend, to enjoy today. Identifying the truly wealthy in America is difficult because many people who live in expensive homes, drive luxury cars, and play with great toys do not have much wealth. Many wealthy people do not live in upscale neighborhoods. Wealth is not having a huge credit line that you use up. Wealth is not what you spend. Wealth is how much you accumulate—and keep.

Are you in better or worse financial shape than you were five years ago? Are your debts or your assets increasing? Which is growing faster? Have you planned to protect yourself against losing 6 percent (or more) of your yearly take-home earnings due to insidious inflation? What are your contingency plans if your company fails? Who brings home the bacon if you fall off the roof next weekend, become disabled, and lose your earning power?

Wealth does not depend on luck and good intentions. Success lives at the intersection of Hard Work and Smart Work avenues. You need financial food for thought, solid-ground commonsense strategies to improve your personal money life. You need to learn how the wealthy get richer. You want the truth, not the hype, about what to do with your money—and why.

2. I Plan to Save Like Crazy...Someday

There's always tomorrow. Today, there's mortgage payments, orthodontist bills, your cholesterol level, and more to worry about. Folks can get so lost in daily life that they never get around to planning for their futures.

This is probably not the first money book you have read. What happened to the last set of good intentions to trim the budget, cut credit card debt, and start a monthly savings plan? Let me guess: The next spending crisis came along. Perhaps you convinced yourself that a vacation, a new car, or an addition to the house was necessary, soothing your conscience by promising to start planning first thing tomorrow...next month...next year...after the annual raise...after the kids have moved out.

The things that come to those who wait are generally the things left behind by those who got there first. Opportunity gives every bird its food, but it does not throw it into the nest. Enough words—now win.

3. Paying Yourself Last

Most folks budget upside down. What is the first bill you pay each month? What comes after that? Are you paying yourself last? Make the first bill you owe each month a bill to yourself. Before you pay *anything* next month, before even the mortgage, the rent, or the car payment, put away something for yourself. A part of all you earn is yours to keep. But you have to be selfish and grab it. Just $50 a month in a savings or investing plan can accumulate into a tidy lump sum in a few years. The concept of paying yourself first has made more millionaires than has winning the lottery or selling hot stock options. This easy automatic strategy is the most underrated method of accumulating wealth over time.

Believe you can't afford to save right now? Examine your priorities. If your parents were starving, could you afford to buy $50 worth of food a month for them? Of course you could! Aren't you as valuable? Do you care as much for yourself and your family? Think of that savings or investment payment as a bill you owe to yourself.

Nearly everyone fritters away $50 or more a month. Sign up for an automatic payroll savings deduction or checking plan. Because you won't see the extra savings, you won't be tempted to spend it.

4. No Problem, I've Got a Guaranteed Pension

What's the primary job of the CEO of a company? Raising the price of the shareholders' stock, not guaranteeing the health and welfare of an aging workforce. Workers who spend it all today and depend on Social Security, company pensions, and hope for financial security, lose the power over their financial futures.

Few workers today still believe they are putting Social Security taxes into their own account. Your children may have greater confidence in the existence of UFOs than in the future of government retirement subsidies. A lean retirement purse is more easily cured than endured.

Do you trust that your pension will still be there when you're ready to use it? The solvency of company pensions depends on how much they earn in the markets (ouch!), how much in earnings shareholders want to divert to retiring employees (not much!), and often funny money calculations used to make a pension fund look more secure. If moving operations north, south, east, or west of the border will increase a company's profit margin and keep the current CEO in a job and stock options, your company may close, sell out, or retire to a warmer climate before employees can say, "You can't do that. I'm entitled."

When your father lost his job, they called it a deep depression. When you lose your job today, they call it re-engineering, reallocation of resources, rightsizing, or restructuring, so that you don't see it coming. An out-of-work 50 year old generally has not accumulated enough money over sufficient time for compound interest to grow his or her company retirement plan to maturity.

Seeking another job after age 50 is tough. Unfortunately, most folks are too young at age 50 to stop earning a paycheck and support themselves for 25 or 30 more years.

5. Learn the Golden Rules

One dollar invested at 8 percent per year for 20 years would grow to $4.66. If that same money can grow for another 10 years or for a total of 30 years, that original $1 would multiply 10 times, to $10. If at age 18, you started an investment program of just $25 per month till age 65 and received a 10 percent per year rate of return on your money, you would have an extra $325,000 lying around for your retirement. What if you had invested $50 per month from age 25 on? An additional $318,000 more to spend on your grandchildren or those vacations you promised you would take when the kids grew up. If someone had invested for you $1 per day at a 10-percent annual rate of return from birth until your 65th birthday, you would have amassed $2,500,000 smackeroos! As you can see it takes many years to become an "overnight" financial success.

6. Custer's Last Command: Charge!

In 1876, General George Armstrong Custer received information that a significant number of Indians were gathering at Little Big Horn. Without analyzing the facts, he decided to ride out with 250 men to "surround" almost 3,000 Indians—a serious mistake.

Americans are caught in a dangerous credit crunch, "surrounding" every material good by leveraging their financial futures with weapons of "mass seduction." Their homes have become virtual ATMs with cash-out refinancing available! Instant gratification. When you want that SUV, be assured that some stranger (whom you will make rich) will befriend you. At least until you sign the purchase order. Neither governments nor individual families can borrow themselves into prosperity. Your government has a backup plan: you. Where will you turn when you are down on your financial luck?

A credit card can be a valuable tool, like a hammer to a carpenter, if it is properly used. Using plastic can establish an initial credit history when you are ready to purchase a car or a home. It can allow you to use the credit card company's money for *free* from 25 to 30 days every month if you *pay off your monthly balances in full and on time.* It can also be an emergency card if your car needs towing or breaks down away from home.

But it will be the greatest financial enemy you will ever know if it encourages you to feel richer, to live beyond your affordable means, and to fool yourself into believing you will be able to pay it off with future income. Keeping up with the Joneses who may be keeping up with the Rockefellers is a losing proposition. Today, you can even charge a car with no payments for two years!

People are borrowing against their homes and futures to support astronomical spending habits. High society can mean high mortgage payments, high credit card balances, high monthly payments, living life on the installment plan. If you cannot afford to pay off what you owe now, what in the world are you doing borrowing more?

For all of the talk about family, spiritual, religious, and moral values, the one thing Americans seem to value the most is *stuff*! It takes a marketing genius to convince people to pay more and more for an item that becomes worth less and less as each day passes. How much will you fork over for your home? On a 20-year loan, more than twice the amount originally borrowed. On a 30-year loan, nearly three times the original mortgage debt.

7. Listening to Madison Avenue

You're in China and hungry for a Big Mac. Don't worry that you don't speak Chinese; just look for the Golden Arches. Perhaps you're in Egypt and thirsty for an ice-cold Coke. You can spot the company's distinctive red-and-white design. Like the car parked next to you at the traffic light? Check out the hood ornament if you can't recognize the style. Welcome to the branding business.

Advertising achieves three results:

1. It *sells*!
2. It *costs you,* the consumer.
3. It *guarantees absolutely nothing* about the real value of any goods or service you will purchase.

Remember the bunny whose batteries never wore down? That's marketing at its best!

I'll bet your next tuition payment that in 60 seconds, you could recall at least a dozen advertising slogans, tunes, or logos (trademarks) embedded in your brain and intended to part you from your cash. These advertising ploys are your financial competition, not your friends! You are not a commission. You are flesh, blood, tears, laughter, hope, fear, and dreams. If you are a part of anyone's financial strategy, it should be your own.

If your friendly neighborhood bank were on the brink of insolvency, would the president give you a call to advise you to pull out your deposits? Even if you asked, would they tell you the truth? If your investment company discovered that the accountant disappeared with the entire year's profits, would you expect to receive notice to withdraw your money before they declared bankruptcy?

CEOs of public companies can't lie. If they don't disclose financial problems to the public, they could lose their job, their stock goes down the drain, their options become worthless, they might go to jail, and their mortgaged homes go up for sale. But if trouble is brewing in the company and they disclose financial problems to the public, they could lose their job, their stock goes down the drain, their options become worthless, they might go to jail, and their mortgaged homes go up for sale. Unless you are the CEO's mother, you would probably hear the bad news on CNN like everyone else.

8. Read the *Fine* Print

Jim was walking by his neighbor's house and saw him straddled with a couch halfway through his front door. Jim offered to help, and in no time they both picked up the couch, Jim at one end and the neighbor at the other. Just when it seemed they had made an inch or two of progress, they lost an inch. Exhausted and frustrated, they sat down to rest. "I'm sorry, I just don't think we're going to get this piece into your house," Jim said. "*In?*" the neighbor asked. "I'm trying to move it *out*." Obviously there was a failure to communicate! The details were missed.

Buyers don't read the fine print. The old saying, "The bold print giveth, and the fine print taketh away," is true. Every word in a contract you sign is important enough for the company's lawyer to have included it in the contract. It should be just as important for you to understand. Too many people believe what they are told. You must look further.

Before you sign your name to the dotted line, take the time to read the *fine* print—and make sure that what you're committing to can't be interpreted in any way that could be harmful to you. *It's not what they say but what you sign that counts.*

9. A 20-Percent Return and No Risk?

An old fable reminds us a servant went to the Baghdad marketplace and accidentally stumbled upon Death, who pointed a bony finger in his direction. Anxious to avoid Death's cruel fate, the servant ran home to his master and successfully pleaded for a swift horse to flee as far away as possible. He rode all day without food or water until he entered a city called Samara. Feeling safe at last, he dined heartily and soon fell asleep.

Later that same day, his master traveled to the same Baghdad market. Upon spotting Death along the street, they struck up a conversation regarding the frightful experience of the servant. "I did not intend your servant any harm, nor did I mean a threatening gesture toward him," the Dark Angel protested. "It was only that I was astonished to see him in Baghdad this day, for I have an appointment with him tonight in a town called Samara."

Sometimes our efforts to run from one risk may lead us to another, perhaps even greater, peril. Check your risk tolerance. Are you more focused on making money or on not losing what you have already gained? Of what value are short-term profits if you cannot hold onto them? The lure of easy stock market returns ultimately proved the undoing of many investors after the tech wreck in 2000.

Tortoises are slow but sure travelers. They know their race is not a 50-meter dash but a long marathon. Today's rocketing stock or mutual fund may fall hard tomorrow. When you purchase mutual funds, you are not buying a lottery ticket. You are participating in the capitalistic system that favors wealth-building. Some succeed because they are destined to; others because they are determined to.

10. Taming the Tax Beast

Some folks will do nearly anything to escape the wrath of the tax beast. They will purchase poor quality investments and accumulate tax-deferral time bombs that explode in the future. They will buy illiquid investments they don't understand with restrictions on their money and large surrender charges for early withdrawals. They will pay huge internal commissions and high ongoing costs that reduce their overall returns for the privilege of temporary tax deferral, and they will run like lemmings toward a hot tax strategy before examining the inherent risks to investment capital.

Tax-deductible, tax-deferred, and tax-exempt are magic marketing monikers that put billions of dollars into insurance company and real estate coffers. Such investors never stop to research the actual risks of the investments or contemplate how well they will work in adverse investment markets. Control of the money should be your first priority, followed by finding the best set of investments for your financial goals. Then look for tax advantages that will enhance the first two objectives.

Tax planning shouldn't begin on April 1, just before the tax deadline. It should start on January 1 of the prior year, when there is time to plan. Tax planning should remain a part of your financial life, but not the major focus of every investment transaction. Become tax smart, not tax driven.

11. Passing On the Family Tree

Generations can pass down traditions that do not work. More than likely, your parents didn't drink or gamble their money away; they charged a home and burned the mortgage when it was paid for, put some money in low-interest bank accounts, bought U.S. savings bonds, and handed leftovers to the insurance industry through neighborhood house-to-house insurance agents. Today's millionaires watched over their own money, owned their investments such as mutual funds and stocks, understood money management principles, bought homes that they could afford, and made their money work harder than the inflation rate through the years. Buying a house can make you much poorer. Chapter 8 will teach you how to purchase the roof over your head without breaking the bank.

12. Inertia

In George Orwell's classic novel *Animal Farm*, there is nothing but misery, cruelty, and injustice for the oppressed farm animals owned by farmer Jones. So, they plot to overthrow their master and join forces to build a better farm life where all animals are created equal. By the end of the story, loyal hardworking horse Boxer has died from overwork; his pal Clover is practically blind and of no use to the new system of government; and Napoleon, kingpin of pigs, and his plump comrades inhabit the farmer's house. In place of the original seven commandments immortalized on the barn wall, there existed only one commandment: All animals are equal, but some animals are more equal than others.

Were these animals hostaged by an unfair system of government? Or could they have worked the surrounding political environment for their own purposes instead of living in the moment, trusting the rhetoric, believing their system would take care of them?

What makes some people more equal than others? It's not social class, born poor or to wealthy parents. In America, everyone has some opportunity to rise above their humble beginnings, to be hunter rather than prey, to be master instead of servant, to be a financial winner. You have lots of control over your destiny. The choices you make today will dictate your life. No pain, no gain? The only muscle you will need to exercise is your brain.

13. At Last, a Free Lunch!

Before you jump into an attractive-looking product, ask what hidden costs are involved, especially for leaving it in six months, one year, or five years. Many products have severe penalties for withdrawing: deferred charges, backloaded expense fees, early distribution charges, and preretirement penalties. If I sold you a car and told you it was free if you drove it for seven years, would you believe me? There is no Santa Claus, no tooth fairy, and no such thing as a free lunch. There are, however, gullible customers who buy such bunk.

14. Stinking Thinking

Who wouldn't walk 10 blocks to save $75? Assume you're shopping for a fan and enter a store. The price is $125. Then you overhear someone saying that the same fan is on sale for $50 down the street. Do you go to the second store to get the lower price? Your mother would have. You might, too.

But what if you were looking at a $1,000 refrigerator instead of a $125 fan? Would you stop the sales transaction and drive some distance to save $75 at a store 10 blocks down the street? Maybe not. This is called mental accounting—how we justify our actions (or inactions) by the voice in our head that says you deserve it, you can afford it, you should have it, it's too much trouble to work for it, it's too hard to wait for it, you have earned it.

Mental accounting is particularly dangerous when you receive a windfall lump-sum bonus, a tax refund, or an inheritance. A financial windfall may seem more like a gift than part of your hard-earned paycheck, and therefore, less valuable and easier to spend on items you would not ordinarily indulge.

It doesn't make any difference where the money came from. It all has the same value. In fact, a one-time lump sum may be even more valuable as an investment stake to get you closer to your financial objectives.

6 Keys to Financial Success

1. **Invest in yourself.** Your improved earning power through continuing education is your most valuable asset. A $21,000 per year boost in salary is equivalent to a 6-percent rate of return on a $350,000 lump-sum investment. Maybe a better job is easier to achieve.

2. **Protect your family against life's biggest risks:** serious illness, early death, or disability. Term life insurance provides a less expensive method of insurance than others and you can use the difference as a premium for an investment program. Disability is an expensive risk to an insurance company. So be sure to know the specific definitions and exclusions in case you make a claim later.

3. **Borrow sparingly.** Use credit only when you know that you can repay the loan from other assets or income. Learn to pay cash. Take advantage of the credit card company's grace period before you send your check in full each month.

4. **A part of all you earn is yours to keep.** Pay the first bill each month to yourself. Invest regularly and use automatic methods that put your savings habit on autopilot.

5. **Diversify, diversify, diversify.** Don't swing for the bleachers. In investing, as in baseball, those who aim for the outfield also strike out a lot. Avoid volatile stocks or mutual funds and structure your portfolio for comfort, not for speed. Continue to invest no matter what the market outlook. Diversification is boring—that's the point.

6. **Create a better world.** Your own well-being depends on the physical, spiritual, and financial health of others in your community. Share your good fortune by donating money or service. Teach children respect for life in other forms, for if all the beasts were gone, man would die from a great loneliness of spirit. A child can plant a tree, feed a hungry bird, adopt a dolphin or manatee, and improve the world around them.

Times have been so good for so long that we have forgotten how we got here. Become a lean, mean money machine. The meek might inherit the earth, but the smart will always retain the mineral rights. Don't wait for your ship to come in. Swim out to meet it.

CHAPTER 3

Remember the Golden Rules

Do you ever wish that life came with a guidebook? For example, you would know when to switch your 401(k) from stocks to bonds? Or that you were guaranteed 20 more years' work at your company with a promotion and a yearly raise? Or that you knew your children would get a free ride through college, while your company paid your retirement, your life insurance premiums, and your medical insurance premiums for the rest of your golden years?

The universe is stacked against some events. Blame it on Murphy's Law: Whatever can go wrong will go wrong in the worst possible way at the worst possible time. By understanding how Murphy's Law works, you can improve your odds of becoming wealthier.

Bread always seems to land buttered side down when it falls on the floor. Bad luck? No: Murphy. Given the height of tabletops, there isn't enough room for a tipped piece of bread to make a full rotation before it hits the floor. We must adapt to our environment or Murphy will get us.

How does this relate to becoming wealthy? The odds of picking a winning stock out of more than 13,000 public companies are extremely low. One hundred securities in an investment portfolio are much safer than only a few. That's why I see mutual funds in your future.

Even the supermarket checkout line holds an investing lesson. You may think your success rate is a function of how well you size up the lines. But your odds of winning are predetermined. If three cash registers are open, the odds that you will pick the fastest line are only 33 percent. Two-thirds of the time, on average, one of the other lines will end up moving faster. With four lines to choose from, your odds of picking a winner get worse. So to choose the right stock you must be very lucky. If you pick a loser, you will work longer until you can retire.

Murphy is not heartless. He also invented some investing truths to use on your journey to wealth.

Compound Interest: The 8th Wonder of the World

It has been said that Albert Einstein was once asked to recount his most notable observation. His answer? Compound interest—the miracle and magic of compound interest.

Whether or not the story is true, it's a powerful motivator. The businessperson most familiar with compound interest is not the CEO of a large conglomerate or a corporate accountant working daily with cash flow charts. It is the grocery store owner in your neighborhood. Poor man. His markup on shelf items is puny per sale. Most large corporations would have collapsed on such a stingy profit margin.

But how long does that can of soup or bottle of milk stay on the shelf? The store owner may make only a tiny profit per item, but he does it over and over in a relatively short amount of time, and each time, the profits are converted into new inventory for sale.

Because of constraints on space, personnel, and limited markets, no business can increase profits indefinitely. But your money has only two restrictions: the rate of return you receive and the time the money can compound before it is needed. If you give money enough time to work, and choose the optimum investment mix, it will produce the profits you need to fund what you desire most.

How powerful a concept is this? Consider the man who applied for a one-month term of employment. His new employer allowed him to choose the form of his salary: $300 per week for the next month or a pay by which he would receive one cent for the first day, that amount doubled the second day, and each day's pay thereafter doubled again for the rest of the month. Which option would you choose?

A penny may not seem like much in comparison to $300 (which is 30,000 pennies), but because of compound interest, if you took the penny-salary option, at the end of 30 days you would have earned a paycheck of $10,737,418.23.

No real employer would offer such a deal. But it effectively illustrates how awesome compound interest can be.

One dollar invested at 8 percent per year for 20 years equals $4.66. If that $1 can grow for another 10 years (for a total of 30 years), the original $1 would become $10.

Time Value of Money

Ben Franklin preached frugality right along with freedom and democracy and an early bedtime. Though you can't predict the outcome of tomorrow's investment headlines, you can control the outcome of your savings and investing habits.

I can think of no better example of compound interest coupled with the aid of time than the story of twin brothers Bill and Bob, 23 years old.

Bill decided to take care of retirement early and invested $2,000 a year, paying himself first in a retirement IRA account for seven years, investing a total of $14,000. Then, he stopped investing and moved on to other financial goals, letting his money compound at the same annual rate of 10 percent per year.

Bob, however, was more interested in fast cars and an even faster lifestyle. He saved nothing for the first seven years. But as he grew older, he began to worry more about retirement. So at age 30, soon after Bill *stopped* contributing to his IRA, Bob began putting $2,000 per year into an IRA account at the same rate of return, 10 percent per year.

By retirement at age 65, each twin had accumulated nearly $600,000.

This nest egg cost Bill only $14,000 because he started earlier, but Bob was forced to invest $2,000 for 35 years—a total of $70,000—to accomplish the same goal. Would you rather spend $14,000 or $70,000 to make approximately $600,000?

Age	Bill's Investment	Bob's Investment
23	$2,000	0
24	$2,000	0
25	$2,000	0
26	$2,000	0
27	$2,000	0
28	$2,000	0
29	$2,000	0
30	0	$2,000
31	0	$2,000
32	0	$2,000
33	0	$2,000
34	0	$2,000
35	0	$2,000
36	0	$2,000
37	0	$2,000
38	0	$2,000

39	0	$2,000
40	0	$2,000
41	0	$2,000
42	0	$2,000
43	0	$2,000
44	0	$2,000
45	0	$2,000
46	0	$2,000
47	0	$2,000
48	0	$2,000
49	0	$2,000
50	0	$2,000
51	0	$2,000
52	0	$2,000
53	0	$2,000
54	0	$2,000
55	0	$2,000
56	0	$2,000
57	0	$2,000
58	0	$2,000
59	0	$2,000
60	0	$2,000
61	0	$2,000
62	0	$2,000
63	0	$2,000
64	0	$2,000
Total Investment	$14,000	$70,000
Amount at age 65	$586,548	$596,254

The Rule of 72

Obviously, the higher the rate of return (interest) you receive on your money, the faster it will grow. But how fast? And how can you predict what you may be able to accumulate in the future?

The Rule of 72 is a ballpark method of determining how quickly money will grow at a certain interest rate. When you divide the number 72 by the rate of return you expect to receive, the answer tells you how many years it will take to double your money. The following examples should help:

At 3 percent per year, your money will double every 24 years (72 divided by 3 equals 24).

At 6 percent per year, your money will double every 12 years (72 divided by 6 equals 12).

At 8 percent per year, your money will double every nine years.

At 9 percent per year, your money will double every eight years.

At 12 percent per year, your money will double every six years.

Using the number 72 is a fairly accurate way to predict future returns.

Let's examine how this principle applies to real dollars. As an example, I have figured the interest per year on a $2,000 investment that could be invested in an IRA. Taxes were not considered for this illustration, and the money was contributed at the beginning of each year.

Under the Rule of 72 and dividing the number 72 by the comparable interest rates below, let's examine how this principle applies to real dollars. As an example, with a compound interest calculator I have figured the interest on a $20,000 investment per year, which could be invested inside an IRA. Taxes were not considered for this illustration, and the money was contributed at the beginning of each year.

Contribution	$2,000	$2,000	$2,000	$2,000
Percent return	6%	8%	9%	12%
After 12 years	$4,024	$5,036	$5,625	$7,792
After 24 years	$8,098	$12,682	$15,822	$30,357

Two points are critical. First, the higher the interest rate, the larger the account value over time. More importantly, doubling the interest rate *more than doubles the return* over longer periods of time. Look at the 6-percent and the 12-percent columns. After 13 years, the difference in account value between them is more than double. And the gap continues to widen. At the 24-year mark, there is a difference of almost four times the return between the 6-percent and 12-percent investments.

Now let's see what happens to your money when you loan it out to institutions such as banks and insurance companies. According to the Rule of 72, at 15 percent, money doubles every 4.8 years. At 20 percent, money will double in 3.6 years.

	Your Return	Their Return	
$2,000	@ 6%	@ 15%	@ 20%
12 years	$4,024	$10,701	$17,832
24 years	$8,098	$57,250	$158,994

If you think this comparison is unfair because no one could possibly be making that kind of return on your money, check out your credit cards, finance company rates, and the 30-year indentured-servant plan you refer to as your mortgage.

Now that you understand how important the Rule of 72 is to your financial future, strive to get competitive returns on both short-term and long-term savings. The Money Game teaches one very sobering lesson: Use it or lose it.

Perhaps you are muttering to yourself that this concept is great for your children, but it comes too late to keep the wolf from *your* door. The concept remains the same, whether you are age 5, 35, or 65. The only difference is that the less time you have, the harder your money must work. If your time is more limited, you have no time to lose.

Sit down tonight and explain the story of Bill and Bob to your children. That may even be a better idea than funding medical or law school. Children can make time their friend, because the longer their money can compound, the less money they will need to invest to reach their goals and the greater their future money piles. Money gains momentum with the help of time like a snowball rolling downhill.

Einstein's theory of relativity may have great benefits to science, but in the race to beat inflation and provide those dreams and goals you have promised yourself and your family, the theory of compound interest has greater "relativity."

Inflation: The Silent But Deadly Money Killer

If I told you that, as one of my best clients, I would offer you a special investment opportunity that was worth $1,000 in 1945, had steadily declined in value each and every year since then, and was now selling at $180, would you be so anxious to purchase it? That is what just 3-percent annual inflation has done to the American dollar!

Inflation is lurking in your refrigerator with rising costs for food, your heating ducts with rising heating costs, your car's gas tank in rising gas taxes, and waiting in your next real estate tax bill. Inflation is the deadliest money-killer over time, just as dangerous as losses from a miserable stock market.

If inflation is trotting along at 6 percent per year, you must earn 6 percent (after taxes) on your money just to stay in the same financial place you began the year. If inflation is greater than 6 percent, you must receive an even higher return just to continue treading water. Folks now are not investing because they want to. The fun of logging on to the Net to see how much richer they were than last month disappeared with the crash of 2000. Prudent consumers continue to invest because they have to and so they can outpace inflation.

Want guarantees? If you buried your money in the backyard because you were afraid to invest it, 12 years and 6-percent annual inflation later would guarantee a loss of 50 percent of its original value.

Let's look at the effect of inflation on savings. Assume you have $10,000 working at 3 percent interest with a 6-percent inflation factor working against you.

How Inflation Hurts Savings

Original savings investment at beginning of year	$10,000
Interest @ 3 percent minus inflationary loss of money @ 6 percent	$283
Taxes on $300 interest (28-percent bracket)	($84)
Taxes and purchase-power loss at end of year	(<u>$367</u>)
Total purchasing power left at end of year	$9,633

Carry over these losses to the next year and the bottom line will keep shrinking. The longer your money works below inflation, when living on a fixed income, the more principal you use up each year just to live in the same lifestyle. Each year you gain less interest because there is less money to receive interest on. For elderly couples living on the income that their money generates, it's no wonder they might fear shrinking nest eggs more than a root canal or a colonoscopy. Medical science now has the ability to control many of the effects of aging. If only outliving your retirement money were one of them.

The effect of inflation on wages is even more unsettling. If it takes $30,000 per year today to keep your family and home going, in 10 years at 6-percent inflation you will need $53,725 per year to retain the same purchasing power. In 20 years, it will cost you $96,214 per year. Where are you going to find that kind of money? Are you planning to get those kinds of raises at work? Have you told your boss?

If you are thinking of packing in what's left of your investment portfolio and taking it to the bank for some safety, you will get one guarantee you didn't count on.

The same Rule of 72 that works for compounding future values can work against you when inflation robs you of purchasing power over the years. Using the Rule of 72, if the average rate of inflation is 6 percent, your money will shrink in half every 12 years (72 divided by 6-percent inflation equals 12 years). After 24 years, it shrinks in half again. A $100,000 nest egg today will reduce to $25,000 worth of purchasing power with inflation hounding it for 24 years. Today's nest egg will hardly purchase tomorrow's birdhouse. This is why bank CDs won't keep a roof over your head, three meals in your stomach, and your prescription bottles filled.

The most dangerous financial mistake a new retiree can make is to gather their money around them as if they had six months left to live and to invest for income when they really need growth. You must investigate other financial life forms and learn how to manage risk to stay wealthy.

No matter what your age, you must beat inflation with your future retirement money. Learn to seek growth without undue risk on your long-term money. Fixed income vehicles such as bank products and insurance annuities have not generally kept pace with inflation over time.

Inflation and College

For the cost of supporting your student through an ivy-covered college experience, you would think the school could name a dorm or student center after you. A public university can cost $15,000 or more per year. That figure won't keep your kids in designer clothing, but it will pack enough educational skills into them so that they can ultimately find another source of revenue than you.

Present college costs are escalating at 8 to 10 percent per year. So let's assume education expenses increase at 8 percent per year.

If Debbie is starting college next year and you intend to pay two-thirds of the total tuition cost, your four-year expense will be $45,061. You'll have to lay out $71,506 for 12-year-old Bruce. And cute 6-year-old Zelda will cost you $113,471. No wonder she frowns a lot. She knows she's got an uphill battle to coerce you into handing over that much money.

Now, that is public education we're looking at. If the Ivy League is on your college menu, you will need to double or even triple these outlandish numbers. (See Chapter 11 for a more detailed discussion of college funding.)

Confidence or Competence?

You can't control the markets, but maybe you can control yourself. *Confidence* is an attitude about one's self and the world around him. You can be confident about your health, your job, or your future. Confidence is the essence of the American spirit. But confidence can be dangerous. Confidence took small investors for a whirlwind ride to the tech wreck in 2000, and proved again that stock markets have no memory.

Competence implies that you have mastered skills that allow you to perform certain tasks. A competent investor understands fundamentals, uses risk management strategies to reduce losses, and institutes disciplined policies such as regular investing and diversification. Increased competence replaces confidence as you improve critical-thinking skills and ignore the crowd.

Confidence is easy to achieve. Just think positive thoughts. Competence takes hard work and time to develop this education. Maybe that's why more folks practice confidence than competence. Choose competence over confidence to win your money game.

If you're not sure where you're going, "any road can take you there," as the old saying goes. Vague ideas won't solve your financial challenges. Solid financial planning, and using the strategies in this book, are the solution.

Time Can Be Your Friend

Assume that your goal for when you reach age 65 is to accumulate a lump sum of $100,000, and you expect you can earn 10 percent a year on any money you invest.

If you start at age 25, you will need to contribute only $16 per month.

Wait until age 35 to start saving, and you will need to fork out $44 per month.

Starting at age 45 and it will cost you $131 per month.

If you follow the most common retirement plan, you will wait until you're 55, at which point you'll have to sock away $484 per month.

The same rate of return over longer periods of time makes the difference. By letting time and compounded interest do most of the work for you, you can achieve your $100,000 goal much more easily and with less money.

Opportunity Knocks

What's the difference between buying a $15,000 car and a $20,000 car? A whole lot more than $5,000, as we shall see.

Most car buyers purchase their cars on credit. So when interest is applied to the original cost of the loan, the total paid out over time is more than a $5,000 difference. What if you bought the cheaper car and invested that $5,000 difference at 8 percent over 10 years? You would have accumulated nearly $11,000 and still would have had transportation. Over 15 years at the same 8-percent return per year, that original $5,000 investment could grow to more than $23,000.

A dollar works either for you or for the person you gave it to. It's called *opportunity cost,* and it's one of the best ways to build wealth over time. Ready to purchase a new-to-you (a.k.a. used) car? You could save thousands of dollars and get more than four wheels in the bargain. Opportunity might knock only once. But it passes by your door every day.

CHAPTER 4

Show Me
the Money

At the beginning of each day, it's all about possibilities. At the end of the day, it's all about results. And everything in between will help or hinder your journey to greater wealth.

Completing and analyzing the following are essential:

1. Your short-term financial plans.
2. Your long-term objectives and financial goals.
3. Your current income and expenses.
4. Your total net worth.

The worksheets in the Appendix will help you compile this information.

According to Chinese tradition, the world contains cosmic energy, known as ch'i. Ch'i needs to flow smoothly and freely in order to create harmony. Harmonizing your financial surroundings is easy and produces personal power. Use the checklist "Do You Know Where These Documents Are?" in the Appendix to organize your financial history.

Fuel the Right Plan

A young boy confided to his grandfather that he often felt like there were two dogs inside him. One dog was fierce and mean, hated people, was hard to control, and barked all the time. The other dog was kind and obedient, a joy to have around. His grandfather asked, "Which dog do you think will win the struggle?" The boy replied, "It depends on which one I feed."

Developing a financial plan involves shutting off the TV and, if you are married, holding a family council. If they will work with you, include your children as part of your team.

Step 1: Establish Your Goals

Start with the "Current Status Financial Goals and Objectives" worksheet in the Appendix. Decide what you *need* versus what you *want*. List all your specific objectives under each of the major categories: retirement, estate, education, income, and other.

What are your family's most important short-term and long-term goals? Short-term goals have a time span of three years or less. They may include establishing an emergency fund, reducing consumer debt, purchasing a new car, taking a summer vacation, or paying college tuition. Long-term goals, more than three years away, may include savings for retirement, starting a college fund, beginning a small business, or purchasing a first or next home. *Where the money should be invested depends on the length of time until the money is needed, not on the nature of the goal itself.* For example, the biggest mistake new retirees can make is to try to protect their investment principal at the expense of long-term growth. They may invest in fixed-income investments because they believe these are safer. But they really need growth so that their money will last during their long and expensive retirement years.

Short-term money for goals less than three years away should *protect the investment principal, while long-term goals should protect the purchasing power*. As you will see later, the investments suitable for each time period are vastly different.

For singles, a single parent, or sole family breadwinner, careful planning becomes even more vital. Make your goals more specific than "keeping your head above water," "staying ahead of the tax man," or "becoming filthy rich."

Step 2: I Owe, I Owe, So Off to Work I Go

Consumers often ask me what spending limits are reasonable. Is "reasonable" getting dressed in clothes that you buy for work, driving through traffic five days a week in a car that you are still paying for in order to get to the job that you need, maybe hate, so you can pay for the clothes, the car, and the house that you leave empty all week long in order to afford to live in it?

Many folks wish they could simplify their lives. There is a definite relationship between money and a simpler life. If you don't want to work so hard, don't spend so much money.

Multiply your annual take-home pay by the number of years you have been working. Then look at what you have been able to keep. Are you working for a living or for a life? Whom are you making rich? Maybe everyone else in town.

The next step is to create a cash flow statement, which will show you where your money is going. Use the "Monthly Budget and Expense Sheet" in the Appendix.

Creating a written budget may be time-consuming, boring, even depressing, but it is also necessary!

Look at the "Monthly Budget and Expense Sheet." At the top is a line for net take-home pay. This figure should reflect your monthly income based on a regular work week, not including overtime unless you know you can depend on the extra funds month after month. Gather your current pay stub, prior year's tax return, or employee earnings statement, and use average figures from a normal work week.

If you are paid weekly, multiply your take-home paycheck by the number 52, then divide by the number 12. If you are paid every two weeks, multiply the net take-home by 26, then divide by 12. Both methods will give you your monthly income.

Do not use your *gross* income figure in these calculations—*gross* is not what you have to manage; gross is merely what your employer promised when you interviewed for your job. You don't see gross in your paycheck. You don't manage gross. You manage *net*.

Next, go through each expense category and write down what you spend per month—as realistically as possible. Utilities may vary each month. Average the bills including the highest months, typically winter or summer depending on where you live. By pretending you are spending the same amount per month on certain items, you can pay current bills that may be smaller and have the extra money ready in your checking account when you need to write a bigger check later.

Items such as clothing, entertainment, car maintenance, and house maintenance are harder to predict. When in doubt, estimate higher. A newer car, like a newer home, generally requires less upkeep than an older one. But tires, oil changes, and other incidentals add up each year. Older vehicles also need water pumps, temperature gauges, and radiators.

Include a separate category for Christmas, other gift-giving events, and vacations and add them to your budget. That way, you won't overspend at one time, then take nine months to pay off credit card charges from the previous year.

Though Christmas clubs usually pay an abysmal interest rate, I often recommend them if it is otherwise impossible to save ahead. If all else fails, use the envelope system to "stash the cash" for such special events.

Total all monthly expenses and put that amount at the top of the page after "Monthly Expenses."

Subtract your net expenses from your monthly income. Hopefully, there is more money coming in than going out. I call that "fritter" money. "Fritter" money is unconsciously spent and depletes a great portion of your wealth over time. But you can redirect that amount toward a financial goal and make it a budget item. This is your wealth-building money for savings, college, retirement, your own business, or other future goals. This is one bill you pay to yourself each and every month.

This payment to yourself can create your emergency fund, start a college fund, or add to retirement goals. It is not as important what vehicle (bank savings, credit union, or money market mutual fund account) is utilized, as long as the money is protected from loss and you can get it out at a moment's notice. Just put something away each and every month. As your income increases pay more to your monthly savings or investing plan than to your spending plan.

Occasionally, the difference between what comes in and what goes out is a *negative* number—you are spending more than you make, month-in, month-out. You are "out of financial order." This requires immediate attention and extra effort to reduce expenses as quickly as possible. More borrowing, such as a consolidation loan is *not* the answer. That's why you already have a debt "overload." Chapter 6 will teach you how to reduce credit card debt and increase your savings at the same time.

Plan only with dependable current income. Do not depend on future raises or bonuses. Stay within your budget allowance for each expense category. If possible, try to save 10 percent of net income. The ideal mortgage or rent payment (including property taxes and homeowner's insurance) should cost no more than 22 percent of take-home pay. Consumer debt (including car payments and credit card charges) should stay under 18 percent. Disposable income expenses (food, clothing, utilities, and other costs to keep body and soul together) will likely require 50 percent or more of your income, maybe more if you are raising and educating children at the same time.

Once the cash flow statement has been completed, star any budget category that can be reduced. Insurance premiums—auto, homeowner's, health, and life—can often be reduced by raising deductibles or getting rid of an older car that's not really needed. Some expenses are fixed (mortgage or rent payments, utilities, gasoline, and food), while other areas can be reduced (telephone, clothing, vacations, dining out, entertainment, gifts, and miscellaneous) if every family member cooperates.

Step 3: Develop A Budget That Pays You, Too

What is the first bill you pay each month? If you answered the mortgage or rent, think again. The first bill you pay is to Uncle Sam, who takes your money and redistributes it to others. You can move yourself to the number-one spot if you establish an Individual Retirement Accounts (IRA), a 401(k) plan at work, or a retirement SEP, SIMPLE, profit-sharing, or other type of pension plan.

Most folks pay bills in the following order: the mortgage or rent is usually paid first. Then utility bills, car payments, and food are paid for. Finally, there is a scramble to cover the monthly minimums on credit cards, time payments, and miscellaneous expenses.

Let's try a different approach to budgeting. Make the first bill you pay a bill to yourself. Even if you can't save 10 percent of your net income—the amount I recommend as a target—save *something*. If your emergency fund is low, make *that* your first bill and build it up before directing funds to long-term investing goals. Every household needs a rainy day fund.

The second bill becomes the mortgage or rent. Then, as you prioritize them, all other necessary expenses will be paid. What you have done by paying yourself first is to recover the fritter money that became wasteful spending. Now it works for you.

Paying yourself first is the most underrated way to accumulate wealth over time and is a powerful wealth-building habit.

Step 4: Identify Your Net Worth

Finally, list your assets: short-term and long-term savings, bank Certificates of Deposit (CDs), U.S. savings bonds, stocks, bonds, mutual funds, brokerage accounts, employee retirement plans, other types of securities, real estate, and insurance policies. Use the "What Are You Worth?" worksheet in the Appendix.

Step 5: Commit to Your Plan

It is vital to think out and discuss paying for major expenses. Put your budget up on the refrigerator as a commitment to your wealthy future. It will be a daily reminder of the promises your family has made.

Review your plan at least once a month. Hold an occasional family meeting to praise those who have made an effort to keep the budget in check and to find weak spots on which to improve. Make each member of the family responsible for some part of the plan's success. If your teenager, for example, has reduced the number of telephone calls to a long-distance friend, recognize her sacrifice and offer praise.

Make up your mind to stick to the plan. Improve it over time. If temporary emergencies occur that make the plan impossible to stick to, start budgeting again as soon as possible. (Emergencies do not include getting your hair colored so you can be seen again in public or buying new golf clubs because you are entertaining your boss on the links.)

And next time you see Harry over the backyard fence, drool over his leased BMW and his doubly mortgaged home, wave enthusiastically as he heads out to the mall for another weekend with his friends, Visa, MasterCard, and Amex, and remember how you are building wealth for your future. Harry is compromising *his* financial future for *yours*. What a guy! Spenders sacrifice their financial futures for investors who benefit from the wealth-building forces of capitalism.

You may not be able to control your health, your children, or your job, but you *can* control the outcome of a successful saving, spending, and investing plan.

Now They're Calling It Reengineering

What's a seven-letter word for merger? The answer is *layoffs*. With more companies restructuring, rightsizing, and downsizing, no worker is immune to layoffs, job elimination, or even early retirement pressures. How well you survive receiving a pink slip depends on how well you plan for your future. Follow the following steps to stay fiscally fit, no matter what your company does.

1. **Expect the unexpected.** Don't wait for a warning from your boss to get your financial house in order. Companies often want employees to remain as long as possible before termination notices go out in order to maintain continuity and profitability.

2. **Protect your home.** Avoid home equity lines of credit with demand clauses, borrowing against your 401(k), or refinancing a larger cash-out mortgage. If you lose your job and can't make the monthly payments, you could lose your home.

3. **Prepare for retirement** as if your last day of work is tomorrow. A lean retirement purse is more easily cured than endured.

4. **Build a "sock" fund.** Keep a generous emergency fund to pay the bills if you have to look for a new job. You don't want to depend on taxable distributions from your pension, 401(k), IRA, or other long-term investments. Stash this cash in guaranteed accounts.

5. **Dust off your resume now.** Draft a current resume and beef up your skills while you are still employed. Your company might even be willing to provide free continuing education in your field.

6. **Keep your eyes on your employer.** Most downsized workers could have seen their demise beforehand. Watch for changes in your job description, serious health problems for you or for a family member, budget-cutting trends in your salary range or department, shrinking department size, training of new (and cheaper) personnel, outsourcing production lines or support services, loss of company contracts, and merger rumors. All may be signs of lean times ahead for both your company and you.

7. **Become a lean financial machine immediately.** Defer large purchases unless you can afford them—even if your job disappears.

8. **Know your employee rights.** Request an employee benefit handbook today. You may be able to negotiate a better severance package.

Bankruptcy: A 10-Year Shadow

When debts seem overwhelming, bankruptcy may look like the fastest—or only—way out. But the process, the toll on your self-esteem, and the financial aftermath aren't as painless as you may believe.

Job application discrimination, family conflicts, and the loss of future credit are byproducts of declaring bankruptcy. A lawyer can maneuver the legal process for $500 to $1,000, but you may pay dearly in hidden costs not explained beforehand.

If IRS taxes are your major financial problem, a tax repayment plan usually can be arranged.

If debt is becoming too heavy to handle, stop spending at once. Get to a nonprofit consumer debt counseling service and assess your options. Cut up your credit cards or "put them on ice." Then, write to your credit card companies requesting a cancellation of future charge privileges and to discuss a payback plan.

Make sure you request from your legal advisor a balanced presentation regarding the pros and cons of bankruptcy—before starting the process. There may be options for repayment that you have not considered. Because you are walking away from a debt you voluntarily incurred and leaving your creditors in the dust, the stigma of bankruptcy entirely never goes away.

Bankruptcy is a very serious issue. Get as much information and professional guidance as you can before using this debtor option.

How to Profit From a Recession

1. **Stash the cash.** Keep the balance in your rainy-day emergency fund high. Don't worry about low rates of return. The bigger your financial backup, the more power you will have to choose a new job if you get a pink slip. Put long-term objectives on hold (such as buying a new home or funding a retirement plan) until you have enough savings for three to six months' regular expenses.

2. **Protect your budget.** Don't go window-shopping. You will be tempted to buy. Instead, use it up, wear it out, or do without for a while. Defer all large purchases until next year. Buy what you **need**, not what you **want**. Learn to live **beneath** your financial means.

3. **Protect your home.** Don't upgrade your residence now. Stay where you are—unless you bought too big of a house, cannot afford it, and need to sell quickly. Buy new-to-you durables (used) instead of brand new. This includes cars, computers, and even clothing. Haggle for lower prices and, if you believe the cost is still too high, walk away, asking the store manager or owner to call you when the price goes down. Wait as long as you can before purchasing expensive items.

4. **Keep your credit card under control.** Make a list and check it twice before parting with your money. Losing a job is stressful enough without worrying about how to make mortgage and car payments and feed your family. Prepare for such an emergency and unexpected setback.

5. **Prepare for retirement as if it were here today.** During bad economic times, many older employees are forced to retire because they cannot find new work. Use every method now to bolster your emergency funds or to fund long-term financial objectives. You can divert the funds either to cash or to your long-term investments as your needs dictate.

6. **Don't envy the neighbors.** The bigger the house, the bigger the monthly mortgage payment. The newer the cars, the more likely they are leased or charged for many years. No worker is immune to termination in a bad economy. The more they owe, the harder they may fall. A full cabin is better than an empty castle.

CHAPTER 5

Your Piggy Bank

What are banks for?

To make money.

For the customers?

No, for the banks.

Why doesn't bank advertising mention this?

It would not be in good taste. Now go off and open a bank account.

Wouldn't I do better to go off and open a bank?

Feeding Your Piggy Bank

The Federal Reserve (the Fed) determines what banks charge each other for short-term overnight loans to each other (the federal funds rate). They indirectly influence what banks will pay for borrowing money from the Fed itself (the discount rate), what banks charge their best customers (the prime rate), and what banks must pay to the Federal Deposit Insurance Corporation (FDIC) for a type of insurance in case the bank fails.

Without you, banks have no money to loan. But because they don't remind you how much you are needed, you may be intimidated by the local shrine where they keep the vaults and (supposedly) the large piles of cash.

When the Fed wants to stimulate the economy, it can lower the federal funds rate, demand that banks sell securities to them in exchange for money, and expect that lenders will loan out this extra money at lower rates to bank customers.

But nobody explained this last part to bankers. With bank deposits and interest rates the lowest in nearly 50 years, some credit card interest rates are as high as ever.

Credit card borrowers with a poor credit history, who can't transfer to cards with lower interest rates, may pay even more, though interest rates on mortgage and other loans are among the lowest in nearly 40 years. Knowing that these consumers are trapped in minimum monthly payments, lenders can charge rates as high as their states and usury laws allow.

Piggy Banks Act In Their Own Interest, Not Yours

Why do we believe that lending institutions are our friends? Because they *package their deals to look like gifts*. By advertising a lower mortgage interest rate, then adding points, closing costs, and other fees, customers thinks they have saved money while, in truth, they have likely purchased a larger debt by refinancing their home. Most folks don't pay the extra costs such as points and closing fees with up-front cash. They are added to the new loan amount. If the institution can pitch disability, life insurance contracts on auto loans, and private mortgage insurance (PMI), the institution can sell more products to the same customer. That strategy is called *cross-selling* and it is very profitable for the bank. And to add more to their profits, banks now charge for services that used to be free, such as ATM usage, low-balance accounts, check-cashing, returned checks, and monthly clearing service charges.

I Get No Respect

Rodney Dangerfield made this line famous. There are millions of Rodneys firmly ensconced in passbook savings accounts paying low rates. Customer inertia keeps money in low-yielding accounts.

The primary purpose of bank products should be safety of principal, not yield. Short-term bank deposits can be a foundation for your investment portfolio (like the foundation under your home) to cushion the ups and downs of securities markets. Both Savings and Loan Thrifts and commercial banks can be backed by the FDIC today. Shop for the best short-term products and be sure they are FDIC-insured. Technically, the FDIC is *not* the U.S. Government, but instead, one of its agencies. As a result, it is assumed that Washington, D.C., would step in and refill empty bank coffers should a banking disaster of major proportion occur.

Most bank customers understand basic products such as savings accounts, NOW interest-bearing accounts, and CDs. Avoid brokerage CDs, callable CDs, or CDs offered by bank credit card companies. Brokerage CDs may pay more, but they may have long lock-in periods not disclosed to you at the time of sale. There may also be a huge penalty for early withdrawal. Callable CDs can be terminated early by the institution. So you have no control of how long you can lock in an attractive interest rate. There may be enormous penalties for early withdrawals, as some callable CDs don't mature for 20 years or more.

Confine your banking to your own neighborhood where you may hear information to alert you to an institution's financial troubles. If your CD is from your credit card company bank in Alaska or Texas cow country, you won't hear what's happening to the institution or the local economy and you won't have the opportunity to protect yourself. Time deposit periods vary between bank institutions.

Can You Bank On It?

Are your bank deposits safe? Generally, the FDIC insures deposits up to $100,000 per depositor, per financial institution. (A bank with five branches is one institution, not five.) However, the rules can get tricky with different types of accounts and multiple accounts held at the same institution. Ask for the deposit insurance rules before setting up an account. Don't get greedy by trying to register accounts differently to take advantage of some type of special rate. You could be ruining your estate plan. If a banking industry failure should ever occur, it may take some time to sort out customers' liquidation options. So diversify your savings among several institutions. Even a short-term bank closing could crimp your lifestyle. Stash some emergency cash at home (small bills only) to pay daily bills (food, gasoline, or utilities) until your government makes your bank deposits available.

CD Strategies

During periods of falling interest rates, it may be wise to lock in longer CD maturities. When interest rates are on the rise, however, the opposite strategy may work better. Short-term maturities of 30 days or less allow depositors to reinvest at higher rates when interest rates are climbing. Predicting the direction of interest rates is a losing game, however, even for the experts. You may be able to see a trend—up or down—developing to tip you off whether to lock in your deposits for a longer time (if interest rates look like they are declining) or use shorter time deposits (if interest rates are on the rise), and you don't want to be locked in at a lower rate when you could have higher interest on your money in just a few months.

Today's short-term interest rates are so low and so volatile that I currently recommend CDs maturing one month or sooner along with liquid accounts that have no time lock-ins. Don't tie up your savings in long-term time deposits unless a banking institution allows you an emergency escape hatch *in writing* (such as allowing you to withdraw your IRA CD without penalty because you are older than age 70).

Work In Your Own Interest

Request a brochure for short-term savings products and cost-effective checking options before buying any bank product. Bank personnel may be motivated by commissions, quotas, referral fees, or other rewards for selling certain bank products. Some employees have monthly sales quotas to meet. They are working in their own self-interest. Employees are paid to earn profits for the bank, not to impart customer strategies to beat the bank at its own game. Bank safety and competitive interest rates should be your priority. Convenience, friendliness, or ATM machines are secondary issues.

Beware of high yields that sound too good to be true. An institution may be experiencing temporary solvency problems or soliciting funds for short-term operational expenses. There is little real money in the vault. It has been loaned out to strangers (whose names you do not have) in the hope they can maintain a job long enough to pay it back with interest. You are interested only in guaranteed money.

Be sure to diversify your banking activities. Weigh paying service charges on a "regular" checking account with "free" checking offers that require a minimum balance. You may be able to net more money by paying service charges on one bank product while depositing other funds with a competitor.

Don't put large amounts of savings into the same bank through which you have your mortgage or other loans. Your contract probably states that they can grab that money if they fear you are either an impaired risk or you cannot make your regular monthly loan payments. If a bank should shut its doors, and funds for your monthly mortgage payment comes out of the same bank, how will you make your monthly mortgage payments?

Don't accumulate more funds than necessary in required minimum balance accounts if you can do better elsewhere. Deposit only enough money to get the "free" service or benefit unless the yield is competitive.

Ask how minimum balance accounts and interest rates are calculated to avoid penalties. If your account value dips below a minimum for just one day, you could be charged a low balance fee.

As Safe As Money In the Bank

Don't confuse FDIC-insured *bank money market accounts* with *money market mutual funds* sold by the bank but *not* FDIC-insured. Money market mutual fund pros and cons for short-term funds are discussed in Chapter 17.

Not all CDs are backed by the FDIC. Private corporations can create debentures (IOUs) or "certificates" backed only by the bank's assets. Promissory notes can also be sold as "safe." A higher-advertised yield is not necessarily smarter banking. Ask if your CD will be insured by the FDIC. Get the answer in writing. Look for an FDIC insurance sign on the institution's exterior doors or near the teller's window. *Don't assume that all products sold inside the building or by the company will be FDIC-insured against loss of investment principal.*

Bank IRAs and Rollovers

Short-term funds should guarantee your *principal*. Long-term money should guarantee your *purchasing power*. IRAs are long-term money that must outpace inflation. Bank CDs sold as IRAs lose the race against inflation over time. IRAs represent long-term money, and their primary goal should be conservation of purchasing power—to match or beat the damaging effect of inflation on your money.

Lenders spread the news about the benefits of IRA accounts, but they seldom tell customers about inflation-fighting mutual funds. IRA accounts must protect future purchasing power. At the next deposit maturity, consider transferring your funds to conservative mutual funds so the tax-deferred benefits of an IRA account can work even harder.

Collateralizing a CD for a Loan

Suppose you want to pay cash for a used car and you stop by your lender to withdraw your $10,000 CD. Your lender may discuss another option with you. If you take out your CD, he advises, you will lose the future interest (say, at 5 percent) that you could make on that investment. If, instead, you keep your CD intact and use it as loan collateral, you could borrow $10,000 for the car at 8 percent—only 3 percent higher than your CD is paying, he continues. An 8-percent car loan minus the 5-percent interest from your CD is like borrowing at 3 percent, almost stealing from your lender. Really? Let's examine what's going on here.

The formula for compounding the annual effective yield on your CD is probably quarterly, while the interest on a simple loan at 8 percent is compounded monthly. The difference between the interest on the CD and the interest you pay on the loan will be larger than what the simple interest sales pitch implies.

You are borrowing at 8 percent, not 3 percent. This sales technique is called *anchoring*—fooling you into thinking that the loan is less expensive. Your best option is to pay cash for the car, even though you will lose the interest on your CD. You would lose even more money in the end if you financed the car at a higher rate than your bank CD is paying. A collateralized CD is hostaged anyway, until full payment of the loan has been made. So you don't have access to your CD money until the loan balance is paid off.

The lender keeps your deposit on site, talks you into an additional loan, and has protective custody over your CD for a longer period of time.

If you pay cash for the car, then start directing the same monthly payments you would have sent to the lender into your own account, you will be richer at the end of the proposed loan period.

How Can I Charge You?

Let us count the ways: home mortgage loans, home equity loans, auto loans, credit cards, credit card transfer balances, return check charges, low-balance account fees, ATM fees, brokerage fees and commissions, and monthly service fees.

If your bank charges fees for services you believe should be free, complain to management. If your complaint falls on deaf ears, move your business to a cheaper institution. Good financial consumers shop for money carefully.

This Little Piggy Now Has Roast Beef

Some banks have entered the insurance and investment business with insurance annuities and other CD-like investments. The operable phrase here is "CD-like." *No CD-like investment is backed by the FDIC. This is marketing hype.*

Watch out for a sales pitch similar to this one:

> *"We are _____, and although we're not really the bank, we are very closely associated with the bank, and even may be owned by the bank. We would like to show you our CD alternative we sell here in the bank building. It is not insured by the FDIC, but we have researched it and feel that this company is very* safe *for your money, or we certainly wouldn't be showing it to you.*
>
> *"It has a* much higher return *than our bank CDs can offer—and look at all this* tax-free *income you'll accumulate every year until you take it out! And if you never take it out, the money will keep compounding* tax-free *until it goes to your heirs,* probate-free.
>
> "You certainly qualify for tax relief plus the higher interest rate.
>
> *"We don't want to push you into anything. We especially don't want to restrict you to the bank's* low *yielding, taxable* CDs."

Most customers are going to remember three things from this sales pitch: *safe, high yield,* and *tax free.*

Investments sold on bank premises that are not bank products are not backed by the bank or by the FDIC, even if they mention words such as "safe" and "guaranteed." *No mutual fund, insurance annuity, bond, or stock is FDIC-insured.*

Just because a product is sold on bank property, by a bank employee sitting on bank furniture, and sold on forms provided by the bank—even managed by a company that may be a bank subsidiary, with the bank getting part of the product commission—doesn't mean that this sale has to be bank business. (How could you make that kind of mistake?)

The Investment Expert

Your banker wants to manage your money. Banks have acquired mutual funds and brokerage houses. They want management fees, too. Some may market managed accounts, while others pitch their own brand of mutual funds, insurance annuities, and individual securities.

The credentials of the salesperson may be limited to a sales license (vice president means little), relying on the credibility of the institution to bring in customers. Some may let you believe that because their products are sold on bank property, your investment principal is safe. Separate your banking and investment needs. Even if they know more than you will after you finish reading this book, they are simply selling investment products, not advising you in your best interest.

Diversify your savings into several banking institutions, and remember to stash a little "green" at home, just in case.

CHAPTER 6

The Credit Card:
Friend or Foe?

"When a dog has a bone he don't go out and make the first payment on anything. First payments is what made us think we were prosperous, and the other 19 is what showed us we were broke."

—Will Rogers

Imagine for a moment that you could purchase only one item at a time on credit. You could charge nothing else until you had finished paying off your credit balance. What would you purchase first?

If your answer was your home, how would you get to work every day? If you said your car, how would you have purchased it? Would you give up your home in place of the car? What about holiday presents or other gifts, clothes, college tuitions, vacations, pools, furniture, appliances, hospital and doctor bills? Is it difficult to imagine your lifestyle without credit? Is it impossible to imagine a reasonable life without it?

Credit is so convenient. Buy now, pay later. Have it delivered today. You earned it. You owe it to yourself. Why wait? No payments for a full year! Zero-percent financing for a whole year! Buy a lot now, pay just a little...for a lot longer. Live life to the fullest. You could be gone tomorrow.

Credit cards, in a nutshell, are a company's permission to you to buy something you really don't need right now at a price you really can't afford right now with money you don't have right now. A credit card can be a valuable convenience, but it can also become a dangerous financial nightmare if it makes you feel richer than you really are and encourages you to spend beyond your current income.

What Do You Really Owe?

Many consumers don't know the total debt they owe and are not anxious to find out. They are encouraged to deal in monthly payments instead of considering the total price at the time of purchase.

The more debt you buy (you are buying money at a price per dollar per month), the more wealth you are transferring, and the more adversely this loss of money will affect your future goals. Debt encourages impulse buying and overspending. Debt lowers your future standard of living. Debt avoids facing realistic lifestyle decisions. Debt places the power of compound interest at work against you.

The installment payments for your family, excluding mortgage payments but including car payments, credit card loans, time loans and student debt, should total no more than 18 percent of your take-home pay. How do you measure up to that figure?

Use the "Credit Card Management Strategy" in the Appendix to make a list of all of your credit cards and monthly installment loans or obligations. Include appliance contracts, cars, and anything else you have bought on installment payments, excluding home equity loans. Fill out all of the columns, then compare each card with the others to see which one offers the best terms.

But I'm Paying Every Month!

If your consumer debt level consumes more than 18 percent of your take-home pay, you must trim it immediately. Paying minimum monthly payments endears you to the card companies because many cards are designed never to be paid off as long as you continue to use them. In fact, some companies' monthly minimum required payments are less than the interest due for that month.

Assume the minimum payment this month is $20. If you examine the interest column, you may discover that this month's interest is $25. If you pay only the minimum, there will be an extra $5 of interest left unpaid. This $5 will be added to next month's balance, which will charge you interest on the loan balance and on the unpaid $5.

Card Games With a Fixed Deck

The annual percentage rate (APR) on your credit card statement is derived by multiplying the monthly interest rate by 12 (months in a year). For example, if the monthly interest rate is 1.5 percent, the annual percentage rate is 18 percent.

But this is simple interest, faulty arithmetic. If you carry a balance on a card for an entire year, you will pay more than 19 percent for the use of borrowed money. Here's how: Each month, after crediting your payment, the company charges 1.5 percent on the remaining balance. The following month another 1.5 percent is charged on the remaining balance. At the end of the first year, because of the effects of monthly compounding, you really paid 19.561 percent, not 18 percent simple interest. Compound interest, in this case, works against you.

Hey, Our Card Is Free!

Beware of an offer for a free lunch. A company that charges no annual fee may have a higher interest rate. Other companies advertise no annual fee for six months or a year, then tack one onto your monthly balance when the initial period is finished. Review the fine print that comes with your monthly statement.

Zero-Percent Financing and No Payments For Six Full Months!

A company that advertises a low initial interest rate is probably planning to raise that rate in a few months. It is banking on the fact that it may be several months (if ever) before you figure out you are paying higher interest rates.

Some low-interest credit cards charge from the point of sale (from the moment you purchase your item) and have no grace period whatsoever. By the time you receive your bill at month's end, you already owe interest. Avoid these cards because this money will never be free.

Most credit cards charge on a variable interest scale, even if they promise a fixed interest rate at first. If interest rates in the economy spike, the credit card interest rate rises fast. If interest rates drop, it takes substantially longer (sometimes never) for the lender to drop its interest rate.

The interest charged on a cash advance generally starts ticking from the moment you receive the money, not from your closing statement date or the date you receive your monthly statement.

My, What Large Fees You Have!

Watch for these new fees designed to separate you from more of your money:

1. Monthly instead of annual maintenance fees.
2. A reduced grace period and strict enforcement of payment due dates.
3. Higher annual fees; higher penalty fees for late payments.
4. Fees for paying less than the minimum monthly payment.
5. Higher interest rates (from 2 to 10 percent more) as a penalty for late payments.

6. Termination of your account resulting from infrequent use.

7. Increased penalties for over-the-limit purchases until your balance falls under the maximum credit limit.

8. Transaction, cash advance, or transfer fees on convenience checks.

9. Balance transfer restrictions on number of transfers or the amounts allowed.

10. Rising interest rates on variable-rate cards.

11. No grace period before your payment is due.

12. Vanishing bargains and changing terms when credit card companies are sold.

13. Penalty fees for transferring balances greater than your maximum credit limit.

14. Double-cycle billing where the issuer calculates interest retroactively on the previous month's balance before applying your current payment.

15. A two-cycle average daily balance billing method that adds the previous two billing cycles' averages together before assessing interest for the current month.

16. Higher interest rates on cash advances or balance transfers than regular purchases; cash advance fees.

17. Miscellaneous costs on balance transfers from other issuers.

18. User fees for previously free services.

19. Promotions that cost money but are marketed as spending awards.

20. Fewer "freebies" designed to lure you away from the competition.

Tucked in among the bills may be a replacement credit card from a gasoline company or local department store, or so it appears. You pocket the card and when you use it, you get more than you bargained for: a full-service Visa or MasterCard. Or perhaps you receive what you believe is an annual updated credit card replacement. However, the new, upgraded card comes with a brand new set of rules. *Read them.*

Just say no to the "free from monthly payment" ploy. At Christmas, when you are pressed to find money for presents, it is easy to rely on using credit cards. But in the long run, it can become more difficult to pay your normal monthly payments. Just in the (Saint) nick of time, the credit card company comes to your rescue and offers to defer your monthly payment until next year. It, too, has a big heart.

The credit card company didn't stop computing interest during that time. They just held off sending you the unfriendly bill. Your following month's bill comes with a larger interest payment stuck to it.

Here's another ploy. When your credit limit is raised, you might feel like they gave you an A+ on a test. You are proud to be a valued customer, and you may experience a sense of pride (and greater wealth). Out you go to shop! This sales technique, coupled with a large spending habit, can increase your debt. If you can't afford to pay off now what you owe, why are you adding even more debt?

Credit card companies solicit insurance, securities, CDs, and other financial products through their monthly statements. Never buy financial products from a credit card offer. You have no way to check the quality of what you're buying. Calling the toll-free number they provide isn't going to help.

Before shopping for a lower interest rate card, call your current issuer and request a reduction in the monthly interest rate. While you're on the phone, ask them to waive the annual fee. Tell the issuer that you would like to stay but that you will not pay more than the going industry rate. Then, compare their new, reduced rate with other low-interest cards on today's market. This industry is competitive, and a new lender may waive some charges to get your business.

Before transferring debt from one card to another, ask about extra charges or fees levied on the new balance. "Checks" that card companies send are loans with instant cash advance interest rates.

Don't collect credit cards. Each open line of credit is shown on your credit report. If you look like you could, at any moment, charge enough to retire in style, you may tarnish your chances for a more important loan that you may seek. When switching credit companies, close out your old account and request they report its termination to their reporting agencies. That way, it won't count as open available credit on your record.

The $15 Phone Call

Credit card companies will happily sell you credit card loss protection against theft for $15 to $59 per year. The company (after notice from you) will contact every company with which you do business so you will not be liable for any fraudulent use. How does it know where you shop and how many cards you own? You would have sent a list for its files.

This product is unnecessary. You are generally liable for up to $50 of unauthorized purchases made on most credit cards, even if you *never* notify the issuer. (Debit cards do not share this automatic protection.) Maintain your own list of credit cards and emergency phone numbers. If your wallet or purse is stolen, call the companies yourself (they all have toll-free telephone numbers). Save the $15 for your own pleasure. Organize your credit card information with the "Credit Card Register" worksheet in the Appendix.

Out of Financial Order

The following credit card debt danger signals must be addressed immediately:

1. You don't know how much credit card debt you owe and are afraid to add it up.

2. You juggle the monthly budget to keep up with incoming bills.

3. You have reached maximum credit limits on your credit cards.

4. You are frequently late paying some or all of your monthly bills.

5. You have borrowed more money to pay for an overdue debt.

6. You are considering consolidating debt.

7. You are applying for additional credit cards to increase your borrowing power.

8. You have little or no emergency money.

9. You are drawing from savings to pay regular bills.

10. Creditors are sending overdue notices.

11. You postdate checks so they won't bounce.

12. You hurry to the bank on payday to cover potential overdrafts.

If any of these symptoms describe your present debt picture, you are a prime candidate for the following prescription:

Pay down your consumer debt slowly but surely. Target the card with the highest interest rate first and pay only the minimums on the remaining cards. The size of the balance due does not matter as much as the cost for each dollar of borrowed money (the interest rate). Use the "Credit Card Management Strategy" worksheet in the Appendix.

Total up your budget and subtract all monthly take-home income excluding overtime and bonuses unless you *know* those dollars will be dependable. The remaining funds are "fritter money," leftover dollars slipping through your fingers. Recapture their value by dividing those extra dollars in half and putting one-half into a savings vehicle and the other half directly toward the card with the highest interest rate.

When you have paid off the credit card with the highest annual percentage rate, tackle the next highest card and continue to pay only monthly minimums on the remaining cards. Remember to keep saving the other one-half as directed above. Defer *all* major purchases until your consumer debt is under control.

Number Games You Can Win

How many credit cards should you have? Two major credit cards are usually sufficient. If you own a business, the business should have its own set of credit cards so you can keep business and personal expenses separate. The more debt you have, the fewer cards you should own because buying on credit can become obsessive.

Borrowing Money: Know the Risks

Loans are often too easy to obtain and too hard to pay back. Before you borrow money, you need to fully understand the risks.

1. **Retirement plan loans.** You can often borrow money from your 401(k) or employer savings account. The interest rate may be reasonable, and you may be told you are paying the interest back to yourself through payroll deductions. But if you borrow, you will have to repay the principal and interest with *after-tax money*. If you are terminated, most companies expect the outstanding amount of the loan to be repaid immediately. And by robbing Peter to pay Paul, you are spending investing dollars and spoiling the long-term magic of compound interest, which your money needs to grow for your future.

2. **Home loans.** You can deduct home mortgage and home equity loan interest (within limits) if you itemize your tax deductions, but you have to give up the standard deduction when you itemize. So, you trade one kind of deduction for another. Worse, this type of debt is secured by your home, meaning that you could lose your house if you default on the loan. Many home equity loan agreements contain demand clauses so that the lender can demand the full amount of the loan anytime they feel you are an impaired risk, even if you are paying the monthly payments on time.

3. **Credit cards.** What could be easier than pulling out the plastic? Charging more when you are already carrying a balance on your credit cards is dangerous to your future wealth.

4. **Tax loans.** During tax season, to tide yourself over until your federal tax refund check is in the mail, you may be solicited to take out a short-term loan. Refund anticipation loans (RAL) can bite hard. They can carry outrageous interest rates and fees. For example, you could end up paying up to $200 extra for a $500 refund loan payment. Avoid these at all costs.

Identity Theft: It Could Happen to You

Years ago when someone picked your pocket, he took the cash and threw the wallet in the trash. Today, things are much different. Thieves look not only to steal your cash and credit cards, but your identity as well.

Don't...

- give out your Social Security number as identification; offer a driver's license instead.
- print more than your name and address on your checks.
- give personal information over the phone to a stranger.
- throw away old checking or deposit bank slips without shredding them first.
- leave outgoing mail unsecured.

Do...

- tear up pre-approved offers that come in the mail.
- shred or burn all paper trash.
- call your credit card company if your bill is late.
- call to see why different information, such as a wrong address, appeared on a new card.
- get an annual credit report to see who may be using your credit.
- keep your wallet thin to avoid too much information being stolen in the event of a theft.
- review your bills as soon as they arrive.

Whose Big Brother Is Watching?

Every year, thousands of upstanding, financially fit consumers are turned down for credit or whose credit is otherwise damaged by incorrect, misleading, and downright erroneous credit data. Have you checked your credit score lately? Because credit, lending, and other financial institutions may know more about your personal financial affairs than you do, it is vital to schedule an annual credit checkup to correct inaccurate information hazardous to your financial health.

What is a credit score and why is it important? A credit score is a number calculated by a credit bureau, lender, or other company and is intended for use by lenders in making a decision on a loan application or other product or service. For example, many lenders use a system developed by Fair Isaac and Company called the *FICO* score. Think of credit scoring as a point system based on your credit history, designed to help predict how likely you are to repay a loan or to make payments on time. Everyone with a credit record has a credit score.

The Fair Credit Reporting Act provides consumers with some protection regarding the information contained in their credit bureau files. The Act is intended to ensure consumer credit rights and guard against errors made by credit grantors and credit bureaus.

You can request your credit rating for a nominal fee. Each year, you can and should request a current printout of your credit history. If you find errors or omissions, contact the agency in writing, request proper adjustments, then request a copy of the new corrected report. The most popular credit reporting agencies are Experian, TransUnion Credit Information, and Equifax. Check your telephone directory for local listings.

If you are plagued by a poor credit history, you can include in your file a 100-word statement to tell potential lenders your side of the financial story.

The most effective remedy for poor credit is to tighten your financial belt and pay off what you owe. *Late* payments are more favorable than *no* payments. Then, charge small items on a regular basis, and pay them off *fully* and *on time* each month. Your new credit history of disciplined spending will, in time, offset your earlier one.

Debit Cards: Who Needs Them?

Bankers are ingenious in persuading customers to adopt new products. You can use the debit card a lot like a credit card except the money is automatically deducted from your checking account within a day or two. This method reduces the number of checks people write, saves banks a bundle in processing expenses, and gets the money to the vendor faster.

Debit cards don't have much to offer consumers unless your money management skills are lousy. Your credit card is accepted most anywhere debit cards are, and you get free use of the bank's money for up to 30 days. What's more, debit cards don't carry all the protections (or reward benefits) credit cards offer, such as the ability to charge back a transaction that is unsatisfactory.

A Credit Card Checklist

Shop for the lowest-cost dollars. Brand name credit cards such as Visa or MasterCard come with individual agreements, and the terms can vary a great deal. Comparison shop. Here are some questions to answer before you sign up:

1. What is the annual fee? When can it increase and by how much?
2. What is the annual percentage rate charged for purchases? For cash advances? For balance transfers from another credit card? Is the rate fixed or variable?
3. How is monthly interest calculated? How long will it remain fixed at that rate?
4. What is the grace period on purchases before interest is charged?
5. How much are the late-payment fees?
6. Are there transaction fees for balance transfers from other credit cards or cash advances? How much?
7. Is the minimum monthly payment lower than last month's interest charge?
8. When does interest start for a cash advance?
9. Is there a separate charge for each cash advance?
10. Is there a charge amount limit?
11. What is the penalty for over-the-limit purchases?
12. Have you read all of the fine print?
13. Did you understand every word you read?
14. Have you made a copy of your signed application for your records?
15. Can you afford another credit card now?
16. Will you save interest (not just lower your payments) by transferring existing debt to a new credit card?

17. Does your budget allow for this new expense?

18. How much credit do you need?

19. What credit limit can you afford?

20. How will this new financial obligation affect your existing loans?

21. Will this card encourage you to spend more than you can afford to pay back?

22. Do you realize this represents an emergency and convenience option and not a method of living above your means?

23. When was the last time you checked your credit record?

When you cancel a credit card, be sure it's listed as closed on your credit report. Otherwise your ability to borrow later may be reduced. Ask for written verification that the cancellation has been processed. A month later, ask for your credit report again. If the report still shows the account is open, inform the credit bureau and send a copy of the verification letter. By law, credit bureaus must correct disputed information within 30 days.

Once plain vanilla, credit cards now come in flavors. You can get credit cards that earn free airline tickets or rebates toward cars or trucks; refund cash back at the end of the year; deposit money into an insurance annuity; put money in a college savings plan for your child; gain coupons toward toys, shoes, or other retail items; and even pay for tax-return preparation.

Consumers are biting. They charge groceries, fast-food lunches, dry cleaning, and movies. Be sure the deals are better than you can negotiate for yourself. Airline credit cards, for instance, may require you to use points within a certain period of time. Some deals can change before you can earn enough points to qualify.

Be sure you will use the product (reward) you are trying to earn. Airlines often have price wars, so you may find a cheaper price elsewhere—without the credit card deal.

Debt Consolidation: Is It a Con?

Are you receiving letters from friendly credit card companies or finance corporations offering you the chance to trade those higher credit card balances for smaller monthly payments? The first three letters in "consolidation" are "c-o-n," and most offers to refinance debt to reduce your monthly payments should be ignored. Finance companies can charge horrendous interest rates. They reduce the size of your monthly payment amount by lengthening your payoff time.

It's not the size of your monthly payment that matters. It's the price per dollar of borrowed money. Eight-percent loans are cheaper than 10-percent debt, even though the latter may offer a cheaper monthly payment if the loan is stretched out over a longer period of time. Debt consolidation helps *only* if the new compounded annual interest rate is lower than what you are currently paying—and will remain lower in the foreseeable future. Some loans or cards offer an initial introductory rate that will be increased over time. As general interest rates rise, so do the loan company's interest rates.

It is easy to determine whether you will benefit from refinancing your consumer debt. If the annual percentage rate is less than what you now pay, you have found a lower cost for borrowed money, especially if it is offered at a fixed rate. Look for lower interest rates, not lower payments.

Credit Card Smarts

A credit card can be a valuable tool, like a hammer to a carpenter. With it you can do such things as rent a car or show dependability for future car and home purchases. Keep it handy for convenience and emergency use. But don't start buying everything in sight with tomorrow's income that has not yet been earned.

Credit isn't a birthright. It's a privilege to protect. Savvy customers learn to use borrowed money, paying off their balances in full before the end of the monthly grace period. Every credit card in America should have the following label printed on it: "Warning! Overuse can be hazardous to your wealth!" Learn to use the privilege and you're off to protecting your wealth.

CHAPTER 7

Insurance:
Cover Your Ass-ets

You wouldn't buy a typewriter with half the keys missing or a set of "pre-punctured" tires, would you? But many people pay exorbitant insurance premiums while not protecting themselves from dangerous perils. You can pay a lot for premiums, yet not be properly insured.

You cannot rely on what an insurance agent tells you. The words in your contract—not the promises made during a conversation over your kitchen table with a commission looming in the air—are what you have bought. It's not what they say, but what you sign, that matters. There are no fair or friendly insurance contracts.

Where Does It Hurt?

Insure yourself first against those losses from which you could not recover—death, catastrophic medical costs, permanent physical disability, and danger from the other guy (liability). How easily could you recover from a $1-million personal-injury lawsuit against you, your assets, and your future earnings?

Next, protect yourself against those losses that would cause substantial economic harm to your financial future. For example, a total loss of your dwelling and vehicle would adversely affect your financial life.

Finally, the areas you should insure yourself against, before the insurance payoff kicks in, are the small, but pesky, claims. For example the repair of a scratch or fender-bender of your vehicle is not catastrophic (unless the car is a Lamborghini).

Everybody Sues Somebody Sometime

My clients frequently ask how much liability insurance coverage is enough. I first must know what kind of accident they are planning to protect themselves against. The more wealth you have, the more the "deep pockets" theory applies. You should prepare to handle a claim against you for more rather than less. What is the monetary worth of an arm, a leg, or an eye? The answer: Whatever the lawyer in the courtroom can convince a jury it's worth. The loss of material goods is a subordinate risk to liability exposure.

Liability insurance protects you if you are held responsible for another party's loss or injuries. An umbrella policy of $1 million above and beyond your regular underlying auto and homeowner insurance policies may not be enough. Attorney fees and medical bills can add up quickly. Your liability risk increases if you own a pool, a pond, or a recreational lake, swings or other playground equipment that will attract neighborhood children; a boat that guests will enjoy on a lake or that you will trailer from place to place; an old shed or dilapidated barn; an old car; or a decaying tree. Insurers rate these items as attractive nuisances that, if guests (invited or not) are injured, could generate negligence lawsuits against an owner. A pet dog, cat, or horse could unintentionally cause damage to a stranger who might sue for injuries or other damages. Vacant land in another location or a vacation home or cabin are viewed as riskier than your primary residence because the owner does not live on the premises.

Personal liability coverage is generally limited to individual ownership, not business pursuits or rental activities. Don't expect your basic homeowner policy to cover a home occupation, special business, or rental property. If you own a building or storage facilities that you rent out, or real estate investment property, you may need special coverage.

Always report losses as soon as possible, whether you intend to collect from your insurance or not. If a claim or lawsuit is later filed against you and you have not reported the event, your company need not defend you.

An umbrella policy should be considered for the following:

1. Homeowner liability.
2. Auto liability.
3. Auto uninsured/underinsured liability (in case an uninsured/underinsured driver's actions cause you to be sued).

The parts of each of the three umbrella coverages should complement your underlying homeowner policy by insuring the next higher dollar of liability above your regular insurance contract, and auto liability and auto uninsured/underinsured riders and can be added above your basic auto coverages for a relatively small annual premium. *Never risk a lot for a little.*

Health Insurance

Health insurance is changing rapidly. Follow the same rules that are outlined earlier in this chapter. The main elements of any policy are:

- The maximum lifetime payment (how much in your lifetime the company will pay regardless of how high your medical bills climb).
- The co-insurance provision (the percentage of the bill you pay).
- The stop-loss limit (the amount at which the company starts paying 100 percent of all eligible covered expenses).
- The definition of eligible covered expenses.
- A listing of what drugs and procedures are excluded from coverage.
- The annual deductible amount.

There is no inexpensive quality healthcare available in this country. Costs will continue to skyrocket. Plan on having an extra $100,000 to $200,000 in your retirement nest egg to pay for out-of-pocket items that insurance refuses to pay for (such as a drug-coated stent that currently costs $3,500).

Don't automatically opt for the less expensive premium before analyzing the treatment benefits and choice of doctors. You may want to pay higher premiums to maintain the ability to choose your doctors and to have fewer procedures on the "rejected" list. Don't scrimp on your health plan. No matter what the advertisements claim when soliciting new customers, *the bottom line in healthcare is its bottom line*.

Do You Have a Record?

Whenever you apply for individual life, health, or disability insurance, a brief summary of the medical information you agree to provide to the insurer can be sent to the Medical Information Bureau. This coded record indicates key risk factors such as health-related conditions and hazardous sports activities that other insurance companies can access, review, and confirm.

You can access your records by making a written request to the Medical Information Bureau and authorizing it to release to you all medical information contained in its files. Contact: Medical Information Bureau, P.O. Box 105, Essex Station, Boston, Massachusetts 02112. If you discover inaccurate data, contact the Bureau immediately.

Disability Income Protection

The loss of future income is the most commonly overlooked risk. If you fell off your roof next weekend, who would work for you and bring home the family paycheck? If you were seriously injured in an auto accident tonight, who would feed your family until you went back to work? If you never worked again, how would you support yourself and your family?

Disability coverage is divided into two major categories: short-term (three or six months from the time the policy's benefits start) and long-term (from six months on). Companies tend to offer better short-term disability packages because they are less costly to the employer. Especially if you are young, you need a secure, long-term disability program. But if the disability definitions and contract restrictions are significant, you could pay good money for few benefits.

There are many definitions of "total disability":

1. Your inability to perform *one or more* of the primary duties of your present occupation, called "primary occupation."
2. Your inability to perform *all of the duties* of your regular occupation, called "own occupation."
3. Your inability to perform *all of the duties of any occupation* for which you are suited by reason of training, education, or experience, called "any occupation."
4. Your inability to perform *any gainful employment* (including broom-pushing, envelope-stuffing, and dog-walking).

Check to be sure you will actually qualify for benefits under the terms of the contract before you buy.

Accidental Death Insurance

An accidental death and dismemberment policy pays a lump sum in the case of your death from an accident. Most policies pay off only as a direct and independent result of an accidental injury, excluding any medical complications or sickness. By the time you get to the emergency room and expire, you likely would have died of natural causes. Claim denied! *These are rarely worth the money spent.*

Long-Term Care: Guarantees or Nursing Home Hype?

The fear of losing all your assets to pay off a nursing home bill or becoming impoverished with no one to care for you in your golden years is real. The insurance industry's solution to this crisis may not be as "guaranteed" as they would like you to think. Nursing home costs are not so easily insured. Insurance companies aren't stupid. They know that long-term care insurance attracts higher-risk older customers, often predisposed to acute or chronic medical conditions that may last for many years. Restrictive contract language could allow companies to reject claims in the future. The insertion of the words "and" or "or" can mean the difference between coverage or denial of a claim. It is certain that premiums on existing policies will increase over time.

Your most likely scenario will be to remain at home for as long as possible, where the bulk of the home healthcare benefits qualifications become murkier in today's insurance contracts.

If you decide to purchase a nursing home policy, consider forgoing a short elimination period (the length of time before the policy benefits kick in) for a larger daily amount of coverage. Increasing some benefits may subtract coverage from more critical areas in another part of the contract.

Is the Policy Non-Cancelable and Guaranteed Renewable?

The younger you are, the cheaper the current premiums because the company has longer to invest your money for their benefit until they are expected to pay out. But you will pay longer and, in the meantime, the company is working your money. Long-term insurance contracts carry lots of caveats.

Compare policies from several companies. Request a boilerplate contract so you can read it over carefully to see exactly what you're buying. If you decide to return the policy within the free examination period, mail it return receipt to the company, not to the agent's office.

Life, or Death, Insurance?

I prefer to call this coverage "death" insurance because of what it does. Who needs it? Your dependent beneficiaries. Don't have any? Maybe it's time to dump your policies. The most common reasons to need a policy are to provide a dependable income for your family, to pay off debts, to protect a business from insolvency, and to pay funeral expenses, a mortgage, and other postmortem expenses. Everyone gets solicited for life insurance, regardless of real need.

When you are young, a serious concern is your mortality, *dying too soon*, leaving a family and spouse behind with little economic means of support. At retirement, however, your concern becomes *living too long*. Your need for death insurance at that age should be minimal, if any. However, if you feel that you have so few assets to cover your early demise and you would be buried in a wooden box without a marker, a small term insurance policy or your basic group insurance at work should be sufficient.

The Good, the Bad and the Much Too Expensive

Which is better—*cash value* life insurance or *term* death insurance?

Cash value insurance (otherwise known as whole life, ordinary life, paid-up life, single-premium life, limited-pay life, single-pay life, universal life, flexible-premium adjustable-benefit life, variable life, and variable-universal life) generates higher commissions to insurance agents and costs the buyer more than term insurance. That, in itself, should make these policies suspect.

Your first question should be: How much death insurance do I need? The second question: How much do I want to pay?

There are basic necessities such as food, clothing, shelter, utilities, a college education, and the retirement you and your spouse look forward to, as well as paying off a large home mortgage balance. If you are cut out of the picture, where will the money come from? Eight to 10 times your annual salary is a guesstimate of how much you will need.

Most young families need death-insurance protection of $500,000 or more per breadwinner to provide sufficient income while their children are young. Even if the more expensive alternative, cash-value insurance, was within grasp, a young couple could not afford to properly insure their earnings liability. Term insurance is the only affordable and sensible option.

What Is Term Insurance?

Term insurance isn't designed to make you rich while you are living or provide you with any retirement benefits. You get nothing back while you are living. Just like your homeowner and auto insurance, if you don't have a loss, you don't receive benefits.

When you purchase death insurance, you are protecting your family or other dependents against the loss of your earning power, which pays the bills each month. You buy insurance because you don't have the money on hand to support your family properly. You are a money-making machine for your family during those years when the investment portfolio is lean and your paycheck is vital.

As you grow older, your dependent liabilities decrease and your need for living expenses increases. *Buying cheaper term insurance and investing the difference* can help self-insure your loss of income in the immediate future and, at the same time, develop wealth for your old age.

You can't invest efficiently and die cheaply at the same time when you buy a cash-value insurance contract. When you buy cash-value insurance, you are purchasing both a death benefit and an internal savings or investment account called the cash surrender value in the same contract. But in the end, you only get to choose one: If you die, the company retrieves your savings back to them because the cash-surrender value really belongs to the insurance company for the length of your insurance contract. If you take the cash, your death benefit and the insurance policy expires. Paying for two things and getting only one benefit or the other, is a rip-off. The longer you hold a cash-value insurance contract, the more you are self-insuring yourself over time.

Term insurance is criticized because it gets more expensive as you get older, to the point where you can't afford the coverage. But as you get older, you should have fewer liabilities to protect, so you should be decreasing your insurance to match those liabilities and using the difference in premiums to invest. As you decrease your amount of coverage, you can reduce the premiums in order to make the term insurance remain affordable. When you become age 65, would you rather have a $100,000-insurance policy sitting in your lockbox or $100,000 in an investment? Keep in mind when answering that you have to die to get to the $100,000-death benefit!

Term insurance isn't encouraged by the insurance industry on the whole. Most agents don't want to sell it to you because term insurance pays out smaller commissions.

We're Here To Help You Save

The sales pitch that states that if the insurance company doesn't force you to save, you probably wouldn't save anything may be valid. Cash-value policies become a type of forced savings for some Americans. So when you buy term insurance, invest the rest. Use the strategies in this book to make the remainder of your money work as hard as you do for your financial future.

Why the Stuff at Work Is Cheap

Group insurance purchased at work may appear less expensive, but you never get a real policy or guaranteed contract to depend on if you lose your job or if the benefit is later cut by your company. The benefits are temporary and should not be confused with or used as a substitute for a personal insurance contract that can't be terminated—so long as you maintain the premiums.

Group insurance companies can walk away from their customers at any time even if you keep your job because there is no long-term contract between your employer and the insurance company. The insurance company or your company could become insolvent, you could be terminated, or you could terminate your present job and lose the coverage. The price for your group coverage is not guaranteed and will increase as your work force grows older. Finally, if your company should decide to terminate this worker benefit, the coverage is gone. If you are uninsurable at any of these times, your family will suffer if you later die. But group conversions to individual policies are generally only allowed when converting to expensive cash-value policies, which severely limits the death protection you can buy, dollar for dollar.

Term insurance is cheap, even when purchased outside the workplace. If you are not insurable, however, group coverage may be important because it generally requires no medical underwriting.

Good and Bad Terms

There are three basic kinds of term insurance:

1. Annual renewable or yearly increasing premium term.
2. Level term.
3. Decreasing term (sometimes called credit life or mortgage insurance).

Annual Renewable Term Insurance

Annual renewable term insurance has a constant death benefit, but the annual premium increases each and every year. You are charged for one year's mortality at a time. If your insurance coverage need is longer-term, its cost will eventually outpace a family budget, especially once you hit age 40. It is, therefore, most appropriate for a short period, such as two or three years. Taking out a large *short-term* loan for a business or other purpose? This type of term insurance is the most cost-effective way to repay a short-term loan in case of your death.

Level Premium Term Insurance

Level premium term insurance has a stated unchanging benefit at a level premium for a stated period of time. This is most appropriate for folks who need death protection for longer periods, such as when raising a family. It can be purchased for five, 10, 15, 20, or even 30 years of guaranteed premium without an increase in cost. The longer the guaranteed premium, the higher your annual premium. After the initial period of coverage, quality term policies can be renewed automatically until the age of 95 or even age 100. Be sure the contract states that you will never have to take a physical again.

If you have a young family, buy a policy with the longest price guarantee period that is affordable. If your children are older and your future need for death insurance is rapidly decreasing, the shorter time periods may be your best buy.

Review the attached premium illustrations that come with your new policy to be sure that the company states that the premium is guaranteed for the full time period. Some companies sell insurance with projected or assumed premiums but don't guarantee them, hoping they won't have to raise those rates in the future. You want rates guaranteed to remain level for the entire term period.

Be sure that the contract, not the agent, guarantees you will only have to show evidence of insurability during the initial period and not to qualify for the next term period, providing you still need the insurance coverage. Some companies offer inexpensive initial term, but expect you to pass a physical exam to requalify after the initial time period (called *reentry*). Don't take the chance that your health won't deteriorate before then. Buy a policy today that guarantees you can renew without requalifying.

A waiver of premium is usually available, however, the definition is very broad. Basically, if you became totally and permanently disabled, the company would pay your premiums after an elimination period of six months or longer. If you are young, this option may be inexpensive enough to purchase.

Decreasing Term Insurance

Decreasing term (also commonly known as *credit life* or *mortgage insurance*) is heavily promoted by banks to new homeowners. This is the most costly form of term insurance and is the poorest value.

The death benefit in this type of policy decreases as your mortgage does, but the premium stays the same. Near the end of the term, you are paying the same rate as in the beginning, but you are getting very little coverage for your money.

There is a more serious drawback to this type of insurance: The lender is commonly the beneficiary of your insurance policy, not your spouse or family. Your family will not see one penny of the death benefit. The lender has automatically covered its loan risk, even if there are few other assets to keep your family fed and clothed.

Lenders may demand that you have death insurance sufficient to cover the amount of the mortgage loan, but they cannot demand you buy it from them. When buying a large debt such as a new home mortgage, skip the credit-life sales pitch and add an additional amount of insurance coverage for the amount of the new mortgage.

You may want the mortgage paid off, but shouldn't your heirs or spouse be the judge of who gets paid and has enough money to eat: the mortgage banker or your family?

I Can't Die for Two Years?

The *incontestability clause* states that if an insured makes a material misrepresentation (lies) on the insurance application, then dies in the first two years from the original policy issue date, the company can refuse to pay the full death benefit and, instead, refund your total premiums paid. Any material misstatements are considered fraud, and reason for nonpayment of the death proceeds.

Fibs, sins of omission, or "little white lies" have no place in this arena. The stakes are too great for your family.

Where's My Check?

If you are an insurance beneficiary, instead of receiving a death benefit check, you will likely receive an insurance account booklet with check-writing privileges. These funds are safer in an FDIC-insured account while you make investment decisions. Call the company to get a current value of the account, then write a check to the bank of your choice. If the account is more than $100,000, the current amount of FDIC government insurance per account should a bank fail, diversify your funds among more than one banking institution.

Designer Life Insurance

You never see ads with future projections for a mutual fund. It's illegal, and your government forbids such deceptive sales practices, even on late-night TV. But across America, such insurance pitches are commonplace.

Agents come prepared with their crystal ball "dream sheets," nonguaranteed projections of future death benefits and cash-value accumulation accounts. Their computer software generates the "guaranteed" column, the only promise the company intends to back up. But these numbers may be buried under the agent's elbow or are at the bottom of the last page, and you never get to see them.

These contracts are sold as universal life, adjustable-premium, flexible-benefits life, variable whole life, interest-sensitive whole life, graded-premium whole life, and variable universal life. The common link among these labels is that the insurance policy contains an internal cash value savings element, whose illustrations won't predict the future any better than your goldfish can.

When the illustrations sold don't match the actual investment experience of the underlying account, it can represent a greater increase in the internal costs than your cash value. In other words, the extra costs needed to sustain the policy are taken from your cash account until it has been drained dry. Then these policies self-destruct, leaving the insured (and beneficiary) with no coverage unless huge premiums are paid to keep pace with the constantly rising internal charges.

Variable whole life or variable universal life is similar to a universal-life policy, but is internally funded by investments of your insurance sub-account(s) that you choose as your underlying "investment" vehicle(s). You probably don't want your death benefits riding on the whims of the stock market, which is exactly what this type of insurance will do. You purchase insurance in the first place to transfer risk to the company. A better bet is to buy a guaranteed-premium term policy that puts investment risk on their side of the table.

"Churning," or borrowing cash value from an old policy to fund a new one is a deceptive insurance agent practice. Agents may promise you more insurance for the same price, maybe even for free. Such offers don't make sense. In return for more coverage, your current policies may be internally "doctored."

When buying death insurance, consider your *need,* not your *greed.* When you purchase the policy illustrations instead of the policy guarantees, all you have bought is thin air. Only in illustrations do designer policies generally look better than term insurance and a quality mutual fund by your side.

You need pricing you can depend on. Purchase *guaranteed-level term insurance* so you know exactly how much insurance you will have for how long at a predetermined price.

The Winning Death Insurance Strategy

Reexamine your financial position every three to five years. As your debts decrease, your assets increase, and your children get closer to maturity, you may want to reduce the death benefit accordingly. Then, use the reduction in premium money to increase your investment program. Every time you reduce your death benefit, add the premium difference to your regular investment payment program. You will gradually transfer money spent on *dying too soon* to the impending problems of *living too long*.

Trusting Them With Your Money

Fixed-insurance annuities sound attractive because they offer guarantees of safety and tax deferral. Today's *variable annuities* are created to look like mutual funds with an insurance wrapper offering tax-deferred benefits, which makes them sell even better.

Unless you have been living under a rock, you should know that insurance companies can close their doors and lock up policy owners' funds while state agencies and potential new buyers sort out their options. In the meantime—sometimes for years—policyholders are stuck and cannot get their money back.

An insurance annuity is a subordinated IOU that is dependent on the financial health of one company. You are loaning the insurance company your money in exchange for some contractual promises. There are large penalties for early withdrawal to replace (the agent's original commission) called *surrender charges*, and can be as much as 15 percent in the first few years. In addition, there is a 10 percent tax penalty on early withdrawals if taken before you turn age 59 1/2.

Insurance annuities, fixed or variable, are one of the most inflexible and restrictive investments you can purchase, even if the company remains in business. I would rather invest my money where it can be truly diversified, where I can monitor it on a daily basis, choose more than one company to invest with (how many dollars do you want resting on the financial solvency of one private corporation?) and have *access* to it at a moment's notice, without surrender charges, early withdrawal penalties, or long periods of time before my money arrives at my doorstep.

The solvency issue should be of great concern. A company with a decent rating today may deteriorate tomorrow. Why anyone would accept all these restrictions on their money simply for the privilege of temporary tax-deferral that grows into a future tax bomb is a tribute to an insurance agent's or broker's presentation motivated by large commissions.

An annuity provides you with *temporary* tax relief only. All monies you withdraw will be taxed at your highest ordinary income tax bracket until all earnings have been liquidated. If you hold the contract until you die, your heirs get stuck with the taxes. In 2003, Congress provided tax reductions for dividends and capital gains, *but annuities are not part of that favored group*. Annuities generate middle-class taxation consequences. The agent gets a whopping commission for a successful sale. You have little say regarding how your principal is invested. You get the risk if the investment later goes south. Good for the agent, bad for you.

If the insurance company drops dead, your agent will trot across the street, sign with another company, and start peddling new products for new commissions. As the owner of a fixed annuity, where will you go? Don't risk dubious guarantees and temporary tax avoidance. Instead, opt for real mutual funds, not separate investing buckets inside an insurance company contract, and *own* your own investments.

Flavor of the Month

Today, you can find every color of the rainbow annuity options, some with internal investment accounts managed by big name investment companies, through variable annuities. A once hot insurance investment product, variable annuities may be inaccurately sold as tax-deferred mutual funds.

They are a variation on the same annuity concept. They often have small asset bases that are harder to diversify prudently. Higher internal mortality and expense fees have added to investors' losses in the past few years, and the internal sub-accounts tend to own higher risk securities.

A *separate internal insurance company account*, not the popular mutual fund you may believe you are buying, is the underlying investment vehicle. It may take 20 years *or more* for this laggard to catch up with a similar mutual fund, even with a head start tax-deferral advantage.

An insurance annuity, variable or fixed, is still a highly commissioned, inflexible, restrictive product with large internal expenses, egregious surrender charges, hefty withdrawal penalties before age 59 1/2, lack of ownership, and a lackluster alternative to a tax-efficient mutual fund.

Checking Out Your Insurer's Health

To find out how solvent an insurance company is, you may want to check with an industry rating service. Most rating companies are paid by the insurance companies themselves to rate them. The grading systems are not comparable and may be biased. Check with more than one rating company before buying a specific brand policy.

Never purchase a contract on the basis of a state guarantee. Most state agencies are not funded (they have no money to repay you now). It could take years before you receive any of your funds. State guarantees only kick in when a company goes bankrupt, and insurance companies can select rehabilitation, instead, which invalidates any guarantee.

CHAPTER 8

Home Is Where
Your Money Pit Is

It's a symbol of success, a sign of status, and a source of pride. Once a key component of a democratic society and a sign of social achievement, today it is a national obsession, a tax shelter, and a virtual ATM. A lender of first resort, a quick method of freeing up cash, your private castle, and a roof over your head. It's your money pit! It's home.

There are few subjects that evoke as much emotion and patriotic defense as the concept of purchasing a home, the cornerstone of the American dream. Home ownership invariably represents the largest single indebted purchase most of us will ever make. Whether you are purchasing a home, a melon at your grocery store, or a used car, the success of the sale may depend more on the quality of the sales pitch than on what the product is really worth.

Home Sweet Investment

Say good-bye to the notion that a house always beats inflation, that purchasing a house is a risk-free investment, that you should mortgage the largest house you can get a lender to accommodate, and that your house should be the first large, leveraged purchase on your investment list.

Whether you decide to own a home or rent an attractive appliance carton for the next 20 years is not the issue. The point is that proponents of home ownership have their own agenda. Buying your personal residence will make you poorer and slow down your quest for personal financial wealth. It will also make everyone else in town rich on your behalf.

It is generally the largest commitment of debt you are likely to make. Buying a home is a lifestyle decision and should be viewed in comparison with additional financial goals and objectives. A large house could threaten your future financial wealth.

Seize the Day!

Ask most real estate agents, brokers, or lending institutions when the best time to buy is and their response will usually be, "Now." If interest rates are low, buy before they go up. If rates are soaring, buy now before they go higher. Can't afford a reasonable down payment? That's what creative financing, private mortgage insurance (PMI), jumbo mortgages, and government subsidies are for. Don't know how long you will stay in an area? Buy that house now and count your profits when you move, or keep it and rent it out for a steady monthly income.

Haven't saved up a reasonable down payment? Lenders will loan you more. Can't fit the hefty monthly payments into your budget? Then spread them out over a 30-year indentured servant plan, which will give you lower payments along with a life sentence of payments.

Thinking about renting for a while first? You're throwing money down the drain. You don't get anything back when you rent. Look at all the equity that you could be building up in a home instead of making a landlord rich.

The real estate industry makes its money by moving real estate around from seller to buyer. It profits from pitching the advantages of home-buying. When money is deposited into a bank, it must be loaned out as soon as possible. What can the average American do with a big chunk of loaned money? He or she can buy real estate. So, the lender benefits by extolling the virtues of home ownership.

The federal government must find ways of keeping the country expanding and workers employed. The nation's economic health is closely tied to new housing construction and existing housing sales. So, Uncle Sam also has a vested interest in encouraging you to purchase the American dream.

The building industry uses the real estate industry as a middleman to turn over its housing inventory. This feeds the banking industry, which then turns to the government for guaranteed backing (something the government gets from us by selling home mortgages to investors). The insurance agent, the furniture store vendor, the county tax assessor, and the landscaper are just a few of the businesses that benefit when you commit to a home mortgage.

Homeowners are pitched so-called benefits from mortgage interest tax deductions, tax deferrals on profits from the price appreciation of their house over time, VA (Veterans Administration) and FHA (Federal Housing Authority) federally subsidized mortgage loan programs for homebuyers with little down payment. GNMA (Government National Mortgage Association, or "Ginnie Mae"), FNMA (Federal National Mortgage Association, or "Fannie Mae"), and FMAC (Federal Agricultural Mortgage Corporation, or

"Farmer Mac") are lenders willing to guarantee mortgage funds back to the original lender should a homeowner default. Community rehab loans and a plump $250,000 profit per-person tax-free exclusion every two years if the house sold is your primary residence usually clinches the home sale. The home-buying industry has an expensive and powerful agenda designed to keep its bottom line healthy.

Everyone Wants You to Own a House

You often hear the attractive spiel: With a home, you have status; an inflation hedge; tax deductions; tax-sheltered growth; a sound, low-risk investment; increased home value through improvements; a safe investment over time; easy purchase plans; U.S.-government assistance; marketability; the pride of ownership; greater family privacy; control over the roof over your head; and a proper environment to raise a family. After all, this is the American way.

But compare real estate to a bank CD as an alternative investment. Can you sell your home as fast as you can cash in a CD? Does a personal residence generate monthly or quarterly income, or any other type of guaranteed interest? Can you purchase a home as cheaply as a CD? Is the principal in your home guaranteed like the backing behind a bank CD? There are greater risks to owning real estate than meets the eye.

What about liquidity? Are you guaranteed a return on every dollar you sink into your home at sale time? The costs associated with buying and selling, and improvements and maintenance over time must be subtracted from any ultimate profits.

What if your house loses value because markets decline? Real estate doesn't always go up in price. Some homeowners have suffered major losses by buying at the top of their regional property markets. Profits they were depending on never materialized. A CD is protected from loss of principal by an agency of the U.S. government.

Can you move at a moment's notice like you can redeem your bank CD? When you rent, you are bound to stay only under the terms of your lease. The most you could lose is generally your security deposit. Do you need a job, good credit, a mortgage loan, and the promise of continued employment to buy a CD like you do to buy a house? The costs of borrowed money over the life of the mortgage are not even whispered in hallowed mortgage departments.

Can your real estate keep pace with the return on a bank CD? Probably not. On a conventional 20-year loan, you will fork over *twice* the amount of loan you borrowed. Over 30 years, you will pay back nearly *three times* the original debt. A home would have to double in price every 20 years just to keep up with that cost alone. For a 30-year loan, you would have to net three times the price you paid. The average home cannot keep pace with a bank CD when you include the costs of ownership.

Even if your home appreciates handsomely over time, there are other expenses to consider. You don't have to buy fire or theft insurance for your CD, pay property taxes or assessments or buying and selling costs, make improvements, bring your CD up to code, worry about its safety during tornado or hurricane season, or spend more money to maintain it.

Your home may be the *priciest* purchase you ever make. But generally it won't be listed among the top-10 *smartest* investments. It may even rank as one of the *worst*. Think of a home as a roof over your head, a place to hang your hat, and a lifestyle decision, and *not* as a shrewd financial investment.

7 Reasons Not to Shop for a Home Right Now

1. Mortgage interest rates may stay relatively low as the recession winds down over time. When there are fewer customers, lenders have to keep mortgage rates low to attract buyers.

2. Home prices are beginning to decline in many parts of the country. As more workers lose their jobs and relocate or suffer financial setbacks, they may need to sell quickly, increasing housing supplies and further reducing prices of homes.

3. Many new homeowners are unprepared for extra associated costs of owning a home. A down payment is just the beginning. A house is a financial mouth to feed.

4. Could you afford to keep your new home if you lose your job? Costs for heating, maintenance, real estate taxes, as well as gasoline, a new car, college tuition, and healthcare will increase, while bonuses, pay raises, and longer working hours may turn into layoffs, plant idlings, and forced retirements.

5. Real estate is illiquid. You can't get out or sell quickly like you can liquidate a bank CD or a mutual fund portfolio if you discover you have bought too much house. You may have to unload your home for a lot less than what you paid. You buy real estate on a *retail* basis with extra costs paid by the new buyer.

6. If the major breadwinner should die, the mortgage loan may come due. Even with a life insurance policy, a surviving spouse may not have enough funds for an immediate mortgage payoff or may divert insurance or retirement assets intended for future living needs.

7. Renting is a respectable and less expensive method of providing a roof over your head until you make the lifestyle decision to own a home. You can avoid the hassle of the "joys of ownership": the associated costs, the maintenance, the remodeling, the gardening and grass cutting, and the upkeep. You can pick up and leave for parts unknown at a moment's notice, relocate for a better job, or vacate the area if the toxic waste dump moves in next door. If the pipes break in the middle of the night, you call someone else to fix them at no charge.

I Have to Live Somewhere, Don't I?

Buyers have bought large mortgages at the expense of their emergency funds, their IRA contributions, company pension plans, even their college savings.

Before you become convinced that I am anti-American and don't support private home ownership for individuals, let me explain. If you can *afford* a Rolls Royce or a Ferrari, by all means, spend the money. If you can *afford* to spring for a yacht, then reward yourself or your loved ones. If you can *afford* a home, purchase one to raise your family in. But to buy the most expensive home you can possibly squeeze into your budget with the belief that you are beating the tax man and investing well through personal real estate is sheer folly.

A Real Estate Lesson

Harry and Harriet visited a brand-new housing development on a sunny Saturday afternoon. The friendly salesperson showed them through several model homes. And then the sales pitch began.

"How much for the combination brick and wood colonial with the mahogany paneled great room?" Harry asked.

"The price tag on that baby is $300,000," the salesperson answered.

Harry did some quick mental calculations. They already had $50,000 in home equity locked into their current house. If they used that as a down payment, they would need a $250,000 mortgage loan. That sounded expensive, but if they financed the loan over the next 30 years, the monthly payments would be more affordable, $1,580 per month.

"We can afford this home," he whispered to Harriet. "We're making a terrific investment in our financial future."

The salesman was thinking, too. If Harry invested the $50,000 profit from the sale of his current house at a hypothetical 8 percent per year for 30 years instead of spending it as a down payment on the house, he would accumulate $503,133. A $250,000 mortgage loan at 6.5 percent for 30 years would cost the couple another hot $568,861.22. All totaled, Harry was about to fork over $1,071,994 of his hard-earned paycheck to purchase a $300,000 house! Unfortunately, Harry would never make enough in his lifetime to fund this expensive a roof over their heads *and* the remainder of their future financial goals as well.

But what about the home mortgage interest tax write-off? If you are currently paying federal taxes in the 28 percent tax bracket—spending a dollar to get a 28-percent rebate—*you are still losing 72 percent of each interest dollar*. In other words, for every dollar you spend on mortgage interest, you become poorer, not richer, even if you get to deduct the loss on your taxes. *A tax deduction is a method of easing the pain of lost money, not a method of making money.* Never borrow money to get a tax write-off. You only gain part of the lost money back. The rest of the money still ends up in some stranger's pocketbook and works for them forever.

I am not suggesting that you rent forever or live on the streets. I want you to understand the absurdity of passing off the roof over your head as the wisest investment you can make. Most people never do the math and don't discover how they have been duped. They continue to buy again and again, each time a bigger home with an accompanying bigger mortgage, right up to the day they retire. Then they wonder where all their money went!

Low interest rates are helpful, but do not purchase a mortgage you are not otherwise ready to commit to just because interest rates are down. Purchase your money pit when you can afford it, not because interest rates are low.

Think of your home as you would any other lifestyle purchase and ignore foxes who assure you how well they are protecting your financial interests. Foxes don't protect hen houses—or financial nest eggs.

Singing the Money Pit Blues

You are not wealthy because you sport a large house and a large mortgage. You are wealthy when you have money. You have limited dollars in your lifetime to make work for you. Even though you can currently deduct interest payments from your tax return, mortgage payments are made with after-tax dollars, right out of your take-home paycheck. Did you know that when you own your home (your mortgage is paid off) you can get an even better tax break on your annual 1040 tax return? It's called the Standard Deduction, and you lose it when you write off your interest payments on Schedule A as a special expense.

Bubble, Bubble, Toil and Trouble

In the financial markets as in *Macbeth*, talk of bubbles means that someone's up to no good. Right now the talk is about a real estate bubble. Having been burned badly in the stock market bubble of the 1990s, American investors are setting their sights on a new investment mania: residential real estate. Admittedly, buying a home allows people to feel satisfied with their shrewd "investment," which justifies the big "box" they now live in and accompanying mortgage. But just as the promise of ever-escalating stocks turned out to be too good to be true, the idea that you can't lose money on real estate may be setting some up for a fall. Residential real estate prices tend to mirror the health of the local economy. While some locales are hot because industry and business are moving in, other areas are suffering from loss of manufacturing, service, or technology jobs. More houses than buyers? Prices go down to make the sale.

What About Pride of Ownership?

Owner pride and neighborhood status can't be itemized in a column of numbers. But that intrinsic lifestyle value comes with an awfully large price tag. Buy the home you need, not the biggest and best that your mortgage lender or piggy banker qualifies you for. Then invest the rest of your precious dollars somewhere else.

Getting Your House In Order

How much should you spend on a home so that you can give your family a nice place to live in a safe neighborhood with good schools?

Look at the *take-home* pay figure on the budget you completed in the Appendix. Multiply that figure by 22 percent, and subtract expected costs for real estate taxes, PMI, and homeowner insurance. The remainder is the monthly mortgage payment you can afford without sacrificing other financial objectives. Fifteen or 20 years is a sensible loan period. Only serious criminals should get 30-year sentences.

Determine the type of loan that's best for you—fixed rate or one of a variety of adjustable mortgages currently being marketed. Adjustable rates have an attractive low initial interest rate, but payments can increase substantially if you remain in your home for many years as general interest rates rise. The longer you intend to live in your new home, the more important a fixed mortgage rate may become.

When shopping for your home, it is vital to prequalify for borrowed money. That way, when you spot must-sell situations by sellers due to bankruptcy, divorce, relocation, or death, you will have additional leverage if the owner knows you can buy the house quickly.

Defend your pocketbook against lenders and real estate agents who may encourage you to purchase more house than your budget show you can really afford. Even if these institutions reassure you that your dream house is affordable and you "owe it to yourself," remind yourself who will pay each monthly mortgage payment and taxes and maintenance and insurance and other expenses, and of the other goals you may be sacrificing by tackling a bigger pile of debt.

Bottom line: Look for one of the least expensive homes in an appreciating neighborhood. The bigger and more lavish houses on either side of yours will appreciate yours by association.

Playing Hard to Get

You are no more expected to pay the list price for a house than to pay the sticker price for a new car, even though you have heard about bidding wars on homes in upscale areas of the country. Don't be afraid to put in a low bid. Better to hurt the current owner's feelings than to pay more and hurt your financial future.

If you start your home search at your kitchen table with the family budget in hand, determined to keep your mortgage payments plus real estate taxes and homeowner insurance less than 22 percent of your dependable monthly take-home pay, you are ready to proceed with caution.

Why Do You Want So Little?

Visit your favorite lending institution, preferably with a 20 percent down payment in hand, and prequalify for a 15-year or 20-year mortgage using your budget as a guide, even if the lender assures you that because of your splendid credit record and secure employment, you could have a much bigger pile of money to take home with you.

If the lending institution makes you feel like pond scum for asking about points, closing costs, rate caps, truth-in-lending statements, settlement costs, and how your mortgage will be calculated, you are in the wrong institution. These items will all cost you money over the years, and the sales process is designed to get your signature on the note, not to provide you with a comprehensive education regarding how much you will have to turn over in the process. Talk to more than one lender.

If you are planning to live in an area for only a few years, consider renting instead of buying. Real estate doesn't always appreciate, especially over short periods of time. Real estate is generally purchased retail and sold wholesale. This means that you generally pay more for the house than it is worth (commissions and closing costs aren't part of the value of the house). Then you pocket less than the market price when you sell (due to similar closing costs). Rent is a less expensive roof over your head than purchasing real estate.

'Tis the Season to House Hunt

The economic climate as well as the season during which you house hunt are important. Housing prices are largely dependent on the economic health of a local area. Supply and demand make or break real estate markets. The more competitors for each home there are, the more money a seller will want. Most buyers house hunt in the spring and summer, when their children are out of school and buyer competition is the most intense. If, however, job downsizing is common in your area, houses may be harder to sell and, therefore, cheaper.

The best season to house hunt may be winter when fewer potential buyers are looking. Buyers with families try to relocate during summer months while school is out and before fall semester starts. In addition, an unexpected job transfer, job termination, downsizing, financial problems, unemployment, family death, or change in health may motivate a seller to lower their target price.

The length of time a home has been on the market can also expose a potential bargain. Ask if your real estate agent will allow you to review their listings book of homes that have been on the market for a while.

Don't be coerced into a bidding war with another buyer. There is always another deal around the corner. Buy with your head, not your heart.

Slip-Sliding Away

What about bank foreclosures and sheriff sales? Because a house is such a large transaction, these could trap an unwary buyer. There may be no opportunity to inspect the home or view the interior of a property before the auction starts, and purchases are generally considered final. These types of sales should not be attempted by the novice.

Making an Offer They Can Refuse

Bidding and counterbidding are part of the Money Game. Don't be afraid to offer less than the agent told you the seller would accept. The agent is legally working for the homeowner (the seller). Even if you have a buyer's agent, chances are that both agents are working for the highest commission, which depends on the final sale price. Most conditions of sale and costs are negotiable, no matter what you are told is traditional.

Not More Insurance!

A title guarantee, as it is called in the real estate business, doesn't really guarantee anything. Title insurance is a *backup insurance policy* that is sold to repay an insured (either the lender or the buyer, or both) up to the limits of the policy in case the new property comes with a hidden title defect. For example, a lawsuit against your rightful ownership by a previous owner, perhaps an elderly widow who claimed her children sold the house to you without her knowledge, could prevail in court and force you to move. A title insurance policy would reimburse you for the value of the loan you still owe the bank or for the value of the property you would lose, depending on the amount of insurance you purchase.

Even though a *title search* is made before your property transfers from the previous owner, *title defects* can be overlooked. The lender will probably require you to purchase an insurance policy naming the lender as the beneficiary to protect its financial interests.

Because lenders usually insist that you pay for an insurance policy (an ALTA policy) in case a claim against your rightful ownership should be made, it makes sense for you to purchase an *owner's* title policy to protect *your* financial interests. Title insurance *does not guarantee* a clear title to you; it merely guarantees that if your home is taken from you due to a successful claim against your rightful ownership, and you must vacate your property, you will receive the insurance proceeds for the original mortgage loan amount you borrowed.

My Lawyer Is Bigger Than Yours

You should engage a competent real estate attorney from the beginning. Otherwise, the contracts you will eventually sign will have been totally written by lawyers paid by your financial adversaries.

Make your purchase agreement subject to every condition you can think of: financing; locking in a specified interest rate; a completion date if the home is newly built; required dates of occupancy; health permits; an independent inspection; FHA or VA requirements; the absence of any encumbrances or liens on the property; and the adjustment of taxes, water, and other prorated bills that may become issues later.

If you are selling one home and buying another, never allow the new buyer to move into your old home before the transaction has closed and the deed transferred. Until the purchasing deal is completed, you are still the legal owner. If the buyer finds a problem with the home, changes his or her mind, or burns the place down, the deal may collapse and the buyer could walk away before the transaction has been completed without owing you one thin dime. If a liability issue arises, you are still responsible.

Handy Games People Play

Be wary of "handyman" specials. Some houses need only cosmetic facelifts, while others may need intensive care units of their own. Be sure you understand how "handy" you have to be in order to make your new home livable.

Home Equity Loans

An equity line of credit (ELOC) is generally easy to secure, is tax deductible as an itemized mortgage expense, is often pitched by the lender who wants a new loan on their corporate books, and is a *big, big problem* if you lose your job, fall off the roof and can't work, or otherwise fall on hard financial times.

The contracts often have *impaired risk clauses* that allow lenders to *demand full payment* without recourse if they believe (or can construe) that you have become a *deteriorated financial risk, even if you are paying every month*. The agreement can become a demand note with all principal and interest due promptly without notice or protest or due process of law.

This tax-favored strategy could be putting your house on the block. The lender can call in the loan at any time *even if you are paying the monthly payment on time* "if they believe you are in a deteriorated financial condition compared with when you originally signed the agreement."

Consumers often secure a home equity loan "just in case." Just in case of what? In a financial emergency, you shouldn't borrow using your home as collateral. I would rather borrow higher interest *unsecured* debt, even at credit card rates, than to risk the family homestead!

Is It Time to Refinance?

Refinancing in today's interest-rate environment may lower both your monthly mortgage payments and total mortgage interest. But hunting for mortgage money in this lending arena takes more savvy than asking about the interest rate. Before shopping the refinance market, you will need to gather the following information regarding your current loan:

1. The full payoff mortgage balance amount.
2. The number of months left on your current mortgage loan.
3. The present interest rate charged by your current lender.
4. Any pre-payment penalties.

Then shop for the following points from several lending institutions:

1. The proposed fixed interest rate over the life of the new mortgage loan.
2. All closing costs. Get a written good faith estimate *before* you sign.
3. The number of points charged to secure each lower interest rate.
4. All extra costs, including application fee, ALTA title insurance premium, appraisal fee, credit check, and prepaid interest and taxes plus the escrow fee you will be required to pay up front.

Have several institutions calculate a truth-in-lending estimated monthly payment including all loan costs *before* you sign. Note all costs *before* you sign. Compare the original loan payoff with the new mortgage loan amount. Have expenses been added without your knowledge? Consider rolling all costs of your new loan into the new mortgage, because whether you pay them up front or pay interest on them, over the length of the loan, you are losing the opportunity cost of the money.

Check the APR of the truth-in-lending statement with what you were originally promised. It will display the compounded interest rate of the new loan *including* all costs. It may be higher than the simple interest rate quoted by the lender when you were shopping around.

It may not be beneficial to refinance at this time. You will save money *only* if you can borrow a *larger* mortgage (with all costs and/or points rolled in) at a low enough interest rate *for the same period of time or less* to compensate for the additional costs of the refinancing. Some new deals can show a lower monthly payment by lengthening the loan period or requesting that you pay certain costs out-of-pocket.

Don't automatically view a lower interest rate as a better deal than what you currently own. Because payments at the beginning of your current mortgage loan were mostly to pay off interest, and payments at the end of the loan period will be mostly principal, you may already have a lower interest rate loan than you could buy.

Get a written interest rate lock-in. Mortgage money moves quickly, and you will want the rate you were initially promised even if it takes several weeks to finalize your new loan agreement.

Don't opt for a balloon mortgage (a loan that starts with lower monthly payments but has to be refinanced in a number of years). This type postpones the inevitable same refinancing problem, possibly at a time when interest rates are much higher than today.

Comparing one mortgage with another is easier if you understand how points and interest rates interact. One point on a 20-year mortgage is equal to one-eighth of 1 percent (1/8 percent) interest. To compare several 20-year mortgage deals with different rates and points, translate each point into 1/8 percent of additional interest.

Try this example: A 6.5-percent interest and 0-points loan vs. a 6.25-percent interest plus 2 points. First, convert the points to equivalent interest by multiplying 2 by 1/8. Then add that 1/4 percent result to the stated interest rate—6.25 percent—which equals 6.5 percent. You can see that *both* offers yield approximately the same size monthly payments, although one may have looked better on the surface—before you did the math calculations.

When you have found the best combination of interest rates and points, look for the least expensive closing costs and fewest extra fees. Negotiate the ability to pay real estate taxes without an escrow account to enable you to work your own money in an interest-bearing account until real estate tax time.

Check your loan agreement to be sure that if your loan is sold, full payment cannot be demanded earlier than your original loan agreement stated, and that none of the other terms of the contract can be changed.

When Should You Refinance?

Consider refinancing when the current interest rate is more than 1 percent lower than what you are paying, *and* when you can recover the additional cost of the new loan (points and closing costs) through lower payments over the length of time you intend to stay in your home.

If you can save $50 a month on mortgage payments by refinancing, but you have added $2,500 to the mortgage balance payoff with the costs of refinancing, divide the $2,500 cost by the $50 per month savings. If you intend to stay in your home for more than four years ($2,500 divided by $50 a month equals 50 monthly payments, or 4.16 years), then refinancing may benefit you, given other conditions above. If you have an adjustable mortgage today, consider refinancing to a fixed mortgage while rates are relatively low.

Escaping PMI

Private mortgage insurance protects the bank if you default on the mortgage note. It is required when the equity in your home is generally less than 20 percent or if you have blemishes on your credit report. The cost of PMI may be $250 to $500 annually for every $100,000 borrowed on a mortgage.

Many homeowners are paying unnecessary PMI fees. If you live in an area where property values have significantly risen, if you have never calculated when you will be able to stop paying PMI, or if you are prepaying regularly toward the principal on your mortgage, you may be able to eliminate the extra cost.

Lenders don't have to notify you when you're eligible to discontinue PMI. Calculate your home equity. Then divide that figure into the approximate current value of your home based on recent sales of similar homes in your neighborhood. If the answer (your equity percentage) exceeds 20 percent, contact your lender in writing and request to have PMI eliminated. The lender may require you to submit a paid professional current appraisal on the property before agreeing to cancel the insurance policy.

Parents as Piggy Bankers

Occasionally, grown children ask their parents to play piggy banker. They may have a poor credit history or insufficient income to qualify for the home they want to purchase. Parents, thinking they are doing their kids a favor and getting a market-friendly interest rate in the bargain, may risk their own financial solvency by liquidating a large part of their own retirement nest egg for a promise of future payments.

They may even financially harm their children by bankrolling such a project, adding financial burden to both families if the breadwinner is downsized, gets divorced, falls ill, or otherwise cannot afford the additional costs associated with buying a home.

If you are the parents, would you be willing to foreclose on your children's mortgage to retrieve your collateral? Do you have enough money for your own retirement needs if the debt defaults? Are you overinvesting in one project at the expense of diversification? If the children's financial condition became unstable, would you be willing and able to foot the monthly mortgage payments and other expenses, including taxes, until they got back on their feet? These are all possibilities to consider when thinking about making such an "investment."

Managing Your Money Pit

The following is a good checklist when hiring agents or contractors to repair roofs, put in new windows, remodel, repair wet basements, landscape, or provide other services.

1. Get two or three estimates before deciding on a specific company or agent.

2. If you have sufficient cash, think twice about financing the work, even if you are offered an interest-free loan for a period of time. If so, offer to pay cash and ask for a discount on the work done.

3. If you do finance the project, you might have two contracts rolled up into one: an agreement to complete the work by the contractor; and a separate agreement for payment with a lending institution or finance company. If any contract-price changes are made or the project is canceled, you must notify both parties to make adjustments or to terminate your outstanding contract. When a contract is completed, request a statement of payment in full on your account from the contractor *and* the lending institution or financing company.

4. Do not sign on the first appointment if a presentation is made at your home. Compare the quote with others. Check to see if the lists of materials are similar.

5. Get everything in writing. Get every promise, all specifications, start and completion dates, and all monetary arrangements down on paper. You and your contractor should have a clear understanding so that the whole project is included in the price estimate.

6. Read through and understand every word in the contract you are requested to sign. If any changes are made in the written agreement, each change should be initialed by both parties and dated.

7. Never let a contractor start work on your premises until you have seen the worker's compensation certifications, a fidelity bond or state license, and a building permit, if applicable. This protects you in case of accident or injury to a worker on your property.

8. Ask for references. Competent contractors will be pleased to provide the names of satisfied customers. Call these people.

9. Pay as little up-front money as possible. Avoid paying the entire bill in full until the project is completed and you have personally inspected it. You will have financial bargaining power if a project is not completed to your satisfaction.

10. Do not allow workers to enter your home when you are absent. Keep important papers, charge cards, Social Security information and checks, and money out of sight while strangers are working on your property.

11. Call your county or city building code department if your project is extensive to see if a building permit has been issued to your contractor. Also, ask if there are any building practices that must be followed and describe the work that will be done.

12. If you are not satisfied as work progresses, contact the contracting company's owner or manager immediately. Workers generally cannot alter previous

instructions. Have all changes or new agreements written either on the original contract or on a new contract signed and dated by both you and your contractor.

Paying Your Mortgage Off Early

Once you realize how long you will be paying off your dream home, you may decide to repay the loan principal early, therefore, saving thousands of dollars in interest. There are numerous clever methods of using additional monthly payments and adding your normal tax refund to the prepayment pot annually. Some companies sell computer software so you can design your own prepayment plan. Other lenders charge startup and monthly fees to achieve this goal. If you decide to prepay your outstanding mortgage early, eliminate financial middlemen by paying extra principal directly back to the lender, not through a financial middleman.

Prepaying your mortgage, however, may *not* be a smart move. Most folks are stuck in 30-year payment plans because they originally bought too much house, then had to stretch the payments out for as long as possible so they would fit into their monthly budget plan. Trying now to correct this mistake and fund the remaining balance faster by paying larger monthly payments will rob you of the opportunity cost to invest or save that money for college or other financial goals that will come along with time. Perhaps you should, instead, invest those dollars in a college or retirement plan.

You will not benefit in the long run if your home is on its way to be paid off early but your job is downsized and the college or retirement funds have suffered in the process. If you can't fund tuition or other life-costs, it's back to the bank for another mortgage at an older age. You will have paid off one loan just in time to sign up for another.

After retirement, you need more than a comfortable roof over your head. The more money that ends up in your home, the more house-poor and illiquid you could become.

Paying off that mortgage with retirement funds can be dangerous. Later, you may need that money back for other expenses. The argument goes that if your home is paid for, no one can take it from you. Not true. If you run out of money in your golden years, you will be forced to sell the roof over your head to pay for the cost of living.

Mortgages In Reverse

For a generation of seniors whose biggest, sometimes only, asset is their home equity, reverse mortgages may sound like the perfect solution. By borrowing against the value of their homes, owners can receive a fixed monthly check from a mortgage lender to supplement their fixed monthly incomes.

Later, after they have moved into nursing homes or have died, their heirs can pay off the debt by repaying the loan or by selling the property.

Because of high fees packaged inside reverse mortgages, plus the negative aspects of older folks taking on additional debt, reverse mortgages should be utilized sparingly, probably limited to the most destitute, those attempting to avoid foreclosure.

Because life-expectancy calculations enter into this issue, the payments to the home-owner based on an appraised value of the home will likely be calculated at a significant discount to what the homeowner would receive if they sold the house outright.

Secondly, the pretense of staying in your home after a transfer of your property to a life estate limits the use of the property to occupying it during your lifetime (with the actual ownership in the hands of a bank) and forestalls a bigger financial problem if the person lives long enough. A better proposition may be to sell the home outright, rent something less expensive, or move in with family, and pay others for room and board upkeep, using funds from the house sale for living needs.

The $250,000 Bonanza Giveaway

Under current tax rules, if you lived in your primary residence for two out of the last five years, you can currently deduct up to $500,000 of taxable gain for couples, or $250,000 for singles. Even if you used the tax break in the past, you can use it again. If you have lived in the house for fewer than two years, special rules apply, depending on your reason for selling.

You can make a second home's profits tax-free, too. Sell your primary residence and take up to $500,000 of profit tax-free. Then move into your vacation home. Two years later, sell that home and cash in again on tax-free capital gains profits from that sale.

By filing jointly with your spouse, you can avoid paying tax on profits up to $500,000, even if your spouse owned the property before you were married.

If you are single and own your home with someone else (say a child or a companion), each owner who meets these discussed requirement tests can exclude up to $250,000 of his or her portion of the profits. Consult the tax code for other special rules.

If your office is in your home or if you rent out part of your house (even to your own business), special rules apply (with different tax rates on the sale) for the portion you have converted to your home office. A competent tax advisor can explain how these complex rules apply.

CHAPTER 9

Your Child
and Money

Did you know that the best savers in America are 3-year-olds? From age 4 on, our children are taught how to spend, and therefore, transfer their wealth instead of building wealth for themselves.

Most teenagers think their parents are wealthy by the material possessions and spending patterns they see at home. They don't know their parents are sacrificing their own financial futures to finance braces, car insurance, summer camp, cell phones, educational outings, party gifts, athletic events, clothing, games, movies, and trading cards. Children learn quickly that their parents can be money pots, for the asking.

Maribeth graduated from college with a diploma, a $20,000 student loan plus interest due over the next 10 years, and a $7,000 credit card balance. This graduate will be a moving target, marketed by the finance industry. "Sign here. Have it all now. Sign some more. Can't afford it now? That's what credit is for. Sign, sign, sign."

Financial habits start at home. Most teenagers old enough to drive a parent's car are also old enough to help pay for the insurance to protect their parents from financial ruin if the child has an accident. If you teach your children that the world is their oyster, once on their own, they may fall apart because they don't know how to reason, plan, and adapt.

When your children are on their own, they will meet many new friends: Visa, MasterCard, and American Express. Sporty cars, large homes, new furniture, clothes, entertainment and vacations, even groceries, income tax, and utility payments will be theirs for the stroke of a pen.

You won't always be there to protect them from overspending, so teach them savvy money skills while they are still home. If they don't learn the basics of personal money management under your supervision, they will be taught some tough lessons from the school of hard knocks.

The Ways to the Means

Young consumers should consider many facts before making any significant purchase:

1. The total price of the item, including all interest paid over time.
2. The quality of the product and how long it will last.
3. How often the item will be used.
4. How necessary the purchase is.
5. The lost opportunity cost of buying a specific item.
6. Whether they can afford to buy this item now.
7. What other costs will have to be paid (maintenance, monthly payments, insurance, or accessories).

Saving and spending are not conflicting goals. Saving is not spending today so you can have more money to spend tomorrow.

If your children have little respect for paper dollars, it may be because the family encourages the use of plastic and checks without teaching how the spending process transfers wealth over time. Checks represent real money that someone has worked hard to earn. Opening a checking account is easier than managing it properly.

Paying Themselves First

Out of every paycheck or gift of money your child receives, a portion should go into savings or investing. Like brushing their teeth while young, saving can become a habit over time. Your children can establish an emergency or rainy-day fund early.

Without a financial backup of their own, they will borrow from their parents or from each other. This is the start of living above their means.

Overspending can become addictive. Inability to pay off excessive debt with their limited incomes, they become content to live life on the installment plan. They buy everything on the easy payment plan, with monthly interest on every payment.

Show Me the Money: Allowances

Many parents believe it is important to have dress rehearsals for adult spending in the form of a regular allowance. They negotiate "pay" for performing chores around the house. Be sure this strategy doesn't bite back. A child can quickly learn that he or she should be paid for everything, and self-interest might become the only motive for pitching in with family chores.

A team family works together without thought of personal gain. If your teenager threatens to strike for a raise while your garbage fills up the kitchen, you have created a money monster.

If they squander their money at first, don't punish them by withholding allowances or reneging on entertainment and activity funds. Valuable lessons come automatically with misuse of their funds. When the allowance is spent and they want to dip into your funds, sympathize, but provide no disaster aid. When they receive their next allowance, encourage them to manage it better. Mistakes teach children about money and how far it can stretch. This is how they will learn to manage it.

The Teenage IRA

Starting retirement savings early is a great achievement. The sooner one starts investing, the longer the money has to compound before it is needed for retirement. In the same manner as some employers match employee 401(k) contributions, you can motivate your teenager to invest in an IRA with part of his or her earned income.

For every dollar your child adds to an IRA Account, you add a dollar of your own (up to a total contribution of 100 percent of earned income for the tax year). Because these dollars will most likely be tax-deductible from their tax returns, your child gets a tax deduction along with a powerful long-term savings vehicle. This activity starts a "pay yourself" plan—hopefully the first of many that your child will initiate.

Prudent money skills can build integrity and independence. Give your children the opportunity to learn and earn at the same time. If you give a fish to a hungry person, you feed them only for today. *Teach* them to fish and they can feed themselves for a lifetime.

Grown-Ups Can Act Like Children

What to do with a grown child who is "out of financial order?" Sit down with him or her and the budget in this book, and show your adult child how to budget money properly. Suggest he or she put credit cards "on ice" and start an automatic payroll deduction into a separate savings account to build up an emergency fund. Monitor your child's progress every month or so. Be firm. He or she needs strong, structured support during this vulnerable period.

Boomerang Children

Every year, thousands of adult children reluctantly return home or turn to their parents because of debt overload. Living life on the installment plan, they may have lost their job or lost their direction in other ways. If your child comes to you for a roof over his head, what should you do?

- *Have a sit-down council to decide how long and under what terms they will live in your household.* Because they are currently not acting like adults, there is no need to roll out the red carpet. They are no longer in diapers. In fact, the more comfortable you make their stay, the longer it may be before they return to the real world.

- *Lend advice instead of money.* Don't immediately reach for your checkbook to bail them out. This is an ideal time to teach them how to save and build a secure financial future.

- *Develop a working budget together.* Sit down with your child and build a budget using the one in the Appendix. Insist they stop using credit cards so they cannot continue to live above their financial means.

- *Sign them up for money school.* Enroll your child in a personal finance course, buy them this book, and have regular family budget meetings to assess financial progress.

- *Teach them to pay themselves first.* Most folks budget upside-down, paying themselves last. By signing up for an automatic savings or investment plan through payroll deduction or automatic checking at the bank, the first bill your child owes each payday will be the payment he makes to himself. Because they won't handle that money, they will be less tempted to spend it.

- *Don't consolidate their debt.* Exchanging short-term for longer-term debt or consolidating debt may lower the monthly payments but cost more over a longer period of time. It is better to work on a monthly payback plan using the budget worksheet.

- *Avoid home equity lines of credit or other personal loans.* Instead of bailing your child out by encouraging more borrowing (this time from you), help her find lower interest credit cards or unsecured loan agreements, and draft a realistic payback debt schedule.

- *Stash the cash.* Those high-debt balances are a symptom of a more serious underlying financial problem: They are living above their financial means. Building a rainy-day fund at the same time they are paying off their debts teaches them how to control their spending and build savings at the same time.

- *Make them pay rent.* If they can't afford it, expect them to perform chores to "pay" their own way. If, instead, you treat them like helpless children, they will generally comply.

- *Teach them the difference between "need" and "want."* Discourage needless spending. They may need transportation to work but that doesn't mean you cosign for a new car.

- *Don't ignore the obvious.* If your child's debt and resulting financial troubles are a result of a drinking or drug problem, the underlying problem must be dealt with. If smoking in the house was not tolerated before, it should not be now. Otherwise you are enabling your child, not helping him rehabilitate back into society. There are rules everywhere in the world, and your home should be no exception. In fact, the less comfy your doormat becomes, the sooner your child may get his act together. And that is what you want.

- *Keep tabs on their progress.* This includes their activities, their spending, and their emotional progress. Continue scheduled family meetings to touch base. Don't lose the structure you have developed. Expect compliance on major issues. Kids, whether adults or not, know when their parents are pushovers.

- *Mark the calendar.* Remind your children that their return to the nest is temporary. Agree on a date when you will be helping them pack. Resist the temptation to offer your home again in the future.

CHAPTER 10

Using Your Kids
for a Change

The joys, the memories, and the celebrations you share with your kids are some of the most valuable times of your life. But along with these joys come great anxieties, responsibilities, and financial burdens.

And Baby Makes $600,000

No, baby *costs* $600,000. That's what bottles, diapers, summer camps, braces, books, enrichment programs, car insurance, education tuition, and wedding nuptials cost by the time today's baby reaches age 25. Never have children just to take a tax deduction. They can be financial disasters.

Children eventually leave home and live off their own paychecks. But in the meantime, how can you afford them? The annual dependent tax exemption is a cruel joke, considering the annual cost of raising a child. Today's hospital bills for childbirth should be a clue to what comes later.

Kids May Still Be Less Taxing

There are many ways to finance future costs of maintaining and educating your child. Not all of them work equally well. If your child is already threatening to sue when you enforce bedtime rules, some methods may sound too risky. Some strategies are geared for specific goals such as college tuition, while others can benefit the entire family, including parents.

Gifts to Minors Under Age 14

The Kiddie Tax affects the income of children under age 14. Taxable earnings such as dividends, interest, and capital gains of up to $750 per year (indexed in future years for inflation) are generally tax-free if the asset is registered in the child's name, if you file a separate tax return for that child, and the minor has no *earned* income (the kind that comes from *real* work). If your child is working and receives *earned* income in addition to *unearned* income from investments, the rules become more complex. Check with a tax advisor or IRS publications for complete rules.

The next $750 of investment income per year is taxed at the child's *highest tax rate*, which may be as low as 5 percent, generally much lower than the parents' top tax rate. Any earnings received by the minor *greater than* $1,500 (amount also raised over time) is generally taxed at their parents' highest tax rate.

Why would anyone gift assets to a minor who, from the time they watched their first TV show, were encouraged to live beyond their financial means? *Tax savings!* Transferring assets to a family member in a lower tax bracket is called *income shifting*.

Gifts to Minors Age 14 or Older

Once your child hits the age of 14, the Kiddie Tax disappears. The first $750 profit on a child's investment portfolio (if no other earned income) is not taxed, and all excess earnings are taxed at the child's, not at the parents' tax rate.

Who pays gift taxes when money is gifted to a child? If you comply with the gifting rules, probably no one. Gifts less than $11,000 for 2004, $22,000 per married couple (if your spouse approves your gifting strategy) can avoid gift taxation. Unless the funds are enrolled in special 529 college savings programs (discussed later in the chapter), gifting more than the amounts mentioned above will require you to file a gift tax form telling the IRS how much over the $11,000 limit per year you transferred to each person.

The IRS subtracts the amount (over $11,000 per year) from your lifetime unified credit, which can cause final estate taxes after your demise. So be careful not to give more than the maximum limits of generosity.

There are disadvantages to every tax strategy. Not all parents want their children to own large piles of money while they are growing up because the age of *majority* in some homes might not mesh with the age of *maturity*. Generally, when you make a completed gift, you can't take it back later. The money belongs to the child permanently, even though you are named as custodian, can control where it is invested, and can determine how it is spent for the minor's benefit until the child becomes an adult.

Custodial Gifts

The Uniform Gift to Minors Act (UGMA) and its expanded version of the Uniform Transfer to Minors Act (UTMA) allow a minor to own money (or property) with an adult controlling the funds until the age of majority. Only one child is allowed per account, and only one primary custodian per account can be named, although a backup (successor) custodian should also be recorded. Each child could, therefore, have many accounts, each with a different custodian. (Note: Not all states allow UTMAs.)

These types of accounts are easy to open and administer. Nearly all mutual funds have UGMA/UTMA programs. Taxation on these accounts follows the Kiddie Tax rules described above. A UGMA account may limit investing to bank accounts, while a UTMA expands what may be bought. Depending on state laws, real estate or even part of a family business or partnership can be transferred to an UTMA.

The funds can be used for lots of expenses other than education, and the child receives what's left of the funds at the age of majority (which may be light-years away from their age of maturity). If you are convinced that you are raising Conan the Barbarian and fear the money will be frittered away when your minor takes control, stop contributing to the account and start spending down the funds beforehand. You can pay for braces, car insurance, band camp, car insurance, special trips, car insurance, and car insurance. You get tax benefits now instead of future promises of benefits like other plans offer. There is no limit on the amount of total contributions (other than annual gift tax transfer rules) to each minor's account. And this program has been around for a long time, while newer programs have yet to be time-tested.

There are no federal or state tax deductions for contributions, and the transfer is irrevocable. Once the accounts are set up, you cannot transfer the assets to another person, even to another child in the same family. The custodian directs the assets, can change investments, can withdraw money for the needs of the child at any time before college age, and can roll over the account into a 529 savings plan, if desired. Custodians may *not* fund a family trip to the Caribbean, purchase a new car for themselves, or attempt to convince a 6-year-old that a 25-foot Searay boat would make Daddy very happy at Christmas. Assets are considered property of the minor for financial aid purposes.

If the custodial parent dies before the child's age of majority, the assets will be included in the parent's estate, although the child legally owns the money. When the minor attains the age of majority, the UGMA/UTMA should be registered solely in the name of the adult child.

Taxable Investing

If gifting money to your child makes you nervous, you can open a taxable investment account in their own name and gift (transfer) funds to a student at college time or send a check directly to the education institution and eliminate the gift tax limitations. You can mentally earmark one specific investment account as a college fund for your future graduates. In the meantime, the money belongs to you.

There is a favorable capital gains tax treatment on the sale if the investment has been held for more than one year. You don't have to deal with changing rules or restrictions that other plans may implement or require. Mutual fund shares can be sold by several accounting methods to mitigate tax consequences over time. The owner controls the funds until they are transferred. There is no limit on maximum contributions to the investment. Funds may be withdrawn for any purpose, not just for the benefit of the child.

When the time has come to spend, gift shares of the investment, not money. Your child can then sell the investment account, pay the taxes in a lower tax bracket, and you have created a "just-in-time" college funding investment that you own until college. In the meantime, the money belongs to you if you need it or change your mind.

Take Credit Where It Is Due

No one can put a price tag on the joy of a new baby, but the new child tax credits can make parents smile.

Contact your tax advisor for the latest rules regarding income restrictions and the kind and amount of credits available in your tax bracket. Some tax credits increase by an inflation factor annually, while others are introduced by Congress for taxpayers under a certain income bracket. Generally, the more income you earn, the fewer giveaways you receive from your government. Get accurate information. These tax advantages are often overlooked.

An income tax credit is more powerful than an income tax deduction (such as mortgage interest and real estate taxes) because it reduces your final taxes by one dollar for each dollar of taxes due. A tax deduction only offsets your final taxes by a certain percentage of tax due, generally 15 or 28 percent. Congress has recently increased these benefits. Do your homework.

Don't Fly the Savings Flag: U.S. Savings Bonds

U.S. savings bonds are widely used as a college savings gift for children. EE Savings Bonds are convenient to purchase and seem like a larger gift for the money spent because they are bought for half of their maturity face value. For example, a bond originally costing $50 has a face value at maturity of $100.

Their major drawback is that their interest rates are so low when compared to the rising cost of college education that, over time, they can't keep up with spiraling costs, even if they can be cashed in tax-free for certain post-secondary education expenses. You can't chase today's college education tuition, rising at 8, 10, or 12 percent a year with a 3- or 4-percent per year savings bond, even with the tax-free benefit. A $25 bond with a face value of $50 will be worth approximately $24 in purchasing power at maturity. Use better-performing investments with greater potential for growth. Growth-oriented mutual funds, not savings bonds, are optimum for funding college tuition.

Mutual Funds, Ahoy!

No matter which plan you use to register your future investment account, you can generally invest in a mutual fund as the underlying investment vehicle with as little $50 per month and then add to it. In addition, this investment can motivate a desire to learn by tracking its progress in the newspaper or over the Internet. With a mutual fund, you can diversify the funds while helping your children to learn while they earn.

At holiday or birthday time, parents or grandparents can donate to the college fund, helping it grow faster. Gifting money to invest is superior to the usual gifts: clothes left hanging in closets because they don't fit or cheap toys broken shortly after the box has been opened.

Stop Pumping Iron and Pick Up That Broom

If you own a business, consider hiring your child to do clerical, filing, janitorial, or other work. There are tax benefits when paying a family member. But when your child works for you, he or she should not be able to then afford a vacation in the Galapagos Islands. You must pay your child reasonable wages for their job description.

Hiring a family member in a lower tax bracket generates tax benefits: a business expense deduction, possible savings on payroll taxes, and income to your child. Your child gets to earn some of their own college tuition, and the parent receives a job done well. Get the details and restriction on this strategy from your tax professional.

Your children can "pay themselves first" by investing part of their earnings into a college fund or an IRA for retirement.

Gifting Securities

Gifting securities to a minor works best with a security whose price has increased significantly. There should be no taxes on the transfer if done correctly. Transfer shares, not dollars, to avoid taxation on the exchange. The minor can sell the security later, paying taxes in their lower tax bracket. *Taxes are due on the difference between the selling price and the price at which* you *originally bought the investment,* not *the price* at the time of transfer *to the child.*

A parent may run afoul of the gift tax regulations if transferring more than $11,000 per year ($22,000 per married couple) in 2004.

Get Paid *Twice* To Start an IRA

Everyone needs a head start on retirement security. A minor can make special IRA contributions up to $3,000 in 2004 or 100 percent of their earned income, whichever amount is less. They must have earned that much income, but the actual dollars contributed could be donated by you. For example, a child with a $4,000 per year after school or summer job could contribute up to $3,000 in an IRA in 2004. If their total earnings are less than $45,000 during the year, that IRA contribution is also deductible from any income tax owed. In addition to the tax deduction, under new tax rules they can also receive a tax credit just for making the retirement plan contribution. Get more information from a tax advisor.

Direct Education and Medical Donations

Large education or medical expenses bigger than the $11,000 gift tax exclusion amounts can be paid directly to the institution on behalf of a minor to avoid gift tax liability by the donor. Be sure the check is paid *directly* to the educational or medical facility and *not* to the minor.

Child and Childcare Credits

Congress has passed a larger child credit so kids can be less taxing on families. In addition, if you pay for eligible childcare while working, you may be able to deduct all or part of this cost from your taxes. A tax credit is more valuable than a tax deduction. A tax credit is worth $1 off each $1 of taxes you are expected to pay.

Check with your tax advisor to calculate your eligibility. The more income you earn, the less credit is usually available. Before-tax flexible spending accounts offered at work may offer tax savings for childcare expenses, but they also reduce payroll taxes paid on your behalf by your employer and, therefore, your future Social Security benefits. More companies are adding this employee benefit as more working mothers fill labor markets and budget departments attempt to reduce payroll expenses.

Don't Take It to the Max

In general, the more control you plan to exert over your assets, the more encumbered and inflexible they can become. A perfectly good tax maneuver today could become a *Wall Street Journal* front-page headline in a few years. Congress can change the rules when it fits their agenda. And they need more and more middle-class income for their budget programs.

CHAPTER 11

The Hassle of the Tassel

Mary Margaret is only 6 months old, but already she is worth a small fortune. In addition to the costs of clothing, feeding, educating, and entertaining her for the next 18 years, her parents will spend approximately $158,000 for her four-year, ivy-covered college experience.

When your student parades down the aisle on college graduation day, you will beam with pride. You may even forget the sacrifices you made to make this memorable event come true. And if you are a middle income parent, between the first day of school and graduation day, you may also forget what steak tastes like, what a new car smells like, and what your doctor and dentist look like. Welcome to the "Our cruise fund just left with our Freshman" years.

This is as good a time as any to realize that you will have four or more years of hamburger surprise, macaroni and whatever-is-left-over, and gluing together the soles of your shoes.

First, the Bad News

The current cost of an in-state, four-year public university education is approximately $45,061.12 ($10,000 per year and an 8 percent inflation cost increase each anniversary). That's tuition, basic room and board, miscellaneous fees, and minimal supplies at a public university. There are no extras in this figure—no pizzas, entertainment, books, airline tickets home, car on campus, car insurance, spring trips, clothing expenditures, health insurance, gasoline, or telephone bills. And that's the minimal cost at a *public* university. For that price you would think they could name a dorm after you.

If you are currently planning a new addition to your family, you will need between $180,000 and $200,000 to fund the same education 18 years from now. Inflation is the number-one enemy of long-term college planning.

The further away your college-expenditure years, the more money you will ultimately need. But as long as your college fund is regularly outpacing the higher costs of education, your goals will become more attainable. You must choose inflation-fighting investment vehicles that will accumulate faster than inflation deteriorates to preserve your long-term purchasing power.

Schools of higher learning operate within the same price pressures you do. There are utilities, overhead, salaries, costs for expansion and equipment to remain competitive with other institutions. All these internal expenses cost big bucks. If you and your student are considering a private school or specialized institution, double or triple the above approximated figures.

Many mutual fund company Websites can help you calculate the future cost of college tuition and the amount of money at certain annual rates of return that must be invested until college time is here.

Parents tend to make similar mistakes when planning for their children's higher education:

1. Waiting too long to start saving.
2. Underestimating how much tuition will be needed.
3. Waiting for a child to decide on a career.
4. Diverting savings opportunities into spending for a child's entertainment needs.
5. Thinking scholarships and grants or the government will fund the tuition bills.
6. Directing too many dollars to current consumption expenses instead of savings.
7. Allowing children to believe financial resources are unlimited.
8. Denying children a partial financial responsibility for their own education.
9. Depending on borrowing money from retirement plans or taking a second mortgage.
10. Expecting to fund college out of paychecks when the time comes.
11. Offering to foot the entire tuition, therefore, postponing saving for retirement.
12. Using inferior investment vehicles such as savings bonds or insurance products.

Now, the Good News

The most valuable gift you can give to your new pink or blue bundle is $50 or $100 per month in a high-quality, growth-oriented mutual fund. Funding your child's college education is a mutual problem. Why not use a mutual (funds) solution?

Now is the time to assert your financial responsibility as a parent. Your *child* might want designer jeans, the class spring trip to Paris, outrageously expensive tennis shoes, a cell phone, and the latest computer game, but your *student* needs a college investing program. If you yield to their demands today for immediate comforts, how will you tell them tomorrow that they will be pumping gas after graduation? You will find a "College Savings and Investment Plans" comparison worksheet in the Appendix.

529 Plans Sound Fabulous, But...

The latest gift from your federal and state governments sounds too good to be true. College savings 529 plans offer tax-free earnings until the funds are withdrawn, no limits on amount of withdrawals, tax-deferred earnings, and tax-free withdrawals if funds are used for qualified higher education expenses (may be subject to state taxes). They can be invested in a combination of stocks, bonds, or other underlying investment securities, can be invested in other states' versions, and you can contribute to both a 529 plan and a Coverdell Savings account (the old education IRA) in the same year. Some states even offer a tax deduction for contributions.

The maximum contribution per year an adult can gift to another without reducing their estate tax credit at death is $11,000 per beneficiary. However, an adult can contribute as much as $55,000 ($110,000 per married couple) in one year and remove that money from their future estate (if still alive after five years). Contribution limits are higher than for most other college savings plans (as much as $250,000 contribution per account is allowed in some states), and an adult can open an education account for themselves. Anyone can fund the maximum contributions allowable by state law, no matter how much income they earn, even if they have no earned income at all. So far, no income limit restrictions have been placed on the tax-free withdrawal provision. The donor does not have to be related to a beneficiary to contribute on behalf of that minor's account.

Investors in 529 plans have been allowed to adjust their asset allocations by shifting money into new investments when naming a new beneficiary for an account. But currently they are also entitled to make two penalty-free changes per year without naming a new beneficiary, shifting assets within the current plan options and/or moving assets into another state's plan. The move must be completed within 60 days of liquidating the funds or taxes will be charged on earnings plus a 10-percent penalty as well. (If the plan has performed poorly and there are no earnings, this is not a problem.) If you previously received a state tax deduction for your contributions, depending on the state, you may have to pay it back if you pull your money out.

The funds are treated as the adult's for financial aid purposes. The minor does *not* gain control of the money upon adulthood, and the account owner (adult) can transfer some or all of the funds to another beneficiary in the same family. Rollovers are permitted one time per year to another state's 529 plan.

Many folks choose their own state's plan because they can get some form of tax deduction or other tax relief. But if the plan is inferior, a tax refund is a hollow reward, considering the college funds might languish for years and lose more money than you gained from the legal tax dodge. Choose the best investment plan first, then consider any potential tax relief available.

Now for the rest of the story. Participants cannot direct their funds into any investment of their choice. States direct the investment options, generally mutual fund look-alikes. If the funds are not used for qualified education expenses, withdrawals are taxed plus a 10-percent penalty. Withdrawals are also penalized if funds are not used for specific higher-education purposes. Withdrawals void college tax credits on your return. Owning a 529 account may eliminate dollar for dollar any financial aid package otherwise available. Qualified education expenses currently do not include cars, travel, or clothing.

If you invest in a 529 plan through a broker, be aware you may be subject to sales charges levied upon withdrawals in the first few years.

Portions of this program are set to self-destruct in the year 2010 along with the EGTRRA estate-tax elimination act. Then, earnings will be taxed at the child's tax rate.

A government middle-class benefit of this magnitude makes one point perfectly clear: Middle-income families had better use every opportunity to fund their future college educations, as entitlement social programs will be focused toward the poor. This is a golden handcuff funding strategy. If the tax rules change after your funds are invested, you could enjoy less flexibility for withdrawals or fewer tax benefits in the future.

Your government could plug up this tax loophole at any time. When the song comes for free, watch out for the accompaniment.

Coverdell Savings Accounts: Alias Education IRAs

Formerly known as education IRAs, there is no maximum limit on total contributions per child over the life of the account. But this plan limits annual payments to $2,000 per minor in 2004. Funds can be used both for elementary and secondary public or private school education. The account can pay for qualified educational expenses, and this program is not currently set to expire in the year 2010.

Annual contributions could be tax-deductible on your state tax return (depending on the state). You can also contribute to a 529 savings plan in the same year. Annual contributions can be made until April 15 of the following tax year (for a previous year), and qualified withdrawals are currently federally tax-free to pay eligible education expenses.

Nonqualified withdrawals are taxed at the adult owner's tax rate, and a 10-percent penalty is added unless withdrawals are made on account of death or disability of the beneficiary.

The value of the account is removed from the owner's estate for estate tax purpose. There are upper-income limits for eligibility to contribute to this program. No contributions are allowed for singles earning more than $110,000 per year and couples earning more than $220,000 in annual income. State tax deductions are generally not available (unlike with the 529 savings plan). The owner makes all investment decisions and can use regular mutual funds, stocks, or bonds as investment vehicles.

The funds are considered the child's assets for financial aid treatment, and this plan can eliminate other financial aid opportunities. Withdrawals are taxed and a penalty is added if funds are not used by age 30 or not transferred to another family child by that time. An amount of funds equal to the amount of any scholarship or other financial aid can be withdrawn without penalty. Contributions can be made up to the child's 18th birthday.

Obvious disadvantages are the limited amount that can be contributed per year and the fragile future of this program due to the popularity of competing 529 plans sold heavily by brokers. This program could be phased out for lack of popularity. Its name and basic tenets have already been altered. It is doubtful that the government can maintain the tax-free future benefit promise, considering the high cost of future entitlements and the general political tendency for government to tax the middle class to pay for the poor.

College Bound With Series EE Bonds

Savings bond earnings are tax-free when used for certain college expenses (not room and board or athletic fees) if their owner has earned less than a certain amount of income in that year. The earnings on these bonds are tax-deferred until they are cashed in. If used for qualified college expenses, the earnings are income-tax free on the federal, state, and local levels. The bond must be Series EE issued after December 31, 1989, purchased in the parent's or spouse's name (no grandparents allowed). The purchaser must be age 24 or older before the bond was issued. Bonds issued in a child's name do not qualify for the tax-free benefit.

A parent can purchase up to $15,000 per year or $30,000 per married couple. The interest is included as a parent asset for financial aid purposes. The principal is guaranteed by the full faith and taxing power of the U.S. government, and interest is accrued over 30 years to final maturity of the bond. Series EE bonds can be redeemed six months after purchase, but, if redeemed within five years of their issue, there is a three-month interest penalty charged.

If your family income is above a certain amount in the year the bond is cashed in, the accrued interest is taxable, even though you bought the bond when you were under the income limit. This limit is raised over time to match inflation. This government program seems focused toward lower-income parents with payroll savings plans at work.

What About Prepaid Tuition Plans?

Wouldn't it be great for someone to take the risk out of college funding? That's what prepaid tuition plans promise. You lock in credits toward a four-year education ahead of time while the trust or investment company sweats over how to keep up with rising college costs.

Under most prepaid tuition plans (either state or privately endowed), a parent or grandparent can contribute payments that will promise a certain amount of education plus room and board. The college fund (usually a trust) manages the assets until they are withdrawn and used at college time.

Many such plans are failing or already in default because they are trying to accomplish the impossible: outpace rising college costs, pay management fees, and invest safely in bad markets. Promises aren't guarantees. Though they are apart from the political landscape, their independent status and upbeat attitude is no guarantee that your student will receive what was promised.

There are restrictions on exiting the programs if you change your mind or they become insolvent. How will you redeem your funds if they become financially troubled? How can someone manage your money safely and achieve an 8- to 10-percent return at the same time? Who will be willing to subsidize the promised education if they are long on promises and short on results?

If your child joins the military instead of enrolling in college, can you get an early refund? What accountants and regulators will be watching day and night to see that assets are properly managed to meet future costs?

What if your child is not admitted to a school in your state? Even if your state's guarantee works, you have no price guarantee in any other state. If the trust funds become taxable in the future, you may be left with less money to pay the bills. During the investment period, you have no control over the funds.

A better alternative might be a Uniform Gift to Minors or Uniform Transfer to Minors plan that invest in mutual funds that you can control.

Campus Crisis

A jointly owned money market mutual fund between parent and student, with one signature required for withdrawal, can produce instant cash during college years for tuition, books, and living expenses. The parent sends a deposit to the fund company. The child redeems what is needed by writing checks on the share balance. (Sounds just like home again, doesn't it?)

Parents can maintain minimal control over the account by limiting the amount they deposit. Some funds offer overnight wire transfers. You can quickly wire money from your local bank or credit union for the occasional campus crisis.

There Is Always Hope

If you have college-bound children or grandchildren and time is on your side, the Taxpayer Relief Act of 1997 makes paying for higher education easier.

As of 2003 the Hope Scholarship Credit was available for qualified tuition and related costs paid to cover a student's first two years of higher education at an eligible institution.

For each student, the tax credit covers the first $1,000 and 50 percent of the next $1,000, for a maximum credit of $1,500 for educational expenses incurred in the first two years of college or other qualified post-secondary education.

The credit is phased out (reduced and then eliminated) for singles above certain income limits; those limits are raised (indexed) each year for inflation.

Parents putting more than one child through school can claim a Hope credit for each student who qualifies but only up to $2,000 a year in total lifetime credits per family.

To qualify, the student must be enrolled on at least half-time basis and attend an accredited college, university, or vocational school leading to a bachelor's degree, an associate's degree, or another recognized post-secondary credential.

Congress Cares Even More

The law also created a Lifetime Learning Credit for students taking courses to acquire or improve job skills. The 20-percent credit subtracted against $10,000 of tuition and fees can be used for any year of education after the first two years, up to a maximum of a $2,000 per year. The Lifetime Learning Credit limits who can take this tax credit through income limitations similar to the limits on the Hope Scholarship tax credit. You can use only one credit per student. Do the calculations to see whether the Hope or the Lifetime credit is best.

More Help From Washington

Never let it be said that procrastination pays off. The tax code offers a number of education-related breaks even for people who haven't planned ahead. There are tax write-offs and tax credits that can whittle down a tax bill, easing the sting of tuition time. Up to $3,000 for tax year 2003 interest was deductible on loans used for tuition and room and board. The tax law allows borrowers who pay for higher education either for themselves, spouses, or dependents to deduct interest paid during the life of the loan in which interest payments are paid. Loans from Grandma don't count, however. You can't double-dip and take a credit and a deduction for the same student. And unlike a tax credit, a deduction reduces only the income upon which the tax is figured, not the tax dollar for dollar itself. Again, there are family income limitations on who can qualify for this tax break. (Interest on a home equity loan is generally also tax-deductible, no matter how the funds are used.)

This deduction is phased out for higher-income taxpayers. See your tax advisor or IRS publications for current income limits.

Old IRAs Are Softies, Too

The 10-percent penalty that applies to most traditional IRA withdrawals before the owner reaches age 59 no longer applies to withdrawals taken for qualified higher education expenses for the taxpayer, his or her spouse, children, or grandchildren. This option is probably the least attractive as you are robbing your retirement fund for current needs. Robbing Peter to pay Paul may solve today's financial problem but creates a more serious retirement fund challenge in the future.

Roth and Roll for College

If you will have a child in college when you reach age 59 1/2 you may want to fund a Roth IRA for college savings. You can contribute up to $2,000 per year, and once the account has been open for at least five years *and* you are age 59 1/2 or older, you can withdraw as much as you want tax- and penalty-free.

This idea is especially appealing if you have other tax-sheltered retirement savings, such as a 401(k) plan or Keogh plan.

Roth IRA owners younger than age 59 1/2 can withdraw their original contributions (principal) tax- and penalty-free for college expenses (or for any other purpose). But if they dip into earnings for reasons other than education, that amount will be taxed. As long as the money is used for college bills, the 10-percent early withdrawal penalty does not apply.

There are short-term methods you can employ. Each strategy comes at a price:

1. Borrowing on the equity in your home is often recommended because the interest can be deducted from your tax return. This is dangerous. You are risking your home, perhaps putting it on the auction block.

Most equity lines of credit are adjustable demand loans written with an impaired risk clause (if your financial picture changes during the loan period, the institution can demand the money back pronto). If interest rates rise, in a few years your payments could be priced above your budget.

With home equity borrowing you are spreading out repayments over a longer time, creating a large debt to pay back. You are purchasing a long-term mortgage collateralized by your home.

2. Stafford subsidized or unsubsidized loans offer a limited amount of borrowing power and seem more viable because the student can ultimately take on the repayment responsibility.

The Stafford loan, subsidized or unsubsidized, is the most common because it is federally guaranteed, and almost any student qualifies. For needy students who borrow, the interest accrued is subsidized (picked up) by the government during the student's school years. The unsubsidized type is also available to any student attending school half-time, regardless of income or credit history. For both types, in 2003, a maximum of $23,000 over five years is allowed. Freshmen are limited to $2,625; sophomore, $3,500; juniors and seniors, $5,500. Independent students can borrow up to $36,000 total. *Warning:* Defaulting on these loans is no longer tolerated. Any student attending school at least half-time may qualify, depending upon need.

3. PLUS loans are granted through individual lending institutions to parents of dependent students attending school at least half-time. Credit must be approved; those with bankruptcies or delinquencies are denied. Interest and payments begin immediately. Limits vary and specific borrowing conditions must be understood. Generally, the interest rate is higher than on Stafford loans. Shop around.

Give yourself enough time for loan processing. If possible, apply several months before the funds are needed. The first application process will be the most confusing. After that, forms will be easier to complete.

4. Cash-value life insurance policies can be borrowed against for such an emergency. But for every dollar you borrow, your death benefit decreases by the same amount at a time when your liabilities may actually be increasing. In addition, you are taking out another loan. You are sinking deeper into debt.

If you are healthy, purchase cheap term insurance, then surrender your cash value (whole life, adjustable life, universal life, or variable life) insurance policy, and use your money for college costs. Then, invest the extra money you save with cheaper insurance premiums (the difference between whole life and term costs) for your next impending goal (crisis): retirement.

If you purchase inexpensive term insurance while your family is growing, you can invest your savings budget into a mutual fund. Then you won't need to borrow from an insurance company and pay interest on your money until you pay the loan back to them.

5. Refinancing a home mortgage may be helpful *only* if interest rates have significantly decreased. The goal is to lower your monthly payment and free up more cash for college *without lengthening the mortgage debt period.* Refinancing is generally beneficial when interest rates have moved down at least two percentage points and your monthly payment over the same time period is less.

6. Interest from a home equity loan is tax-deductible and current rates are low. But you are putting your home on the block if you cannot repay the total loan amount. Some equity lines of credit are structured so that the lender can recall the outstanding loan principal at any time they believe you are an impaired risk even though you are making monthly payments on a dependable basis.

7. Borrowing from an employer retirement plan may be allowed, but the government may become stingier in the future. By the time you need college money, there may be no method of extricating such funds. Don't expect to tap this option far into the future. *If your job should terminate, most 401(k) or 403(b) plans want the borrowed funds back or you will be taxed for an early distribution with extra penalties at a time you can least afford to pay.*

You are snatching your retirement fund and will have to replace whatever money you borrowed, *plus interest—with after-tax money.* And you lose the compounding effect on the funds that you borrowed. You are obligating yourself to more debt, usually not the most prudent solution. *Your retirement plan needs all the help it can get. Your short-term loan solution strategy could become your next long-term retirement crisis.*

8. Terminating an employee retirement fund or an IRA fund is even less attractive. In the previous example, though you are borrowing money, you must pay it back. This option has no automatic payroll deduction method of recouping those lost funds for the future. Unless you possess great financial discipline, this option is not recommended, even though you don't need to pay back the money you withdraw. There may be nasty penalties for early withdrawal and all taxes are due and payable in the year you liquidate your account. The dollars you can use after taxes and penalties may be small in contrast to the damage you do to your retirement nest egg.

9. Borrowing against securities can be effective but if you have stocks and bonds laying around, why not just sell them? Liquidate savings bonds paying only 4 percent per year. This solution may be more appropriate for the corporate executive than for the average college parents considering selling off the family pet to save the weekly cost of dog food.

10. The military (all three branches) have attractive programs to fund an education. These are popular, but there are service stipulations attached to each. A student should explore the various options. Some education benefits allow full education prior to enlisting. Others accumulate a college-fund credit program to be utilized after discharge.

11. Cooperative education can solve an otherwise impossible funding problem. The benefit lies in the self-funding style of the education. The student works part-time and attends class part-time. The work is coordinated with the study curriculum, so sufficient income can be generated to maintain the costs of attending school. A company can hire a fully trained employee after graduation. The student's advantage is obvious. This arrangement generates a dependable cash flow for tuition.

The disadvantage of cooperative education is the length of time to graduation. A typical four- or five-year course is often stretched to six years or longer. A student must be dedicated enough to pursue the longer time frame. But for a persistent student with few other avenues, this option can work out nicely.

12. Some companies offer tuition-paid college courses to high school graduates/ employees as an incentive to improve employee productivity and performance. Classes may even be conducted during working hours. The company may, however, stipulate some type of reciprocal agreement, such as the student's promise to work for the company for a certain time period after graduation.

13. Commuting to a local college may limit the social experience, but from a purely financial aspect, it should be considered. There are hidden costs to consider: a car, gasoline, parking fees, auto insurance, lunches, and the cost of maintaining a student at home. These should be compared to the cost of room and board on campus.

Students must be sure that all credits transfer if they later decide to attend a college away from home. If transferring at a later date causes extra time and tuition, this option may not be so cheap.

Commuting offers a hidden advantage. Perhaps your student cannot currently handle the freedom and lack of structure in a campus college environment. It is far better to successfully complete the first year of college in a community setting than to fail far from home.

14. College students are relying more on private loans to finance their education as tuition and fees soar. In some cases, students are shouldering the financial burden because parents are less able to take on debt in a sluggish economy.

Unlike federal Stafford and PLUS loans, which have interest-rate ceilings, rates on private loans aren't generally capped. Terms can vary widely depending on the lender, the school, and even the student's field of study.

All of the discussed programs and emergency measures have disadvantages and should be researched before proceeding. Call the financial aid offices of the universities you are interested in and the College Board (1-800-874-9390) for additional information regarding financial aid packages.

Double Trouble

Many parents face a double edged sword: funding college and retirement goals at the same time. The answer? Transfer as much debt to your student as possible. Though this sounds cruel, ask your students if they would rather pay back student loans after college or take you in when you are old *and* poor? Upon graduation, the only debts they will shoulder is a car payment and a monthly rent bill. They have one advantage you don't: Time is on their side.

From Ivy League to Big League

Some parents want their students to start their working career debt-free. Your kind intentions, however, may be hazardous to your retirement years and to your child's character. A student who has partially funded his or her own education may place greater value on the experience.

Even if you have funded another child's education in the past, don't feel compelled to do likewise today if your retirement fund is at risk. Guilt can move you from the penthouse into the poorhouse.

For most of our readers, paying for college is a long way off. Larger entitlement burdens for the aging and the poor can alter current tax programs. I generally recommend that you remember these precepts when choosing investment plans for your children:

1. First and foremost, keep control of the funds.
2. Select the optimum investment allocation and retain the power to change investments over time.
3. Current tax advantages may vaporize as our population grows older, poorer, and more expensive.

CHAPTER 12

On a Clear Day, You Can See Retirement

Your father said to plan on working until you're 65.

Your boss said to plan on working late this month.

Your family budget said to plan on working for a long time.

Your inner voice says to plan on not working forever.

Foreign labor says to plan on not working as long as you think.

Maybe it's your money that should be working.

You've probably never seen it marked on a calendar. No one's ever declared it a holiday. But it's a day that can cost you a lot of money. It's called tomorrow. That's when most folks say they'll plan for retirement. After the bills are paid. After the children have finished college. After other personal financial commitments are met. After this year. Tomorrow. Or maybe the day after someday. There's still time, isn't there? You know the answer to that question all too well.

Today, guaranteed pension payments are going the way of the Edsel, the rising cost of staying healthy and the even faster rising costs of staying alive, and the penchant for companies to expect you to shoulder your own retirement benefits are eroding those plans so fast that some retirees are finding it difficult to afford the bumper stickers, let alone the gas for the RV.

The Golden Years: Why Are They Tarnishing?

Medical science now has the ability to control many of the effects of aging. If only outliving your retirement money were one of them. As America grows older and grayer, the retirement picture is changing significantly. Retirees are living longer, getting sicker, costing their employers and the government more, and saving so little throughout their working years that they are a bigger financial burden to the "system" than anyone believed.

To add to the problem of supporting older folks who don't earn paychecks any more, workers are leaving the workforce earlier, whether they like it or not. What do you call a six-letter word for merger? Layoff! With more companies downsizing and restructuring, no one is immune to forced early retirement. Early retirement means fewer years to build up the pension and more years that have to be supported by your personal retirement investments.

Vital retirement funds will come from your company pension (if it is still in place), subsidized by Social Security (if it is still available to the middle class). You will definitely need a Plan B.

Thinking of working longer because your retirement nest egg has taken ill during the last few years? Unless you have future job guarantees from the CEO of your company, you could find yourself merged, downsized, rightsized, restructured, or replaced by foreign job competition—in other words, without a job long before your planned retirement date. Merged companies don't need twice as many employees. Overseas factories don't need American-based workers. Technology advances don't require the human touch to "man" them.

In earlier generations, retirement was a brief, joyful period, then a time of being too sick to work and too well to die. Inflation wasn't even an issue. Retirement was predictable, stable, and between the government and your company benefits, the financial picture was relatively secure. American workers must now accept some hard truths. There is no money waiting in little piles in a vault with a taxpayers' names attached to it, as Social Security implied for many years. No taxpayer has any legal claim to any amount, despite having made contributions his or her entire working life. There is no Social Security trust fund. By the admission of the Pension Benefit Guarantee Corporation (the government agency that backs up defunct pension plans), it is currently obligated to pay more than $8 billion dollars more to workers than it has in assets. You can't predict the future but you can prepare for it.

Retirement Myths Are Hazardous to Your Financial Health

During the initial working phase of your life, your growing children will need braces, college tuition, and possibly at least one wedding paid for. When they move out, do you want them to add nursing home costs for you to their monthly budgets? There is no great insight to retirement planning. If you spend everything today, you will have nothing left for tomorrow. If you transfer those opportunity dollars back to the wealthy through current spending, you may retire in an appliance carton on a suburban curb or eat cat food under a bridge. If you foster the illusion of wealth today by living *above* your means, you and your money will stray so far apart that you might as well be strangers by the time you're ready to retire. The penthouse or the poorhouse? The choice is strictly up to you. Our readers will not pay for your drug-coated heart stent.

Let's test your retirement IQ. The following statements are as hazardous to your retirement wealth as smoking is to your physical health:

1. "Conservation of principal should be my top priority." Dangerously false. The most critical element of any long-term investment plan must be to protect your purchasing power. If you are planning to live for more than three years, you have an inflation challenge bigger than any potential loss of principal by investing for growth. The two primary themes throughout this book are: the time value of money (how powerful money can be when you are working it in your own interest) and how dangerous inflation can be when ignored.

If you earn 10 percent on a bank deposit, but inflation is galloping along at 12 percent, you are still losing financial ground. The most dangerous mistake you can make is to gather your money around you and invest only for income after retirement, losing the potential for future growth to outpace inflation, the deadliest money-killer of all over long periods of time. *Always manage some of your money for growth.* The investing secret is to fund necessary growth without undue risk on your investment capital.

2. "What happened to my parents won't happen to me." False. Your future plight might be even worse. Your parents weren't spendthrifts who mismanaged their paychecks. They were immersed in daily life issues; working long hours; raising children; stretching the family budget; putting some savings away in a bank; trusting that their companies would take care of them when they could no longer work, intimidated by investing jargon, leaving basic financial decisions up to strangers who called themselves experts. Your parents also have you, the taxpayer, to fund their monthly Social Security payments and other entitlement benefits. These systems are eroding quickly and cannot be depended on for your retirement plan.

The only retirees who will be financially comfortable and independent may be those who manage their own money, using inflation-fighting investment strategies.

3. "I will need less money after retirement." False. The closer your retirement, the more ludicrous this myth. You will likely need *more* money than you spend today. The only bills that will stop are current mortgage payments and the debilitating college tuition invoices. Inflation won't stop just because your paycheck has been replaced by a smaller monthly pension with little or no cost-of-living increases, or maybe eventually no pension check at all.

Your dentist won't fill cavities but, instead, will present you with a full and expensive set of teeth. Your physician will exchange some body parts you take for granted today with metal or drug-coated substitutes that come with a whopping price tag that your employer and the U.S. government won't subsidize. Income, real property, school, gasoline, and other federal, state, local, and user taxes will continue upward. Healthcare and other types of insurance premiums will continue upward. The cost of groceries, medical prescriptions, geriatric treatments, and other senior services will escalate as well.

You will live longer, perhaps long enough to outlive your retirement nest egg. Like an older home, you will need more upkeep. To live comfortably, plan on spending 100 percent of today's average monthly income, increasing at 6 to 10 percent per year. Assess your retirement readiness with the "Total Compensation Benefits Checklist" found in the Appendix.

4. "I will pay less in income taxes after retirement." False. Only if you are poorer than you appear today will you pay fewer taxes. To pay for larger social entitlements, federal budget deficits, future costs of healthcare and national security, the price of government (taxes) will increase. If you intend to be in a lower income-tax bracket than you are today, you will be living on less money than you are now. If so, you will be in *worse* financial shape.

Some retirees think it's clever to financially strap themselves by purposely earning less in order to qualify for free Social Security payments and lower federal income taxes. If you end up paying less in taxes, you will be eating less as well.

5. "I have Social Security and my company pension to depend on." Maybe not. As the Baby Boomers deal with early retirement and downsizing pressures, more focus will be placed on each individual's responsibility for his or her own financial success. Guaranteed pensions are morphing into 401(k)-type of pensions called cash balance plans, where you receive whatever the account has earned by retirement time instead of a pre-planned guaranteed monthly income based on your age and years of service with the company. Defined-benefit pensions where workers previously had no responsibility for investing options and stock market losses are disappearing. In their place, 401(k)s and profit-sharing plans are more popular and cheaper for companies to support. Your children will have their own income issues and will hardly be willing to support the older generation's aches and pains and nursing home payments. Companies are finding more ways to unlock retirees from promised benefits. Corporations are terminating older workers and cutting benefits of retirees who produce no direct benefit to the company's bottom line. Much of your macaroni-and-cheese and Laundromat money will be paid by you. Complete the "Retirement Benefits" page in the Appendix to assess your progress.

6. "It will be easier to save for retirement in a few years." False. It may be harder. The fallacy here is the belief that your future will automatically be rosier and you will have extra cash not available today to divert into investing and savings. Unfortunately, inflation and your family's growing pains have other plans in mind, such as funding college tuition or a larger home, raising teenage children, replacing cars, appliances, and furnaces, paying insurance premiums, and funding an increased standard of living. If you can't invest the relatively small contributions today when time is on your side, how will you earmark even greater sums in five or 10 years when time is running out, American job opportunities are limited, your current salary is frozen or reduced, and other financial drains may leave you in worse financial shape?

7. "I'm young, so I have plenty of time." Time can be your friend—or your enemy—in investing. While many people got through school cramming for exams, it is difficult to "cram" for retirement because you have lost your most critical ally: time. Time is money, and compound interest works better the longer the time period. If it takes $30,000 after taxes today to keep your financial house humming, 12 years from now (at 6-percent annual inflation), you will need $60,000. If your budget is $40,000 a year, in 24 years you will need $160,000 in today's dollars just to maintain the same lifestyle. Have you told your boss you expect those kinds of raises? Where will you get that kind of money unless you start today on a regular retirement savings program?

8. "There will only be the two of us." Don't say this out loud. Today's "boomerang" children are moving back home (often with their own children) because of divorce or the death of a spouse, loss of a job, or as single parents. They are also waiting longer to fly the coop, marry, and set up independent households.

9. "My home is my retirement fund." This and other real-estate fairy tales are fostered by everyone who lives off your money pit and encourages you to purchase illiquid, expensive, and leveraged real estate, assuring you of a shrewd future investment gain. See Chapter 8 for an in-depth explanation of why this type of spending makes you poorer—instead of richer—over time.

You are not wealthy because you have purchased a large house—especially one that comes with a large mortgage. You become wealthy when you have money and investments. Real estate doesn't always appreciate in price. At best, your primary residence will keep pace with inflation.

If your home becomes your major retirement asset, how will you unlock its value? Spend it? By selling off a bedroom or bathroom? In addition to a comfortable roof over your head, you will need a comfortable feeling in your stomach from eating three meals per day. Diverting retirement-bound funds toward maintaining the box you live in over the years will cost the opportunity to invest in more efficient and more marketable types of investments such as cash and mutual funds.

10. "I'm enjoying my money now. What if I die tomorrow?" If you save 10 percent of today's income for tomorrow, you'll have 90 percent left over for life's adventures. If you can't live comfortably on 90 percent of your take-home pay, how will you feel if you *don't* die and instead possess only the memories of transferring your potential wealth to strangers to keep you warm, fed, housed, and medicated? Who will you depend on for comforts in your old age? Saving and spending are not conflicting goals. Saving is merely *not* spending right now, today, so that you can have *more to spend* tomorrow.

Saying "Sayonara" Too Soon

Our retirement system is not designed for early retirement. Company pensions, Social Security, Medicare, and Medicaid all depend on taxpayer funds, longevity of a workforce, a short worker lifespan, and a long time for entitlement money to compound before it is needed. Increased longevity, the transfer of lucrative jobs overseas, early retirements, a sparse job outlook for workers over age 50, and the rising cost of senior healthcare are challenging public and private retirement systems alike. As Americans live longer than ever, monthly pension payments to a retiree may be expected for as long as 30 to 40 years!

Thinking of closing up shop early and finding a part-time job for extra income while you enjoy company benefits and federal subsidies promised after your official retirement date? In what job market? You may *not* be able (or be healthy enough) to find part-time supplementary work. Workplace age discrimination thwarts such plans. Even entry-level college graduates are struggling to find dependable work in this contracted business environment. The sooner you leave the work force, the sooner you start eating into your retirement nest egg. The healthier you are, the longer you will need that money.

Time to Rock and Roll

If you retire, become disabled, change employment, or are downsized, you may have the option to leave your pension fund with your company *or* take your pension savings and roll it over into an IRA to manage yourself. Take the lump sum and learn how to manage it. Today's worker-guaranteed pension laws are not as strong as they once were. Lump-sum options may morph into lifetime monthly payment checks.

Use a Trustee-to-trustee IRA rollover method to transfer retirement funds into a money market mutual fund registered as an IRA rollover and leave it in cold storage until you feel comfortable with the investing fundamentals in this book.

You can learn to invest like the pros—perhaps better. Use the "Portfolio Planning Worksheet" in the Appendix to get a picture of how you stand today, and use Chapter 18 to learn how to choose the right mutual funds for you.

Pension Confusion

Planning to receive a rollover distribution from your retirement pension? You must understand a special rollover law regarding pension rollovers. *Lump sum payouts* for basic company pensions, 401(k) accounts, profit-sharing funds, thrift saving plans, non-profit tax-deferred annuities (TSAs, TDAs), and other types of *qualified retirement plans* are affected and restricted in the following manner.

This special law does *not* apply to IRA rollover accounts that were originally set up before January 1, 1993 (even if the funds originally came from a pension fund) nor to Traditional IRA Accounts where the source of the funds has been annual contributions out of your paycheck earnings.

If you receive your retirement funds in a check *made payable to you* (constructive receipt), your check will generally be light by a 20-percent withholding tax penalty. Though this mandatory tax withholding can be returned after tax time of the following year, you must replace those missing funds during the rollover process and send the original amount in whole to your new IRA custodian. Otherwise, the missing withholding tax amount will be considered an *early distribution* of pension funds, subject to federal and state taxes and potential early withdrawal penalties.

Be sure the check is made payable to the new IRA custodian, even if it is sent to your address and not directly to the new IRA Trustee.

To Max or Not to Max? That Is the Pension!

In your list of retirement benefit options, you may have the following choices:

1. A lump-sum distribution to continue tax-deferred if rolled over into an IRA. Some after-tax money may also be sent from after-tax contributions to a pension plan. These after-tax funds can also be rolled into your IRA rollover account.
2. A monthly pension check for the rest of *your* life only—*not* for the life of your spouse if he or she lives longer than you. (This is called a *single-life annuity.*)
3. A smaller monthly pension check for the lives of both you and your spouse (or another beneficiary) with a variety of percentage options allowed for monthly payments.
4. Any combination of the above.

Avoid the Insurance Solution

Beware! Insurance retirement solutions have major drawbacks, large commissions for their agents, high surrender fees, hefty internal charges, and they generally are not cost-efficient at delivering maximum monthly income or growth on your retirement funds.

An insurance agent or broker may recommend that you take the more generous *single-life monthly pension payout*, leaving your spouse with *no pension* if you should die first, then have you purchase an insurance policy to replace the payments your spouse would have received had you chosen the smaller joint- and survivor-annuity payment. The policy, upon your death, would provide your surviving spouse with monthly payments for his or her lifetime. You opt for the larger monthly pension check option, and part of that larger check pays for the monthly insurance premium with your spouse as your beneficiary.

This product may seem a win-win situation: You get the larger monthly retirement check (from which you pay the death insurance premiums) and your spouse gets a lump-sum death benefit check if he or she outlives you. If you outlive your spouse, the insurance policy can be directed to your children.

However, the attractive ledger sheets showing future illustrations of how the insurance policy will work are meaningless. A *universal life* cash value policy that illustrates only hypothetical premiums and hopeful cash surrender values, not the guaranteed figures, may self-destruct over time.

Instead, get *guaranteed level* premium quotes on *term insurance*, a cheaper way to fund a retirement death benefit if you decide to opt for the single-life monthly pension annuity. Be sure that the amount of death benefit you purchase is enough to provide your spouse with the same amount of monthly income over their life expectancy that the joint and survivor annuity option would have provided.

Lump Sums Offer the Most Control

If the lump-sum option is large enough to provide decent monthly payments, consider rolling over the pot of money to invest yourself. That way, you will have access to any or all of your nest egg at all times.

A fixed monthly retirement check represents a lowered standard of living over the years. Inflation and the increasing costs of aging will shrink the payments over time. What if you need medical care that your health insurance won't cover? How will you buy a car when it costs twice as much as today's price? How will you handle a large, unexpected financial crisis? How will you pay for groceries at tomorrow's prices with the same monthly income check you will receive today? How will you combat inflation with a fixed monthly check? Cost-of-living raises are by no means guaranteed to retirees as company shareholders pressure CEOs to reduce retiree benefits. What if your company is gone? Or merged? Or incorporated into a foreign country?

As more workers consider longer retirements, long-term pension promises are tremendous risks. You have no voice in how your company spends its financial resources and no golden executive parachute. How will you manage if today's promises of a comfortable pension fail?

Occasionally, a company's lump sum offer is so paltry compared to the monthly income payment option, that you have little choice but to take the payments. In that case, you have fewer options—and better have a substantial Plan B.

Choosing the monthly income option is an irrevocable election. You can't change your mind later when you realize that today's nest egg will hardly purchase tomorrow's birdhouse. If monthly pension survivor options are your only choice, consider an option that pays your spouse a larger monthly payment when expenses will be higher, taking less money today.

What To Do With Your Company Retirement Plan

Tough times mean tough choices. If you lose your job, retire early, or are otherwise separated from your job, you can benefit from rolling over your company retirement benefit plans to an IRA rollover account. Here's why:

1. You can roll over company funds to an IRA without paying taxes and other mandatory penalties and keep the money growing tax-deferred for a longer period of time. Your children can stretch inherited IRA distributions over their lives as well. Company plans generally do *not* allow this type of "stretch" option.

2. IRAs can be easily coordinated with your overall estate plan. You can name anyone you wish as your beneficiary.

3. IRAs are creditor-sheltered in many states just like your pension funds are. IRA funds are not restricted by federal and state laws as much as company retirement funds are. You have total control of an IRA account.

4. In an IRA you can invest from a universe of investments and are not limited to options offered by the company plan.

5. IRAs have no withdrawal restrictions. You have immediate access to your funds, even if you are under age 59 1/2. You may pay taxes, and if not taking payments under early IRA distribution provision, a 10-percent extra penalty may apply under age 59 1/2. But company plans generally restrict *any* distributions before retirement, disability, or death as well as charge such extra taxes on withdrawals. And if your company is sold, the new employer plan rules may be even more restrictive.

6. Company plans can withhold and restrict your funds (including *your* contributions) after you leave work until your normal retirement age. No such laws exist for IRA accounts.

7. As your government seeks additional funding sources to provide services to an aging and generally poorer population, company plan rules may be changed or drastically restricted. Ownership of your money and total control of your retirement nest egg should be a primary retirement goal.

You May Have More Options

Stock options from your company are a taxing issue. But your decision to keep or sell them should depend on the principles of diversion more than on how to tame the tax beast. Because you are leaving your company, you should take your money with you, including any stock options that either must be tendered when you leave or should be cashed out if they can be exercised.

After you are gone, you will know even less about your company's general direction and business strategies. In case you think every company is on the up-and-up, I have one word for you: Enron!

Whether the options are qualified or non-qualified, get some direction from a tax advisor with experience in this field. You can often make a *cashless* transfer by using a brokerage as a short-term lender while you borrow money to buy the stock, then quickly cash out, pay back the brokerage loan, and split with the cash.

Social Insecurity

Social Security is based on the principle that part of the responsibility for the loss of an individual's income because of retirement, disability, death, or medical needs should be born by society as a whole.

Supported through employee–employer payroll taxes, it is currently a pay-as-you-go program with current workers indirectly paying benefits to recipients. Controversy over how long the program will be solvent should caution future retirees not to depend on this or any other entitlement or social program for their primary retirement financial needs.

Retirement benefits are figured on covered work credits and are related to career employment earnings. A weighted formula is applied for each retiring worker's record. Participation during most employees' lives in the for-profit world is compulsory.

The more you pay into the program, the less you are entitled to receive, percentage-wise. Benefits are not directly based on the amount a worker contributes to the system. Benefits are meant to replace a greater percentage of lower-income workers' wages and are designed to be only a supplemental retirement benefit for middle-income retirees.

Beware of Single Disease and Accident Policies

So-called "dread disease" insurance policies covering cancer or Alzheimer's disease, for example, generally offer limited coverage. No insurance company is dumb enough to attempt to make a profit on the sale of insurance policies that isolate the most dangerous health risks, attract those individuals most likely to contract a certain disease (adverse selection), then sell generous coverage at affordable premiums to customers.

Medicare Part A and Part B, your current company health insurance, an individually purchased catastrophic health insurance policy, and a supplemental Medigap health insurance policy, will cover most health risks. Examine a specimen contract before you buy to determine eligible covered expenses and what benefits are *available* or *excluded* for specific health conditions. Check pre-existing clauses that might reduce the value of any policy. Review Chapter 7 for a more in-depth method of choosing the right health insurance coverage for you.

The greatest cover-up in economic circles today may be the uncontrollable rising costs of healthcare. Access to a white coat is not the same as access to the best medical system in the world. You need to be a smart customer in this arena.

Prepaying Death Expenses

Guaranteeing future costs of a funeral and associated expenses at today's prices may sound appealing, but unless there are overriding reasons (such as qualifying for Medicaid) for paying final expenses early, don't prepay funeral expenses based on today's guarantees.

If the money is mismanaged, who will replace the funds? What if the funeral home closes down or the owner dies? Or the business goes bankrupt? What if the business is sold to someone or to a national chain who won't honor prior contracts of customers? You might decide to move to Arizona and want a local funeral home. The funeral director will invest your money to "guarantee" today's costs. You could do the same and keep the funds until the last minute.

Given a choice between paying for your funeral now and keeping that money to live on as long as you need the funds, I would opt for having your heirs pay funeral expenses out of your estate after you are gone.

Long-Term Care and Medicare Supplements

Medicare, Medicaid, and Medigap coverage can be confusing, misleading, and benefits bought today may be unable to keep up with tomorrow's costs. *Medicare itself will likely be reduced for many retirees, depending on their annual income or total net worth.*

Supplemental medical policies have become more standardized. You can purchase "qualified" contracts and deduct the insurance premiums on your tax return. "Nonqualified" contracts provide no tax write off but offer greater potential medical benefits. Sales abuse is rampant. Do *not* purchase an agent's sales pitch.

Insurance to Cover Your Ass-ets

Making the money and controlling it may be a piece of cake when compared to keeping it safe from others who have spent theirs and want to share yours with you. Lawsuits are rampant in today's litigious world. You will need lots of liability insurance coverage in addition to regular homeowner and auto insurance coverage. If you are involved in a business pursuit, you may need both personal and commercial liability coverage.

Rocking Chair: A Piece of Furniture, Not a State of Mind

It's not the years in your life but the life in your years that makes retirement fulfilling. Your body parts, however, may remind you that they need fewer lawn-mowing and weeding chores, and more time to travel. You may even consider moving into an assisted-living facility or other planned residential complex.

Some facilities provide only assisted-living help, and if your health deteriorates, you must find other residential and medical-care arrangements. Other systems provide several levels of step-up care and promise you can stay with them, whatever your future health. They vary in price, and some have steep initial residential fees plus a monthly association fee that will increase over time.

It may be comforting to believe that higher taxes, increased healthcare costs and other expenses can be someone else's problem. But your upkeep costs will increase over time. So will the expenses of the facility. In addition, costs for greater health expenses by some residents may be spread over the group, similar to insurance risk management. If you remain healthy, you may be expected to pay part of the costs for others to whom the facility has promised respite. If your health deteriorates, you will increase the general cost of the facility.

If the organization becomes financially troubled, how will it continue to take care of you? You are its main source of funds, and government assistance may not be available as America grows older and sicker. If costs soar above expected levels, it can't create money from thin air. Most facilities are for-profit companies, not nationalized social systems. If they can't make a profit, they may sell out and leave the community altogether. If the facility shuts down in the future for any reason—say, a highway goes through the living room—where will you go and how much of your original deposit will you retrieve?

A better alternative might be to rent in a facility close to medical assistance so you can move when you want to and retain your money for your future living-assistance needs. Be aware of all the financial risks you may encounter: early or forced retirement, rising inflation, pension problems, and costly health and long-term care issues. For more on saving for retirement, read Chapter 16.

Medicaid Programs

Medicaid is a last-resort health subsidy currently funded by a combination of state and federal money. It is designed specifically for the financially impoverished, not for the clever and strategic middle class who intend to transfer their assets to their children, impoverish themselves, then apply for benefits under the law. Its regulations are restrictive and its financial coffers are diminishing quickly. To qualify, applicants must have few financial reserves or other types of property.

A common strategy to qualify for Medicaid is to purchase a long-term care nursing home policy that will self-pay from the time folks transfer their assets out of their name to the date they qualify for their state Medicaid program.

As more indigent entrants fill Medicaid rolls, the rules will likely be changed and exclude those who could pay but, through such strategies, manage to qualify for a program designed primarily for the indigent. Be sure you're getting accurate information before pursuing benefits.

Your Retirement Planning Checklist

1. Use your company's handbook to determine when you are eligible to retire.
2. Identify the options of pension plan payouts. They may change in the future without employees' approval.
3. Find out if you can receive a lump sum payment.
4. Make a decision regarding the type of monthly benefit you will choose, such as the *single-life income benefit* for as long as you live, various *joint and survivor* variations for you and your spouse, or a guaranteed period of time your surviving spouse will receive payments if you die (called *period certain*).
5. Analyze your supplemental retirement savings plans. Then calculate how long your money will last. There are many free computer, Internet, or mutual fund company programs that simplify otherwise complicated formulas as you test certain rates of return and inflation rates to determine how long your retirement nest egg will last.
6. Make decisions regarding health and death insurance. *Remember that your company does not guarantee your right to retiree healthcare for you or for your family for your lifetime.*
7. Determine your estimated Social Security benefits. (If you have not received a recent estimate of benefits, call Social Security and request an illustration of your earnings history and an estimated monthly benefit at various ages.)
8. Use the budget in this book to estimate your monthly retirement needs. Use a compound interest calculation to determine how much money you need to stop working and how much retirement will cost.
9. Determine the supplemental monthly retirement income needed.
10. Adjust your investment portfolio for conservative growth, not for speed. Higher risk means greater potential for loss of principal.
11. Arrange for monthly cash to be sent directly to you or automatically to your bank. Mutual funds can simplify this process.
12. Be sure you will have enough money to last a lifetime before you hand in your resignation. *Plan on losing some of your retiree benefits along the*

way. If you lose your retiree healthcare or some of your guaranteed monthly pension check, can you still afford to retire now?

13. Apply for Social Security benefits three months before eligible.

14. Apply for Medicare Part A three months before age 65.

15. Decide whether to enroll in Medicare Part B or use another type of plan.

16. Shop carefully for health insurance, supplemental insurance policies, or long-term care nursing home coverage.

17. Get your estate plan in shape. Use Chapter 15 as a guide.

18. Keep investing on a regular basis, even though you no longer receive a paycheck. The more money you save and invest, the more secure your golden years will be.

19. Evaluate your spending habits now that your regular monthly paycheck will be stopping.

20. Review property and auto insurance policies knowing that your lifestyle will change.

21. Be tax-smart, not tax-driven. Don't purchase investment products for tax advantages first. Use this book to determine the best investments for your retirement needs.

CHAPTER 13

Retirement:
Pensions, Profits,
and Pitfalls

What do IRAs, Roth IRAs, Simplified Employee Pensions (SEPs), tax-sheltered annuities (TSAs/TDAs), KEOGHs, money-purchase plans, profit-sharing plans, employer SIMPLE plans, and employee stock ownership programs (ESOPs) have in common? They are all tax-sheltered umbrellas, turbo-charging your underlying retirement investment capital. The tax label, stamped over your choice of investment vehicles, enhances the power of the underlying securities.

There are two basic types of pension plans: *defined-contribution plans* and *defined-benefit plans*.

Under a *defined-contribution plan* an individual or a corporation (or both) can contribute up to a maximum limit per year for each eligible worker. This type of retirement plan does *not* provide a fixed, guaranteed monthly benefit upon retirement. Examples are 401(k)s, cash balance plans, money purchase pensions, profit-sharing, tax-sheltered annuities, and defined-contribution KEOGHs.

The *defined-benefit pension* offers a traditional guaranteed monthly income check for a vested employee who retires with the required age and service years. Because these plans are currently under pressure to pay out rising payments to retirees and have experienced recent market declines and negative investment outcomes, they are being replaced by cheaper (for the company) defined-contribution plans, where the worker shoulders the investment risk, the company does not have to replace annual investment losses to the funds, and workers provide more of the investment capital needed for a comfortable retirement.

As with all investments, you need to consider the taxes involved. But don't let the tax tail wag the investment dog. Consider tax benefits only as a final criterion in your investment policy.

Setting the Pension Table

While Americans brace for another round of corporate downsizing and smaller employee benefit packages, more individuals are starting small businesses or exploring second incomes. Developing strategies for legally hiding income from Uncle Sam may not be as hopeless as you think.

Even if you own a small business or are self-employed, retirement plans can offer tax-favored savings as well as precious future nest-egg dollars. Associated expenses and administrative fees don't have to gobble up precious investment capital. There are many types of retirement plans that are easy to administer, convenient to install and maintain, and tax-deductible with tax-deferred compounding on annual earnings.

Whether you are incorporated or operate as an individual sole proprietor, a *Simplified Employee Pension* (SEP) plan may satisfy your pension needs.

Employers make all the tax-deductible contributions for themselves and for each eligible employee. All earnings are tax-deferred until withdrawn after age 59 1/2. Payments to the plan are deductible as an employer business expense, and all contributions are immediately vested to the employee.

SEPs are currently portable and can be transferred, rolled over to an IRA, or liquidated completely when a worker leaves. There are no time-consuming annual ERISA, IRS, or Department of Labor reports, which explains why SEPs are popular for small businesses. Underlying investments in a combination of inflation-fighting mutual funds can enhance SEP accounts to help outpace the ravages of inflation.

Maximum annual contributions for 2004 are 25 percent of each employee's compensation, up to $205,000 up to a maximum contribution of $41,000, and 20 percent for individual self-employed persons. Business owners must contribute the same percentage for all eligible employees. Payments are not required for each year, and contribution amounts can be changed yearly, even skipped from year to year. The distribution withdrawal rules for SEP require mandatory distributions at age 70 1/2 and are similar to those for an IRA or other qualified pension plan.

SARSEPs

Starting *Salary Reduction Simplified Employee Pension* plans (SARSEPs) is no longer sanctioned by the government. However, existing SARSEPs are reserved for employers with 25 or fewer employees. Both workers and employers contribute to a SARSEP plan. Workers request a salary deduction from their paychecks, and contributions to the SARSEP are not included in their gross salary for tax purposes. All earnings are tax-deferred until withdrawn.

The primary advantage of the SARSEP over the SEP is that workers can also contribute to their accounts. The main benefit over more complicated plans such as 401(k) and profit-sharing plans is their simplicity of reporting, and therefore, reduced costs and less paperwork. Maximum contributions from employer and employee can total 25 percent of gross compensation, indexed in future years for inflation.

Company owners, officers, and certain highly paid employees may contribute even more than the average deferral percentage. Higher plan contributions can be "legally" skewed toward higher compensated employees.

Tax rules and withdrawal consequences are similar to IRAs, with a 10-percent penalty for early withdrawal except for death, disability, or a lifetime annuity based on life expectancy. Withdrawals must start after age 70 1/2.

SARSEPs are more confusing and a bit more complicated than ordinary SEP plans. A SARSEP can be rolled over to another type of employer pension plan with assistance from companies who specialize in employer retirement plan issues.

SIMPLE Plans

SIMPLE plans were created by Congress to replace the SARSEP. The SIMPLE has few reporting rules and both employees and employers contribute to the plan. The SIMPLE is more fully explained in Chapter 14. It is a variation on a Super IRA. However, the penalty for withdrawing funds within the first two years the plan is in force is a whopping 25 percent. The plan is limited to entities with 100 or fewer eligible employees. Self-employed individuals can also set up a SIMPLE. Contributions for 2004 are $9,000 plus a $1,500 over age 50 catch-up amount. A new plan must be set up by October 15 of the plan year to give ample notice to employees.

Who Says Nice Guys Finish Last?

Employees of nonprofit institutions such as hospitals, service organizations, and schools serve altruistic and charitable goals. But charity can begin at home.

Tax-Sheltered Annuities (TDAs/TSAs), technically known as 403(b)s, are nonguaranteed basic or supplemental retirement plans designed specifically for employees of educational, service, or social service agencies. Employees contribute to the account and employers can add matching contributions. All TSA contributions are made on a before-tax basis. In addition to reducing current salary and, therefore, current income taxes, any value in a TSA/TDA plan will compound tax-deferred, sheltered from federal income taxes until retirement or other withdrawal time.

Withdrawals prior to age 59 1/2 (unless special rules apply) result in a 10-percent federal tax penalty. Surrender charges may apply to some annuity contracts.

You determine how much of your salary (up to a limit of $13,000 with a $3,000 catch-up if age 50 or older in 2004) to contribute and how often (for example, on each payday). By signing a salary reduction agreement with your employer at enrollment time, the contribution can be conveniently deducted from your paycheck and sent by your employer to your chosen investment company.

You can generally change the underlying type of investment vehicle to one of your own choice, even if outside the accepted current vendor list your company offers. You may also change your contribution percentage from time to time. You can stop your contributions at any time, though your specific plan may have penalties restricting how soon you can again begin contributing to the plan in the future. You may choose any mutual fund or insurance annuity company that works with TSA/TDA programs. But your company may have a select list of vendor options with whom you must deal.

Most TSA/TDA plans have attractive loan features while you are working. The loans must generally be repaid in quarterly payment installments within five years, unless funds were used for a longer period, such as a home mortgage. The loan principal and interest are deducted from your paycheck and reinvested back into your own plan. Therefore, it may feel as if you are borrowing from yourself and paying interest to yourself, which may sound like a more attractive option than borrowing from a commercial lender. However, you are robbing your retirement investment that may perform well-above the interest rate at which you have borrowed the funds (usually the prime rate plus a small increase). You are paying the loan back with after-tax money. If you are terminated or otherwise leave your job, how will you repay the remainder of the loan?

You are always 100-percent *vested* in your own contributions, though an employer's matching funds may vest over a period of several years.

If you change jobs, you may be able to roll over your TDA into another TDA plan, an IRA, or leave your TDA with your original investment company. You can even defer taxes after retirement with an automatic withdrawal payout option on a monthly, quarterly, or annual payout basis.

Warning: Even though you have contributed all the funds into the plan, it is a company-sponsored retirement plan. Not all TSA/TDA plans may offer a lump-sum withdrawal privilege at retirement time. Some will eventually offer only monthly income options. Your employer could change its current lump-sum option to a monthly annuity payment format at any time. This plan becomes a lot less attractive if the investment company can keep your funds all through your retirement years while you receive only a monthly retirement check.

Do *not* confuse this type of employer plan with a private insurance annuity investment product that anyone can purchase. This type of pretax supplemental retirement opportunity is available only to employees of certain nonprofit institutions.

You can choose either mutual funds or insurance company annuity products for your account. The greater earning potential of mutual funds makes them popular TDA investment choices. Although past performance is no guarantee of future results, there are many high quality mutual funds that have averaged well above the annual inflation rate.

Do not confuse brand name *fixed or variable annuity insurance company sub-accounts* with *real mutual fund* options. When the product comes from an insurance company, you may be paying unnecessary charges inside an already tax-deductible, tax-deferred investment. Mutual funds are recorded in *shares*. Insurance annuities are calculated in *unit or account values*. Some insurance agents sell variable annuity products inside TSAs/TDAs instead of mutual funds because the commissions are larger. You have no obligation to fund a stranger's retirement years, only your own.

Think twice before you annuitize (sign away the rights to your account principal) in exchange for monthly lifetime payments. The insurance company will then own your funds for life.

Congress grandfathered pre-January 1, 1987 money, which means that account owners don't have to calculate this "grandfathered" money until age 75 along with the rest of their TSA funds for required minimum distribution rules (RMDs).

401(k)s Sell Like Hotcakes

Everybody loves the 401(k): employees, companies, and money managers. The sizzle is appealing: a tax-deductible contribution limit of $13,000 for 2004 plus a $3,000 match if age 50, voluntary matching employer contributions, account earnings tax-deferred until retirement, portability upon termination or retirement from the company, a choice of investment vehicles and tax-favored status at retirement time through an IRA rollover. What more could you ask for?

Many 401(k) plans now have hardship distribution or loan provisions where you can borrow up to 50 percent of your account and pay back the funds with interest to your own 401(k) account. There are no credit checks or lengthy applications to complete.

401(k)s are popular with employers because companies don't have to guarantee any monthly retirement payments. What your account accumulates, you get. If you lose money, you picked the options. And they are generally cheaper for your company to fund than a guaranteed pension.

Employees with one year of service, 1,000 hours of work in a year, and age 18 or 21 may be eligible to participate. Eligibility rules may be more generous. The boss may match contributions up to a certain level. At separation of service, a worker currently may roll over his or her account into an IRA, further deferring tax consequences until after retirement.

Though employees usually grab for the tax benefits, if the investment options are full of hidden fees, up-front commissions, annual year-after-year commissions, and life insurance costs, you may do better over time outside the 401(k), despite the obvious tax shelter assistance.

There is a more ominous aspect to your maximizing contributions to these pension plans: under the federal pension rules of ERISA (who ultimately controls qualified retirement plans), any distributions from your account could be restricted until normal retirement age. Then, your company could further restrict your distribution options to monthly annuity checks and eliminate any lump-sum withdrawal option. Uncle Sam may change the rules so you can "share" your funds with those less fortunate than you via its future entitlement budget program needs. Remember, you are only *vested* in your account at all times. *Being vested is not the same thing as owning your funds.*

I recommend that you invest wholeheartedly outside your current company plan options and consider control of the funds as a priority of your investment plans. If your 401(k) funds become more restricted in the future, you may eat out less often, travel to cheaper vacation spots, and have less to spend on your medical care. Don't maximize payroll contributions at the expense of your annual IRA and other outside investment vehicles, even with the enticement of an employer match. With the future of Social Security, Medicare, and other retirement entitlements so uncertain, your pension funds may look tempting to Washington any day now.

Looking Out for 401(k) Number 1

If you run your own business, you have another retirement savings choice: a 401(k) for one. Called a *uni-(k)* plan, it follows the basic rules of 401(k)s: employer contribution limits of up to 25 percent of compensation up to a maximum in 2004 of $41,000, including a $13,000 maximum employee contribution, plus an extra $3,000 catch-up if you are age 50 or older, and low costs, funding flexibility, and the ability to borrow against your balance. Many mutual fund companies offer setup fees as low as $250 and annual fees from $100 up.

This plan works best for a one-person business (and a spouse who works for the business). It is not suitable for businesses with outside employees.

Already have a SEP-IRA or a SIMPLE IRA? You can roll it into a 401(k), although you must wait two years after funding a SIMPLE IRA to qualify for a rollover without penalties.

Avoiding 401(k) Fraud

Although most of the nation's 401(k) plans are fraud-free, if you spot any of the following, request an explanation from your employee benefits office:

- Your quarterly statement consistently arrives late or at odd intervals.
- A significant and unexplainable drop in your account balance.
- Former employees are having trouble getting their benefits.
- Your statement is missing contributions.
- Contributions don't match your year-to-date pay stub.
- Investments are not in the accounts you originally chose.

- ◆ Frequent and unexplained changes in investment managers.
- ◆ The account statement shows inaccuracies.

If your benefits department cannot satisfy your questions, contact the Pension and Welfare Benefits Administration's nearest regional office.

Cash Balance Pensions

Traditional guaranteed pensions are giving way to cheaper methods for companies to provide benefits for their workers. *Cash balance plans* are controversial because they can reduce benefits for older workers and act like 401(k)s in that they guarantee no future monthly income check, just what the account makes during the employee's working career. They can be created by terminating a company's guaranteed pension plan and removing any "surplus" funds the old plan had before the remainder of funds are put into place in the new plan. This extra cash then works for the company's bottom line, not for yours. Lump-sum withdrawals and IRA rollovers are currently available when you terminate employment.

Profit-Sharing Plans

Employers control most *profit-sharing plan* contributions and how the assets are managed and invested because they contribute all the funds to the plan. There is no requirement that a company contribute every year. Most companies wait until year end to decide whether the bottom line was profitable enough to reward workers. If the company should become insolvent or merge with another corporation, funds could become restricted, maybe even merged with a new company's options. Very little control exists for workers. If there are no profits in a year, no funds are added to the plan.

No benefits are guaranteed, no annual employer contributions are required, and the employer chooses the investment manager.

ESOPs

Employee stock option plans (ESOPs) are a loose variety of stock employee benefits that generally offer some type of company stock. Owning a piece of the company you work for may motivate you to work harder, but if the company becomes unhealthy, you may have a job, a pension, *and* the cost of the stock at risk.

Giving (or selling discounted) stock to employees is beneficial to the company. If the shares are already in the company treasury, it gets a full tax deduction for current market value. It also gets a free loan from the employees to fund future growth or other costs without incurring additional debt. It is possible that the CEO may be selling stock at the same time the employee is motivated to buy. Companies offer pieces of ownership and its inherent risk to workers who refund part of their hard-earned paychecks, further reducing bottom-line employee costs. Companies often match retirement plans with stock. I prefer matching dollars.

It is possible you may give up a high flier. But by diversifying, you will cushion any losses attached to the fortunes of your company.

KEOGHs

There are two basic types of *KEOGH* pension plans. The most popular (and the easiest to administer) is a *defined-contribution plan*, which limits the annual contribution to a percent of income depending on your total annual compensation ($205,000 for 2004).

The other KEOGH prototype is a *defined-benefit plan*, a more complicated prototype administered at greater expense that could actually replace 100 percent of your future income per year after retirement. This plan allows much greater annual funding and must be administered by a third-party pension company.

There are several methods of skewing greater dollars to the most highly compensated or the oldest personnel, or both. All contributions are tax-deductible to the participants and tax-deductible to the corporation. All earnings are tax-deferred like other qualified retirement pension plans.

A new KEOGH plan must be set up by December 31 of the calendar year in which it starts, but contributions to an existing KEOGH may be made until tax time (April 15) of the following year, including extensions.

Penalties are similar to those for IRAs and, in addition, in-service loans are available, hardship distributions can be granted if the written plan allows, and employees may contribute to outside IRAs as well, though the IRA may not be tax-deductible, depending on their adjusted gross income.

KEOGHs are more complicated than most other small business retirement alternatives. Unless a significant amount of funds can be invested to make the extra expenses and additional tax rules worth the trouble, the SEP or SIMPLE plans may be more attractive choices.

Deferred Compensation Plans

Called *Section 457* plans, these cover many public employees. Contributions are voluntary and tax-deductible primarily because *they carry a substantial risk of forfeiture to the worker in the future.*

Contrary to public belief, they are not owned by or vested to the employees themselves but, instead, are held in a trust and represent part of the financial property of the public agency the employees work for. Most fund assets are accessible to the claims of the creditors of the public entity. The funds can be used to pay creditors or other budget purposes.

They are not protected by any federal pension agency, are often informally funded, and are very risky future promises!

Flexible Spending Accounts

Section 125 plans are widely used in the public employment sector. They allow certain expenses to be deducted before payroll taxes, but reduce your wages for other employee and retirement benefits such as Social Security credits. Balance the "free lunch" from tax-sheltered funds today with a potential loss of Social Security benefits tomorrow.

Pension Pitfalls

If you are thinking of taking a loan from your 401(k) or similar retirement plan at work, there are facts you must know.

Although retirement funds are intended for retirement, you can usually borrow up to 50 percent of your vested account balance to pay for excessive medical expenses, a college education, a new home, or the loss of a principal residence.

Loan payments are generally deducted from your paycheck until the loan is paid off, generally within five years, unless the funds are used for a home, when the loan limit is longer.

While you are repaying the account at a market interest rate, your account could be earning much more. In addition, you are robbing your retirement nest egg. Instead of repaying funds back into your account, you could be using that money to fund another future goal. *A loan is a loan, even if you are the banker as well as the customer.*

What if you lose your job and can't pay off your loan? The unpaid balance will be considered an early distribution (if under the age of 59 1/2), and all income taxes and a 10-percent penalty will be due on the loan balance not already repaid.

You may also be able to make special hardship withdrawals from your plan that you never pay back for excessive medical bills, for college tuition, or for the potential loss of your home. Again, income taxes and a possible 10-percent penalty may apply.

If you change jobs and request the check be made payable to you personally, you will be automatically assessed a 20-percent withholding tax and later an additional 10-percent tax for early withdrawal if under retirement age, unless you come up with the extra 20 percent from outside sources to add to those rollover funds. Otherwise, the 20-percent withholding tax missing from your check is considered an early distribution, and an extra 10-percent penalty for early withdrawal may also apply. Be careful that the check is made out to the new IRA or plan custodian for your benefit, not to you personally.

If your account balance is less than $5,000, employers can cash out your plan and send you a check without your permission. At the time you terminate employment, make arrangements for any plan rollovers.

If you retire at age 55 and need immediate income, you may want to leave some funds in your employer plan such as a 401(k), as these can often be tapped at age 55, while an IRA generally cannot be withdrawn before age 59 1/2 without penalty.

Under new regulations, even after-tax money from your plan can be rolled over and remain tax-deferred far into the future. If you need income from your retirement accounts but are under age 59 1/2, there are several methods to tap an IRA without penalty, explained further in Chapter 14.

Because a *guaranteed pension* is tied to your company's financial health, and other employer retirement plans may be temporarily stuck or even diverted in case of insolvency or a sale, read your employer's annual report. Companies are continually lobbying Congress to get out from under their "legacy" costs, the huge promise to their retired workforce that saps funds that could be used for other more business-oriented purposes. Many manufacturing and older pension plans are already under-funded today, a reminder that you must beef up other investments for retirement, even if the HR department assures you that the company pension is "rock solid."

When Will Your Savings Run Out?

The following chart can help you estimate the number of years your current savings may last. Plot the number of years by picking your savings growth rate from figures listed at the left of the chart and your rate of withdrawal on the bottom of the chart. The chart assumes that you do not add funds to your savings. The number at the intersection of these two percentage rates is approximately how many years your savings will last.

(This chart is intended only as general educational material and does not predict or depict the rate of return on any mutual fund. Consult an investment professional for a more specific and detailed analysis of your personal financial situation.)

Withdrawal Chart

Growth Rate Per Year

Growth Rate	2%	3%	4%	5%	6%	7%	8%	9%	10%	11%	12%	13%	14%	15%	16%
15%															20
14%														21	16
13%													22	16	14
12%												23	17	14	12
11%											24	18	15	13	11
10%										25	19	15	13	12	10
9%									27	20	16	14	12	11	10
8%								29	21	17	14	12	11	10	9
7%							31	22	18	15	13	11	10	9	9
6%						33	24	19	16	14	12	11	10	9	8
5%					37	26	20	17	14	12	11	10	9	8	8
4%				41	28	22	18	15	13	12	10	9	9	8	7
3%			47	31	23	19	16	14	12	11	10	9	8	8	7
2%		55	35	26	20	17	15	13	11	10	9	8	8	7	7
1%	70	41	29	22	18	15	13	12	11	10	9	8	7	7	6

Withdrawal Rate Per Year

CHAPTER 14

IRAs:

New and Improved

An IRA is not a specific investment like a stock, a bond, or a bank CD. It is a special retirement tax shelter set up by Congress for individual retirement savings. You can choose a variety of underlying investments and add the IRA tax-shelter label. All earnings in an IRA account are tax-deferred until withdrawn.

Even if your company has a pension and you receive Social Security benefits, you should create additional retirement funds. Company pensions collapse and, as more workers retire earlier and live longer, plans may not be able to pay out larger and longer benefits. We already know what pressures our social insurance system will face.

As of 2004, taxpayers can stash as much as $3,000, or 100 percent, of their compensation (whichever is smaller) into a traditional IRA or a Roth IRA (or a combination of both). Those age 50 or older by the end of 2004 can add an extra $500 catch-up deposit. That's true even if you (or your spouse) are already covered under a retirement plan at work, you work for several employers during the year, you are receiving a retirement pension under another company plan, or even if your spouse doesn't work outside the home. *The only restriction is that you (or your spouse) must have enough earned income during the year to make the contribution(s).*

For IRA purposes, compensation includes wages, salaries, self-employment income, tips, professional fees, alimony, bonuses, jury fees, administrator or trustee fees, and other amounts you receive for providing personal service.

Compensation for IRA purposes does *not* include rental income, interest and dividend income, capital gains, pension or annuity income, deferred compensation, and passive partnership income. The sooner you contribute to your current-year IRA, the longer the money has to work tax-deferred. In addition, you can also contribute to last year's IRA account until April 15, or the tax deadline of the current year.

Congress agrees that being a homemaker and/or a mom is a full-time job. A worker and a non-working spouse can *each* contribute the maximum to an IRA, providing the working spouse or household earns at least the amount of both IRA contributions. Single-wage earning couples can contribute up to $3,000 for each person ($3,500 if age 50) if only one spouse works and even if the working spouse has a pension plan at work. No individual can contribute more than the maximum amount per year, depending on his or her age.

Because the rules don't specify what "non-working" spouse means, it could include unemployed, never employed, or even retired with a working spouse.

Many folks believe if they have a company pension, they are prohibited from investing in an IRA. *This is not true.* Workers with a company retirement plan can still contribute the maximum contribution. *Whether the IRA contribution can be deducted from your income on your federal tax return is another matter.*

Many retirees were previously unable to deduct IRA contributions in the past. But new tax rules make it easier to qualify for a tax deduction. For 2004, if your single adjusted gross income is less than $45,000 and you are active in or eligible for a company retirement plan, you get to take the entire deduction. Income more than $55,000 eliminates any immediate tax write-off. For married couples filing jointly, the phase-out for tax write-offs begins at $65,000 and eliminates any tax deduction at $75,000. These income limits are adjusted upward on an annual basis to compensate for inflation. Even if you have an employer retirement plan, you may still qualify for a deductible IRA, depending on your adjusted gross income.

If your company has no retirement pension or if you are not yet eligible to join, you can deduct your total contribution, regardless of how much "bacon" you bring home during the year.

For married couples, the tax-deduction rules become a bit more complex. If neither you nor your spouse has a pension, you can each deduct a full IRA contribution, regardless of your individual or combined income. If one or both of you are covered by a pension plan, and your income falls within the figures mentioned above (before the IRAs are deducted), the deduction limits are already explained.

If a working spouse is covered by a pension plan, a non-working spouse can *deduct* the full IRA amount as long as the couple's joint income does not exceed $150,000. Between $150,000 and $160,000, a portion of the IRA contribution can be deducted.

Once more than $160,000, there is no longer any tax deduction available for the non-working spouse. (Remember, however, the working spouse with a pension doesn't qualify for a totally deductible IRA if his or her joint income rises above $75,000.)

Even if you cannot deduct your IRA off your current tax return, you can still contribute to a non-tax-deductible IRA if you have earned income during the year. And you definitely should take advantage of the most powerful part of this retirement program: the long-term tax-deferred earnings benefit until you start redemptions or until death do you two part. *Remember: The ability to contribute to an IRA is not restricted by whether or not you have a pension plan at work, just whether you get the tax write-off off your current tax return.*

You can contribute to a variety of deductible and/or non-deductible IRAs (provided you qualify for all types), including the Roth IRA, discussed later. The total combination of your IRA underlying contributions, however, cannot exceed the maximum contribution per person per year.

Old IRAs Just Got Better

The 10-percent early-withdrawal penalty that applies for withdrawals by owners before the age of 59 1/2 no longer applies to withdrawals taken for qualified higher education expenses for the taxpayer or his or her spouse, children, or grandchildren. Nor does it apply to withdrawals up to $10,000 for qualified, first-time home purchases used within 120 days to buy, build, or rebuild a first home that is the principal residence of the taxpayer, spouse, child, grandchild, or ancestor of the taxpayer or spouse. Such penalty-free distributions are limited to $10,000 during the taxpayer's lifetime.

Penalties are also waived for withdrawals due to excessive medical expenses or for health insurance premiums if the IRA owner is unemployed and collecting unemployment benefits for at least 12 consecutive weeks.

Though IRAs accumulated during a marriage may be considered marital property even though the account is in one name only, a divorce may not affect the tax-deferred status of an IRA account, even if an ex-spouse receives part or all of the other spouse's IRA accounts. By properly transferring the IRA to an ex-spouse as a property settlement, the IRA can remain tax-deferred and continue compounding as though it belonged to the new owner from the beginning. No taxes or early withdrawal penalties may be due in that case.

Gadzooks! Another IRA?

Under current tax rules for the Roth IRA, there are no tax deductions for contributions. However, with a Roth IRA, you can withdraw your contributions (not your earnings) at any time, even before age 59 1/2, tax-free, without a 10-percent penalty. Though workers cannot contribute to a Traditional IRA after their 70th birthday, they can purchase a Roth IRA, even if they are taking minimum distributions from Traditional IRAs.

Contributions are limited to a maximum of $3,000 or $3,500 per person per year, depending on your age. Many taxpayers who qualify for tax deductions for Traditional IRAs are being encouraged to choose Roth IRAs instead, paying their taxes upfront to qualify for the tax-free benefits later.

When you compare the compounding power of a tax-deductible IRA with a Roth IRA at withdrawal time, there is generally no difference in account value, unless you are in a lower tax bracket after retirement than today. Because this book is dedicated to teaching you how *not* to be in a lower tax bracket after retirement, if you remain in a 27-percent tax bracket through your working years and remain in the same tax bracket after retirement, you will not be any further ahead by pre-paying your taxes upfront with a Roth IRA. In fact, by choosing a Roth over a deductible Traditional IRA, you could be in worse shape if Congress reverses the Roth tax-free promise in the future and taxes the earnings as with a Traditional IRA.

Wealthy folks don't pre-pay their taxes unless they know they will get something much better in return. With so many elderly needing so much from future benefits systems, it is doubtful that the United States will be able to keep its tax-free promise.

Only two of the following requirements must be met to take a "qualified" tax-free, penalty-free distribution:

1. You must wait five years after the account is open from the first tax year the Roth IRA is started.

2. Either a) distributions are made for first-time home buyer expenses up to $10,000 maximum; b) distributions are made due to the IRA owner's disability or death; or c) withdrawals are made after the age of 59 1/2.

Unlike money in Traditional IRAs, Roth IRA owners can make "non-qualified" withdrawals of their after-tax contributions (principal) tax-free and penalty-free at any time, even before age 59 1/2, even if the above restrictions are not met. The above rules apply only to Roth conversions and earnings on Roth IRAs. Taxpayers aren't required to make Roth IRA withdrawals when they reach age 70 1/2.

In order to contribute to a Roth IRA, your adjusted gross income must be less than $95,000 for a single tax filer and less than $150,000 for spouses filing together for a full Roth contribution. The eligibility for a Roth IRA is eliminated for singles at $110,000 or greater and for joint filers at $160,000 or more.

Under current law, beneficiaries inherit the assets income tax-free if the Roth IRA owner dies. Spouses can roll over the deceased spouse's Roth IRA into their own Roth. Inherited IRA beneficiaries, however, must follow similar rules as for inherited Traditional IRAs. Non-spouse beneficiaries inheriting a Roth IRA will use the Single Life

Expectancy Tables, taking annual distributions from the inherited Roth over their own lifetime. Distributions must begin before December 31 of the year after the IRA owner's death.

Who Can Roth and Roll?

Workers earning $100,000 or less adjusted gross income can convert Traditional IRAs to Roth IRAs (except for married taxpayers filing a separate return). Although not subject to the 10-percent premature withdrawal penalty if under age 59 1/2, ordinary income taxes will be immediately due on any assets previously considered "deductible." In other words, any contributions and earnings that were not previously taxed will be taxable at the time of conversion.

The amount you convert does not currently count toward the $100,000 income limit to qualify for the conversion. If, for example your income is $90,000, you can convert more than $10,000. The amount you convert, however, *does count* toward income limits for qualifying for a *deductible* IRA.

When a Traditional IRA is converted to a Roth IRA, the five-year holding period begins with the tax year in which the conversion was made, or the first time the Roth account was opened, whichever is earlier. Because the conversion is actually a "roll over," the conversion must be completed within 60 days of distribution from the Traditional IRA.

If you convert to a Roth IRA and use funds outside the IRA to pay the taxes, the full account value can continue to compound tax-free inside the new converted Roth IRA and be distributed tax-free, according to the current rules.

You may want to time your taxable conversion(s) to coincide with losses from other investments or convert in a year when your income drops. If you have several IRAs, you may convert one or all of them. You also have the option of converting only part of a Traditional IRA to a Roth Account.

The longer an IRA has to compound before withdrawals are made, the more sense a Roth IRA makes, if Congress keeps its tax-free future promise. Qualified withdrawals are tax-free once the account has been opened for at least five years, a better alternative for young taxpayers in a higher tax bracket when they retire.

To Roth or Not to Roth: That Is the Confusion

Converting to a Roth IRA is not a "no brainer" because the tax bill for the conversion may be substantial, even without penalties. Once switched, assets can only be recharacterized back to a Traditional IRA before October 15 of the following year. The conversion may result in a higher tax bracket now.

Many investors have converted to a Roth IRA and paid taxes on funds that have been lost to the stock market decline. There are lots of considerations before an IRA conversion should be undertaken. The questions few are willing to ponder are: What if Congress changes the tax-free nature of a Roth IRA in the future? What if it doesn't grandfather existing Roth IRAs? Congress could restrict Roth IRA tax-free withdrawal benefits in the future because taxing hundreds of millions of previously tax-free dollars stashed away in Roth IRAs could provide significant revenues for social projects and general budget needs?

Employer IRAs

Small companies may create simplified pensions with *Super IRAs*. Employers can contribute to a plan for their employees who can also contribute for themselves through a payroll deduction plan. Each worker has a separate account and all benefits of a regular IRA. These plans have been generally replaced by more popular choices for small employers.

A Simple Pension That Really Is: The SEP/IRA

SEP/IRAs are ideal for self-employed individuals or small business owners. They follow similar rules for other IRAs, except that they have larger contribution limits, currently 25 percent of wages up to a maximum limit of $41,000. They have few reporting requirements as well. Employer contributions are tax-deferred to the employee until they are withdrawn. Account earnings accumulate tax-deferred until withdrawn as well. Generally, only employers contribute to these plans; employee contributions usually are not allowed. However, for a small business with only a few employees, the SEP can direct many tax-deferred dollars into a retirement nest egg. A self-employed owner/employee may be limited to less than the maximum contributions listed because of special rules and a special formula.

Simple IRA Plans

SIMPLE IRAs are a combination of employee before-tax salary deferrals and required employer contributions. Employees may contribute up to 100 percent of their income to the plan but not more than $9,000 in 2004 and a catch-up amount of $1,500 for those age 50 by the end of 2003, indexed for inflation in future years.

Employers *must make matching contributions* by either matching employees' contributions dollar for dollar to a maximum of 3 percent of compensation, or 2 percent of compensation for each eligible worker. The employer's contribution can be lowered to 1 percent in two out of five years. The SIMPLE IRA is anything but! Employers should seek expert advice so they do not trip over the complex tax rules and regulations. The penalty for withdrawing funds within the first two years after the plan is set up is a whopping 25 percent. New plans must be set up by October 15 of the year they are for to give employees ample notice.

Taking Care of (IRA) Business

Banks originally popularized the IRA phenomenon when interest rates were high, however, what banks sell are CDs to which they add the IRA label.

You can purchase numerous underlying investments such as mutual funds, stocks, bonds, insurance annuities, even certain gold or platinum coins. The bank then adds the IRA stamp to alert Uncle Sam this money is tax-deferred until withdrawal time. You can use any source of funds (savings, a loan, or a gift) for your contribution. You must have earned at least that much income during the year (unless you are a non-working spouse).

You don't need to invest a full maximum contribution of $3,000 or $3,500 per year. Put away what you can, whether a single lump sum or payments on a weekly or monthly basis. You can invest portions of your IRA in more than one place. Investing on January 1st of each year is ideal, but many folks don't recover from holiday bills until spring.

If you invest $250 on a monthly basis starting in January, you will have the full $3,000 (the under-age-50 limit) contributed by the end of the year. To contribute a full $3,500 (the limit for those who are age 50 and older), the monthly contribution needs to be $291.66 per month. Making your IRA investment at the last minute (at tax time for the previous year) is better than no contribution at all. But the longer you wait to invest, the harder your money has to work to make up for lost compounding time. You can invest your IRA contribution in more than one place, such as two or three mutual funds with different investment objectives and different underling securities. That way, you can diversify. If you don't contribute the full amount for one year, you cannot make up for it in the next year by adding it to your next year's contribution.

Whether you have a 401(k), a 403(b), a profit-sharing plan at work, or are self-employed and have a SEP or a KEOGH for your business, you may also contribute to an IRA account, though your contribution may not be tax-deductible. If you have the extra money, start an IRA, too. The more money that can be tax-deferred in one way or another, the better.

If you inadvertently contribute too much to your IRA in any year, remove the excess (and any earnings on those funds) before you file your tax return. If you discover the excess contribution too late to remove it before tax time, the excess amount can be transferred to next year's account. You will be taxed 6 percent per year on the excess funds in the meantime. If you are contributing to more than one IRA Account, watch your investment statement(s) to monitor how much money you have invested.

Robbing Peter to Pay Paul

You may not borrow from your IRA. You can, however, take constructive receipt of IRA funds (the check in your hands) one time per year for a period of up to 60 days to move your IRA funds instead of submitting paperwork to directly transfer your IRA rollover to another IRA custodian. If Uncle Sam believes you are borrowing those funds short-term, the event is considered an immediate distribution of IRA funds, and taxes will be due on all pre-tax money (plus a 10-percent early withdrawal penalty if you are under age 59 1/2).

Simple Estate Planning

The simplest method of passing an IRA to your heirs is to name one or more as primary beneficiaries, and backup contingent beneficiary(ies) as well. You can designate as many primary beneficiaries and backup beneficiaries as you want. In this manner, your IRA will avoid probate. Be sure the IRA Custodial Agreement at your IRA institution allows the beneficiary designations you choose.

Coverdell Savings Accounts: Education IRAs

This IRA is not really an IRA because it's funded through gifts to a minor who doesn't work; its purpose is education expenses, not retirement; and by age 18, you can no longer deposit any further funds. By age 30, all funds must have been paid out or transferred or there is a tax penalty. The popularity of this college savings plan is proof that the public doesn't look a gift horse in the mouth if the marketing is good enough. This account is examined in more detail in Chapter 11. Parents, grandparents, other relatives, and friends alike can contribute a total of up to $2,000 per year for future college expenses per student under age 18.

Although there are no up-front tax write-offs on these funds, under current laws the account grows tax-deferred until withdrawn tax-free to pay for qualified education expenses including tuition, fees, room and board, and equipment such as computers.

The funds can be used for public and parochial elementary and high school expenses as well as secondary education costs.

Additional contributions can be made to a 529 savings plan in the same year. The law may prohibit funding an education IRA in the same year that you contribute to a state-sponsored, prepaid tuition program. There may be limits on using more than one tax-favored college savings strategy in the same year such as the Hope Scholarship credit or a Lifetime Learning credit. See tax rules for complete information.

Under present financial aid formulas the account is considered the child's assets. You may want to use all education IRA assets on one year's educational costs so you can take the tax credits in other years.

Be careful that total contributions do not exceed more than the law allows, especially if Grandma and Aunt Harriet are both sending funds. You can invest contributions in more than one place.

Roll over Rover

Even after age 70 1/2, when IRA mandatory distributions must begin, you can transfer your IRA from investment company to company at any time during the year, by directing it trustee-to-trustee and directly from one IRA custodian to another. Unless your current IRA rollover came from a pension distributed to you after December 31, 1992, you have 60 days from the time you receive the IRA check to manually send it to the next IRA custodian. Tax law allows you to receive those funds only once each 365 days. To transfer more often than that, request a direct trustee transfer of funds to the new IRA investment company custodian. *If your IRA rollover came from a pension plan that was set up after January 1, 1993, you will need paperwork to directly transfer your funds from one IRA custodian to another to avoid taxation of funds on the transfer.*

You have only 60 days to get your IRA to the next IRA custodian. If you miss your transfer deadline, you can lose the IRA tax-deferral benefit, and all money will immediately become taxable as ordinary income.

Keep IRA rollover accounts separate from other mutual fund money and from new IRA contributions. Keep IRA rollover funds from a company retirement plan separate from any other IRAs, even if you plan to invest in the same mutual fund.

A bank CD sold as an IRA can be moved as well. You may want to wait until the CD matures to avoid an early withdrawal penalty. Many lending institutions offer penalty-free withdrawals for depositors over the age of 59 1/2. Ask your bank about withdrawal privileges and penalties.

An insurance annuity is similar to an IRA but is really an *Individual Retirement Annuity*. Its funds can be transferred as well to another type of IRA investment vehicle. Insurance annuities are more fully discussed in Chapter 7.

The $50,000 Mistake

If you are not putting money into a Traditional IRA because it is not currently tax-deductible from your gross income, *you could be making a terrible mistake!!!*

Unfortunately, Congress lets no good deal go unpunished for very long. So, the tax deduction that felt so good and erased a maximum of $2,000 per worker from the gross earnings of all wage earners was maimed by the 1986 Tax Act. But the death of the IRA has been greatly exaggerated. Before you throw away a silver bullet that Congress still allows, consider the following:

Suppose a taxpayer makes an annual $3,000 *totally non-deductible* IRA contribution each year as opposed to merely investing $3,000 per year in a taxable investment. Both the non-deductible IRA and the taxable investment funds are invested in the same vehicle averaging 10 percent per year. The following is the result of each investment at the end of 20 and 30 years. The money was invested at the beginning of each year:

At the end of:	Nondeductible IRA	Taxable Investment*
20 years	$189,007	$127,006
30 years	$542,830	$286,529

*The taxpayer is in the 28-percent tax bracket, plus 5 percent state and local income tax.

The *tax-deferred* power of IRA earnings inside the IRA account over time is far more powerful than any immediate tax deduction. *Even if you cannot deduct any portion of your annual IRA contribution, your earnings grow tax-deferred until you take them out.*

The longer that money can compound, the larger the gap and the difference between the tax-deferred IRA account and the fully taxable investment.

Remember, the IRA account shown above has *no* tax-deduction advantages. Only the benefits of tax-deferred compounding are seen here. If any portion of the IRA account can be deducted, the advantages over time could be even greater.

Considering the current uncertain retirement government entitlement outlook, it is prudent to invest now for the long term. Put in your annual IRA contribution, deductible or not!

Tapping IRAs Without Tears

You can always withdraw funds from an IRA (unlike company retirement plans), even if you are younger than age 59 1/2. However, generally, you cannot withdraw from your IRA without a 10-percent penalty until you have reached age 59 1/2. If you don't need the money, let it continue to compound even longer. Use taxable investments, instead, for supplemental income. The *longer* your dollars work inside the tax umbrella, the *harder* they work.

If you withdraw funds before you reach the age of 59 1/2 (for reasons other than death, disability, or one of the exceptions mentioned earlier), you may incur a 10-percent penalty for early withdrawal plus all taxes due on the amount you withdraw. There are several ways to tap an IRA before age 59 1/2 without paying the penalty:

- ◆ You can withdraw money from your IRA before age 59 1/2 without penalty if you take the money out in the form of an annuity, a substantially equal series of payments based on your life expectancy or over the lives of you and a beneficiary combined together. There are several methods that can be used, and each produces a different mandatory annual withdrawal amount. This is called a *72T withdrawal,* and distributions must continue at least annually for five years or to the age of 59 1/2, whichever period is longer. The remainder of your IRA is not taxed in any way as long as you follow the early withdrawal annuity rules. More information is available under Section 72T of the IRS tax code.

- ◆ You can separate your IRAs into different accounts and use the 72T early withdrawal method with one account while leaving the other IRAs to compound until after age 59 1/2. Seek assistance before implementing this withdrawal method, as the tax penalties for mistakes in calculations are significant.

Taxing Matters

When you withdraw from your IRA, all tax-deductible contributions and tax-deferred earnings will be treated like interest from a CD—as ordinary income. You pay taxes only on the amount you withdraw. The remainder of your IRA continues tax-deferred until you withdraw it.

Keep all IRA records for the rest of your life, or eternity, whichever period is longer. Especially save every tax form #8606 you complete for annual partially or totally non-deductible IRA contributions. These records will provide a clear paper trail if the IRS should ever examine your IRA history. When you start withdrawing from a combination of tax-deductible and non-deductible IRA accounts, a certain percentage of each withdrawal will contain part of a previous non-deductible IRA contribution and will not be taxed again.

I'm 70 1/2! Now What?

Fear grips some retirees when they reach age 70 1/2 and they must withdraw their first mandatory minimum IRA distribution. Every IRA Account owner/investor must start taking mandatory required minimum distributions (RMDs) before their required beginning date (RBD).

Mandatory required withdrawals must start by April 1 of the year *after* you turn age 70 1/2. Even if you wait to make the first withdrawal until the year after you turn age 70 1/2, the first IRA distribution actually counts for the year before, in which you turned age 70 1/2. Therefore, you must take your next year's RMD in that same year as well. Two withdrawals in the same year could put you in a higher tax bracket. To avoid this problem, the initial withdrawal can be made by December 31st of the year you turn age 70 1/2. If you plan to be in a lower tax bracket, however, postponing the first withdrawal until April 1 of the year following your 70 1/2 birthday may lower your overall tax bite. Such decisions should be made carefully and with expert tax advice. You may always withdraw more from your IRAs than the law specifies, just not less. Distributions may be taken as one lump sum annually or in any number of payments over the year, as long as the total mandatory distribution is withdrawn by December 31st of each year you must make a withdrawal. After the first year, all RMDs must be taken by December 31 of that year. Only during the first year are you entitled to the time extension period for withdrawing the first IRA RMD.

Calculation Methods

Under the new, newer, newest IRA required minimum distribution rules, calculating the annual required amount of withdrawal is a breeze. The Uniform Table fits all except when you are married and your spouse for the full year is more than 10 years younger than you, the IRA owner. In that case, the Joint and Survivor Table is used to determine the annual amount to be distributed each year from all of the owner's IRAs. Everyone else will use the Uniform Table. Check the Appendix for the latest version.

Divide the total fair market value of *all* IRAs on December 31 of the *previous* year by the divisor to the right of your age (at the end of the current year) on the Uniform Table. Your answer is the amount of money that must be withdrawn before the end of the year.

The RMD calculations, the amount you must withdraw each year, does not depend on who your beneficiary is (except as outlined above with a younger spouse). Generally, your mandatory withdrawal is not connected to the age of the person you name as beneficiary. The Uniform Table provides all the information most folks will need. For every year after the first, the method is the same, only you will use your new age divisor. All other IRA withdrawal methods previously used have passed on to IRA heaven.

The mandatory withdrawal amount can be taken from any IRA account, preferably from the investment providing the lowest return. Don't forget to add in the value of all IRA accounts. You can always withdraw *more* money. These rules only affect the *minimum* amount you must withdraw after age 70 1/2.

Beneficiary IRA heirs also have required distributions. They use the Single Life Expectancy Table to calculate their annual RMDs. This table is used in the same general manner, using the numbers on this table except that you use this table only for the first mandatory withdrawal. For all of the following years, you reduce the first divisor number by a full round number 1. In other words, if your first divisor was 34.6, next year you will use the divisor of 33.6, and the next year 32.6, and so on down. You do not go back and recalculate using the Single Life Expectancy Table after the first year, and you do not use the same Uniform Table that IRA owners use.

Seek expert advice on the latest IRA distribution rules because they could be changed at any time. The penalties for withdrawing too much are the loss of tax-deferred funds, and the IRS tax penalty for withdrawing too little is 50 percent of the amount you failed to withdraw but should have.

For more information about IRAs, contact your mutual fund service department or shareholder services. You can also request IRS Publication 590 for more details.

Don't forget to add primary and contingent (backup) designated beneficiaries to all your IRA accounts so you can create a "stretch" IRA that can be rolled over to your spouse, then inherited by your children, and even be available to your grandchildren, should your children die before the IRA accounts are empty.

Despite the fact that some people can no longer deduct their IRA contributions, IRAs invested into growth-oriented mutual funds remain one of the best long-term retirement investments you can make.

CHAPTER 15

Estate Planning: You Can't Take It With You

Tax his cow, tax his goat; tax his pants, tax his coat.

If he hollers, tax him more; tax him 'til he's good and sore.

Tax his coffin, tax his grave; tax the sod in which he lays;

Put these words upon his tomb: "Taxes drove me to my doom."

After he's gone he can't relax; they'll still go after inheritance tax.

Passing the Buck

Estate planning for the yachtless is a vital part of every financial plan if:

1. You are married, divorced, or widowed.
2. You have children or other dependents.
3. You own tangible assets (cars, home, personal property).
4. You owe debts or financial obligations.
5. You own financial assets (bank accounts, stocks, bonds, mutual funds).
6. You have a company pension plan or 401(k).
7. You own property or personal assets in another state.
8. Your financial circumstances have changed.

9. Your health has recently changed.
10. You have a disabled spouse or child.
11. You intend to disinherit any of your family.
12. Your plan has not been updated for several years and laws have changed.
13. You will eventually die.

The above list covers just about everyone. The specifics of your estate planning depend upon your unique circumstances, and the inheritance registration vehicles you will use will vary.

A competent attorney should spend enough time with you to outline options and to explore Will substitutes and alternatives for property distribution other than the wholesale distribution of a trust. There are many alternate ways to title your assets that provide relief from the cumbersome and expensive process of probate.

Where There's a Will, There's a Way

No matter how little you own, dying intestate (without a Will), creates difficulties and expenses for those you leave behind. Without instructions to the contrary, state laws will determine who gets your possessions, who raises your children, how your assets will be divided and who your Executor (male) or Executrix (female) will be. Leaving the distribution of your estate up to the legal system is time-consuming and may cost more to settle the estate.

In addition, dying intestate gives tacit approval for your relatives to haggle over your belongings (at your expense) and over your children, who might be attractive if they come attached to a large insurance policy naming them as principal beneficiaries.

You will have two kinds of estate: a *gross estate,* which includes all assets you owned at the moment of your death, and a *probate estate,* which most folks seek to avoid. If you can register your assets so that you can tell who inherits them without going to the Will for a determination, these assets can avoid the probate process and be directed to your heirs sans the expensive time-consuming probate process. A well-thought-out estate plan, using Will substitute titles with a Will to catch assets that don't have a direct transfer plan can often provide an efficient transfer process for your heirs.

Because Wills can be contested, are not cheap to administer, and can become bogged down, you may want to keep assets out of your Will. There are many Will substitutes, which I discuss later, that avoid the probate process and do not require complicated legal paperwork, such as a trust, to implement. Will substitutes do not negate the necessity of drafting a Will. Think of your Will as an instruction booklet for your heirs and the courts to follow with certain powers that your Executor/trix can use to maximize assets to your loved ones and minimize taxes at the same time.

Unless you have a reason to protect your Will from your family, consider keeping your estate planning documents in a fireproof box at home, not in a bank safety deposit box, or at the attorney's office. You can provide others with a copy if necessary for their information and their safekeeping.

When you die, assets that have a built-in transfer plan, such as a beneficiary or joint-owner designation, can generally avoid being included in your Will and, therefore, avoid the probate process. In fact, your Will could leave your heirs *all* your property, while using Will substitutes to register beneficiary designations on your assets could transfer those same assets to other beneficiaries instead, leaving the *heirs in your Will penniless*. Will substitutes are powerful tools that you can use to direct your estate assets more clearly and more cheaply. If your estate is relatively simple, most, if not all, of your possessions can be passed directly, efficiently, and inexpensively in this manner. Know your state's individual laws and probate codes regarding Will substitutes.

The following checklist suggests how Will substitutes, ownership, and estate designations can be used:

1. **Bank savings and checking accounts, CDs, credit unions, bank money market accounts, and savings bonds.** *Joint ownership with rights of survivorship* means either person may withdraw during his or her lifetime with the assets payable directly to the survivor at death. Individual accounts or joint and survivor ownership, with an additional beneficiary registration called *payable on death* (POD), will avoid probate and directly transfer funds to the named beneficiary(ies) upon the death of the owner or co-owners.

2. **Securities such as stocks, bonds, brokerage accounts, and mutual funds.** *Joint tenants with rights of survivorship* means each co-owner has a full and undivided 100-percent interest in every dollar in the account. Both parties must consent to terminating the account or the liquidation of any funds during their lifetime. Remaining funds are payable to the survivor upon death of one of the joint owners. Many states allow an additional beneficiary designation called a *Transfer on Death* (TOD) to be added to security investment accounts. Upon the death of one owner, the surviving owner still receives the funds. However, upon the death of both co-owners, the named beneficiaries (the TOD designees) receive remaining funds outside probate. During the lifetime of the co-owners, these TOD beneficiaries have no control of the funds nor any ownership of the account. An individual can use the same method to pass assets outside probate and outside of their Will by setting up a *Sole Owner* account with a Transfer on Death. Upon the death of the individual owner, a Transfer on Death beneficiary will receive the account proceeds and avoid the probate process. A Transfer on Death is a simple and useful method of avoiding probate without using a trust.

3. **Insurance proceeds.** With primary beneficiaries and contingent (backup) beneficiaries, you can designate certain percentages for each heir you choose. For the benefit of minor children, you can name an adult who will receive

the money as a fiduciary on behalf of the children until they reach the age of majority. (See a further discussion of insurance in this chapter.)

4. **Real estate.** *Tenancy by the Entireties* between husband and wife, if allowed in your state, can transfer the home directly to the surviving spouse and avoid most forms of creditors who may want to lien the survivor's home due to debts owed by the deceased. A *joint and survivorship* deed keeps the property in an undivided interest in both owners' names during their lifetime, then transfers full ownership directly to the survivor(s) after the death of one owner. Real estate deeds can have multiple owners, but unless specifically Tenancy by the Entireties, Tenants in Common, or Joint and Survivor, each part owner's share generally passes to the deceased's heirs named in their Will. *Tenancy in Common* allows each property owner to transfer their proportional property interest to their heirs through their Will, therefore, through the probate process.

5. **Auto and truck titles, RVs, or water craft.** Joint titles or, in some states, Transfer on Death registration titles, allow these types of property to pass directly to either the co-owner or the named beneficiary. In many states, spouses can transfer these assets in the name of the deceased spouse just by re-registering them at the title agencies where license plates are bought, also avoiding probate.

6. **Pensions, 401(k)s, profit-sharing plans, IRAs, SEPs, SIMPLEs, KEOGHs, tax sheltered annuities, and other insurance products.** Each of these types of plans can have beneficiary options that bypass the Will.

Death Insurance Proceeds

Death benefits are often registered with little thought and, therefore, may not provide full benefits for your beneficiaries under state insurance and federal and state tax laws. The greatest advantage a life insurance policy beneficiary designation has is to pass the death benefit directly and quickly to your heirs outside the Will and away from creditors. If life insurance policies are included in a Will, they become part of the probate assets and may be subject to probate and may be contingent to the claims of creditors or contests by unhappy heirs.

Generally, insurance death benefits avoid federal income taxes. They may not always avoid estate taxes or state income taxes.

There are three people involved in every insurance policy sale: the *owner* of the policy, the *insured*, and the *beneficiary(ies)*. The *owner* controls the terms of the policy and can continue or lapse the contract as well as change the beneficiaries. The owner also can pledge the policy as loan collateral or for other purposes. The *insured* is the person whose life is insured by the contract. The insured is generally also the owner. The *beneficiary(ies)* receive the death benefit, whether they are designated persons or entities such as a trust or a charity. *An owner and a beneficiary must have an insurable interest in the insured in order to receive the death benefit.* In order to pay a death benefit to a beneficiary, an insurance company may demand that an insurable interest exists. Otherwise they may direct the death benefit according to state law succession. So if your beneficiary is *not* your spouse or an immediate child, it is helpful to designate on the insurance application why your choice of beneficiary should receive the funds.

Insurance companies expect that beneficiaries have an insurable interest in the policy death benefit, which replaces an economic or financial loss to the beneficiary if the insured should die. An insurance company can easily understand the economic loss of a husband, a wife, or a dependent child. However, if two unmarrieds buy a home together with a mortgage, they may each purchase an insurance policy naming the other as beneficiary to pay off the loan in case of the death of one of them. An insurance company might re-direct the death benefit to someone else unless they understand upfront that the policies were taken out because a financial loss would result to each beneficiary.

If one spouse owns the other spouse's insurance contract, the death benefit can be conveyed to the beneficial spouse *outside* the deceased's gross estate and, therefore, can generally avoid all federal and state *estate* taxes as well as income taxes. Otherwise, a large insurance policy in one spouse's name as the owner *and* the insured could add to the size of the death estate and create estate taxes that could otherwise have been easily avoided. A lawsuit could also attach assets of the deceased, including the insurance that the deceased owned before his or her death.

Check beneficiary listings on all insurance policies (including the one supplied by your employer). A first spouse won't likely hand over a death benefit check to your current spouse if you forget to change the beneficiary after the divorce, although some states have laws that automatically terminate such beneficiaries once a divorce or dissolution has taken place.

Whenever major events occur in your financial, personal, or medical life, you should re-examine all beneficiary and ownership titles to keep them current with your wishes. Always keep copies of all beneficiary designations in your storage lockbox in case the insurance company loses its copy. (It happens more often than you may believe.)

The *primary beneficiary*, usually a spouse, a parent, or a child, gets the entire death benefit first. If more than one primary beneficiary is designated, they share equally unless you have specified percentages in writing. If the primary beneficiary(ies) should predecease (die before) the insured or should die in a common accident with the insured, the insurance proceeds ordinarily pass to the *contingent beneficiary(ies)* named in the policy.

Young children under the age of majority are legally incompetent, so no insurance company is going to write out a generous insurance check to a 3-year-old. Naming an adult trustee for the child's benefit keeps the insurance money out of probate court and away from creditors or court action. If a contingent beneficiary has not been named, the death benefit goes into the decedent's estate, generally through the Will.

If your current insurance policy has been converted from an employer benefit, federal employer plan laws may interfere with your beneficiary plans. Get expert advice.

Who Gets the Kids—And Control of Their Money?

When drafting your Will, don't forget about the care of your minor children. Upon your death, a second spouse may not automatically wish to care for and raise your children from a first marriage.

What if you and your spouse die in a common accident or your spouse survives but is seriously injured? What if you are divorced and feel your ex-spouse would not be a good money manager of your children's inheritance? What if your children's only other living relatives are your aging parents or a friend or relative in another state? What if the solution to your children's future emotional well-being and financial health are two different people? Solutions aren't always simple.

In the case of divorce, will the courts award custody of your children to your ex-spouse, even if another adult is preferable? In cases in which both parents are killed or die, courts could name their own choice of guardian. It is vital to make your requests for Custodial Guardianship (residential custody) of your children in your Will. Courts may also intercede regarding who gets control over a minor's inheritance. Plan to name backup custodians and trustees until the children reach the age of majority or the age of maturity, depending on how you write the testamentary trust. A *trustee* can manage their financial resources under the guidelines you set up in the trust, *even if someone else is raising the children*.

Your death insurance benefit must be sufficient to pay off all of your liabilities plus support your children in another household to adulthood, perhaps even through college.

Taming the Estate Tax Bite

Income taxes may play a part in your estate plan. Transferring appreciated assets to family and friends in a way that favors the recipients instead of the IRS may take some planning. Here are a couple of tax rules you should know about:

Taxable gains may vanish at death. Say you buy stock for $1,000 and sell it for $500,000. Your taxable gain is $499,000. What if your son inherits the stock from you and it's worth $500,000 when you die? He can sell it for as much as $500,000 and report *no federal income taxable gain* because his basis in the stock is *stepped-up* to its estate value.

Gains don't disappear when assets are *given away* during your lifetime. They are given a *carry-over cost basis*. Suppose you give your stock (or your home) to your son today. His carry-over basis is the same as yours: $1,000. A sale for $500,000 would again result in a $499,000 reportable tax gain—this time paid for by your son, the same as you would have paid taxes. Sometimes it is better to hold on to your property during your lifetime.

There are many exceptions to this general tax rule. Be sure you know what the tax consequences are before transferring assets during your lifetime. There is generally *no stepped-up basis* on assets transferred during your lifetime.

Banks accounts, U.S. savings bonds, IRAs, pension plans, 401(k)s, and insurance annuities *do not currently share* this favorable tax advantage, and therefore are not as advantageous as inheritance vehicles in this circumstance. IRAs enjoy other forms of deferred taxation to heirs. Chapter 14 tells you how to create a *Stretch IRA* so you can enjoy your IRA funds as long as possible, then roll them over to your spouse, then onto your children—and finally on to their children.

What If I Become Disabled?

Create a *Durable Financial Power of Attorney* now to name a financial representative so that if you become physically or mentally incompetent, someone you trust can make financial decisions for you. Social Security benefits; money management; disability arrangements; pension distributions; license plate renewal; opening of mail; maintaining homeowner, auto, and life insurance premiums; and paying taxes are a sample of financial tasks that must be carried out for you. You can also designate a backup, a contingent representative, if your primary person should be unable, unwilling, or otherwise fail to qualify as attorney-in-fact.

A *general* power of attorney can be utilized by your representative at any time, while a *springing* power of attorney is valid only after you have become disabled. However, the springing power of attorney may take time to be implemented by the court system. In the meantime, your insurance coverages could lapse, money management affairs may suffer, and tax penalties could be assessed while your financial representative waits for court appointment, perhaps for several months. This document must contain language that it will continue through any disability to remain valid when you need someone to perform financial tasks for you.

This is a powerful document and general powers of attorney can be used even when you are not disabled. So keep the original documents in your fireproof lockbox safely stored away in case it is needed.

The *Medical Power of Attorney* or *Healthcare Directive* is becoming an important addition to today's estate plan. It performs a similar function as the general power of attorney, only in the area of medical decisions. You can name a trusted family member or friend to act in your stead and a contingent person in case the first is not able to qualify.

What If I Become Terminally Ill?

A *living will* allows you to provide written intent regarding withdrawing or maintaining life-support medical care if you are terminally ill or permanently unconscious. Individual states vary in their approaches to this sensitive issue. Some states advise both a living will and a *durable health power of attorney* to cover healthcare contingencies. Contact the legal bar association in your state or county to see what forms the courts will accept and if it has prototypes you can use at little or no cost.

Trust Me on This

Trust-mania is rampant, with some lawyers, especially in heavy retirement states, soliciting documents you may not understand. While there are advantages to trusts in some cases, trusts are not the panacea you may hear about at the free estate planning seminars. Carefully consider why you need a trust when there are so many simpler methods to direct your personal assets and real property outside of probate, minimize taxes, and retain the direct ownership of your assets while you are alive.

Trusts are broadly categorized according to when they take effect and whether they can be altered after they have been drafted. A *testamentary* trust takes effect after death, and may be included inside or outside a comprehensive Will. A *living trust*, or *inter-vivos trust*, takes effect as soon as it is established and is generally administered outside a Will, even though a Will is drafted as a complimentary estate planning tool. Probate may be required even if you draft a trust when the Will is entered in probate court after death. Trusts do *not* take the place of Will documents. They restrict or enhance the Will.

Living trusts are further classified as either *revocable*, subject to change during the lifetime of the grantor, or *irrevocable*, not able to be changed once they are signed into effect. (Even revocable trusts, however, become irrevocable upon the death of the grantor.) Each person's estate planning goals and needs are unique and must be considered in light of both the benefits and burdens inherent in estate planning strategies available today.

Keep in mind that a trust document represents a change in the control of your assets before and after your death. Trust laws change and current language may be a future impediment to the execution of your trust. Trusts may even set up your assets better for creditors, and most trusts can be contested like Wills.

The Tax Man May Not Cometh

Most Americans do not have to worry about federal estate taxes. Surviving spouses enjoy an unlimited marital deduction (no federal estate taxes on the transfer of estate assets to a spouse). State laws often provide tax relief for married couples. Federal estate laws currently exempt transfers to heirs other than your spouse of $1,500,000.

Sometimes 'Tis Better to Gift Than to Bequeath

You could avoid paying future federal estate taxes on certain assets by gifting appreciating assets away during your lifetime before they grow even larger. In 2004, you can currently transfer (or gift) an estate up to $1,500,000 without paying federal estate taxes on the property now or after you have died.

If you transfer more than $11,000 per person per year ($22,000 if your spouse also agrees to the transfer), you must file a Federal Gift Tax Form 709. This tells the government to reduce your unified credit tax exclusion at your death of $1,500,000 by the amount gifted per year over the annual $11,000 gift tax exclusion limit.

For example, if you have a net worth of $1,500,000 and you gift $400,000 during your lifetime above the annual gift tax exclusion limit per year, the additional amount excluded from federal estate taxes after your demise will be $600,000. If you die with more than $1,100,000 remaining in your gross estate, federal estate taxes will be levied. By combining the lifetime gift tax exclusion and the one-time after-death unified credit, plus making annual gifts up to the maximum gift tax exclusion limit per year, you can better direct who gets your money after you are done with it. *Be sure, however, you will not need that money later*. A well-intentioned gift could mean the loss (opportunity cost) of much more at a future date because that money will never again compound for you.

Estate planning measures such as Qualified Personal Residence Trusts (QPRTs), Grantor Retained Income Trusts (GRITs), Q-Tip Trusts, Spendthrift (minor) Trusts, and the more common A/B (Marital Bypass, Credit Shelter) Trusts are complicated estate strategies. Before committing to a major change in your life, interview several legal advisers to separate the sizzle from the steak. In many cases, registering your assets with Will substitutes backed up by a thoughtful Will can solve your estate issues without the need for more complicated legal paperwork and the associated costs.

The Executor/Administrator

If you are named the Executor or Personal Administrator of an estate, interview several attorneys (if needed) for estimates of legal fees. Ask about hourly fees versus set project prices for the whole process. Do not automatically use the lawyer who drew up the deceased person's Will. Get prices beforehand and a written estimate. Because this is likely a new experience for most folks, take your time and ask questions throughout the process.

Executors usually list assets, inventory contents of safety deposit boxes, and locate the decedent's property. They can admit the Will into probate and advertise for creditors. They pay final expenses and estate debts, analyze business interests, prepare and file a final estate tax return, and, ultimately, turn over the assets to the deceased's beneficiaries or trustees.

Executors have a fiduciary responsibility to beneficiaries and to legitimate creditors. You could be personally responsible for paying such bills if you cannot retrieve money given to heirs before all legal creditors have been satisfied.

The most dangerous estate planning mistake is "default" planning—doing nothing. Though not a pleasant activity, planning for the distribution of your assets should help you sleep better so you can move on to living successfully and working your wealth-building plan.

CHAPTER 16

Myths, Legends, and Truths of Investing

Money managers aren't born with a special talent for predicting the future. In fact, many of them lose significant investor money when their strategies fail.

Whether the top-down approach, the bottom-up fundamental strategy, the Dogs-of-the-Dow theory, the efficient market thesis, modern portfolio theory, or the whatever-my-neighbors-and-friends-are-buying method of investing, strategies you hear about can be colorful, varied, and often diametrically opposed. The amazing thing about conventional "wisdom" is the frequency with which it is plain wrong.

You may have heard the top mutual fund is the one that boasts the best past performance; that the more risk you take, the more money you will eventually make; that the younger you are, the more stocks should be in your investment portfolio; that financial institutions are your partners; that no-load mutual funds are free; that paper losses don't count because you don't lose any money until you sell; and that a losing investment can come back. The punch line is that *none* of these so-called axioms is true. Let's expose some myths and substitute some investment *truths* you can build upon.

Determine Your Time Horizon

Decide when the investment money will be needed. Short-term savings are funds you will need within a three-year time horizon. Long-term money strategies are reserved for funds invested for three years or more. Short-term investments should guarantee your principal. Long-term funds must preserve future purchasing power. Using mainly fixed-income investments for long-term investing is like using a screwdriver to change a car tire. You are using the wrong investment vehicles for growth to fight inflation. Always manage some of your funds for growth. Growth investments won't guarantee your principal.

Determine Your Risk Tolerance

Imagine sailing off to an exotic island for a few years. Because you know about the time value of money and inflation forces, you decide to take your investment funds with you.

On this island, there are only two industries to invest in: a suntan lotion corporation and an umbrella factory. You have some information to assist in your investment choice: The sun shines 50 percent of the time, while it rains the other half of the year. Like your local TV weather person, you can't predict when the sunny days will appear. So how will you invest your precious funds?

Risk-adverse investors would choose a 50/50 split of each company's stock. Given the limited bits of real investment information available in the financial universe, when they understand the inherent risks of investing, most folks choose to lose less money, even if it means making less return. That prudent instinct can create cautious and careful money managers.

Conservative investors would rather net lower profits when times are hot and profits look easy to preserve their investment principal from the potential of greater loss when markets unwind. This summarizes the "get rich slow" theory of investing. *Short-term money should guarantee your principal. Long-term funds should guarantee your future purchasing power. The proper diversification of assets for each time horizon can lead to a conservative sleep-tight investment stance.*

Determine the Optimum Investment

Consider the period of time your money has to compound before it is needed. Because short investment time frames demand guaranteed principal, your options are fairly limited to bank savings and other interest-bearing accounts, bank CDs, credit union accounts, savings bonds, and conservative money market mutual funds. These are appropriate for investment periods *less* than three years.

Money you can tie up for a longer investment period—*more* than three years—dictates using a *completely different strategy* to stay ahead of inflation. Consider mutual funds as the optimum investment for long-term capital. Mutual funds can diversify your portfolio like that of a millionaire, allow you to monitor your assets at all times, cut through financial intermediaries for a greater share of profits, and allow access to your funds at all times. Mutual funds are appropriate in taxable accounts as well as for retirement, other tax-sheltered accounts, and college savings vehicles. Nearly every long-term financial goal can be met by using mutual funds in your investment arsenal. So let's learn something about the basic financial ingredients that make up most mutual fund investment options.

My Word Is My Bond

A bond is an IOU, a promise to pay. It can be issued by your government, a private corporation, a non-profit entity, a foreign company or government, or for a public purpose. The bond issuer promises to pay the holder at scheduled intervals a certain *yield* or *rate of return*, and to repay its principal, the *face value*, at a specific date in the future, called the bond's *maturity date*. Bonds are fixed-income vehicles, generally pay a regular rate of return, and, unless the bond fails or is impaired for any reason, you know how much principal you will receive when the bond matures.

There are several common types of bonds:

1. **U.S. Government securities.** Issued or backed by the U.S. government, they have safety from default but not from loss of value during periods of rising interest rates.

2. **Corporate bonds.** Issued by private industry, they can vary widely in yield, maturity, and credit quality. These can default or lose total value, as well as decline in value if their credit quality is reduced by rating agencies and when interest rates rise around them.

3. **Municipal bonds.** Issued and backed by local and state governments, public revenue projects, or general obligations of regional or county agencies, they pay investors lower yields because their income is generally free from federal taxes. If issued in the state where you reside, they may also be exempt from state and local taxes. They could default, and they can lose more principal when interest rates rise because they offer a lower yield than either government or corporate bonds.

4. **Foreign bonds.** Issued by foreign entities, corporations, governments, or financial intermediaries, they can trade in the United States or overseas and may be denominated in a foreign currency. They have volatility because of political and economic fluctuations of the country in which they are issued and risk from currency movements in the global markets.

5. **High-yield (junk) bonds.** Issued by lower-rated companies with poorer credit ratings, they are considered speculative and are not recommended in large doses for high-quality investing. They carry a higher degree of default risk.

6. **Zero coupon (discount) bonds.** Issued at a deep discount from their final face value, these bonds make no semiannual payments of interest. The bondholder receives no money until the bond matures, though they may be taxed

on the accrued interest annually. The bond grows over time from price appreciation. They tend to lose the most value, carry the highest interest-rate risk, when interest rates *rise*. They also gain the most price appreciation as interest rates *fall*. Because we are more interested in *not* losing money than in getting rich quickly, they are considered high risk to principal. If held to maturity and they do not default, they will accrue to their final face value. These are Wall Street creations, backed by actual bonds held by the companies that design these securities.

All investments involve risk, the chance that the result might differ from your original expectations. Bond risks can be categorized as follows:

- **Market risk** is the chance that the bond will fall in value based on market demand for the specific security. When inflation is high, the number of bond buyers may increase. When stocks are moving, bonds may be overlooked.
- **Credit risk** implies that the bond issuer won't be able to make interest payments or repay the principal when originally promised. Rating agencies analyze credit ratings for investors. But a bond issued today with a stellar rating could deteriorate in credit quality tomorrow.
- **Inflation risk** is the danger that bond yields (interest payments) won't keep pace with inflation over long periods of time. This is why a well-diversified investment portfolio must include some stocks as well as fixed-income vehicles such as bonds and cash.
- **Re-investment risk** is the lost opportunity to earn a higher rate of interest when interest rates decline as your bond or bank CD matures, forcing you to reinvest your principal at a lower rate than before. When interest rates are at their peak, investors may lock in longer maturities for longer high annual returns. However, when interest rates are climbing, short-term bonds or short-term bond mutual funds allow reinvestment of principal at higher future interest rates. Bond yields rise with the upward direction of interest rates in the economy and as their prices decline. *The longer the bond to maturity generally the greater the prepayment risk.*
- **Interest-rate risk** occurs when bond prices go down as interest rates climb. Each time market interest rises, the price of a bond held by an investor loses actual value. Unless the bond is held to maturity (which could be 10 or 20 years away), the investor loses money, even if he or she has purchased a U.S. government bond or an insured variety. *The longer the bond, generally the higher the interest rate risk.* As interest rates rose in 1994 and again in 1999, bond investors lost significant investment principal. *Bond prices move inversely to the direction of interest rates.* How to purchase bond mutual funds is discussed later in the book. Because higher bond yields tend

to reflect higher inflation, when interest rates rise, bondholders lose in two ways: lower locked-in rates and an additional loss of value from inflation.

◆ **Default risk** means that corporate or municipal bonds could stop paying the interest to bondholders, and may even call the bond worthless, leaving you with no yield and no principal. The penalty for municipalities and other public debtors defaulting today is *nothing.* Economic uncertainty and recessions increase the likelihood of bond defaults as state and local budgets become tighter. *Time increases default risk: The longer the bond, the more likely its future default (excluding the U.S. government and U.S. agency varieties).*

As you can see, bonds can be nearly as dangerous to safety of principal as stocks. For most investors, bonds should be purchased only through mutual funds where such risks can be reduced through geographic and security selection.

If you buy two bonds and one defaults, you have lost half of your investment. If, instead, you hold 100 bonds through a bond mutual fund, and that single bond should fall off the face of the earth, you are still in the bond business with 99 other issues. Because interest rates are constantly moving based on numerous factors, it is impossible to consistently predict the direction of interest rates. To reduce many types of risk, choose shorter duration mutual funds (explained in Chapter 18).

"Safety" of Stocks

Stocks move up and down with even fewer warnings than bonds. Scandals, accounting irregularities, internal upheaval, labor strikes, bad products, lawsuits, reduced sales, industry competition, and rising interest rates are factors affecting stock prices.

There are no *safe* stocks. Those who bought IBM, AT&T, Ford, or GE did not fare a lot better in the last three years than investors who jumped into large technology stocks in the last few years.

Stock picking is a game of master psychology. Tomorrow's performers rely on how large investors will react (what they will buy or sell) in response to major market events that have not yet happened. Summit corporate meetings, which the general public is not privileged to, are held behind closed doors. No wonder you can't predict the future! No one can. Stock markets have no memories. They don't have to come back. You can't buy last year's returns.

"Trust Me. I'm the Expert."

The financial industry's mission is to help itself. Their greatest expertise? "A B C": "Always Be Closing." To do that, sales forces have to convince you that they know the future and their product benefits outweigh the cost of the investment. Where are their customers' yachts? If they are successful in their careers, is it because they do so well for their clients or because they make a lot of money on their clients?

"Who Cares What It Is If It Saves You Taxes?"

Tax-deferred, tax-deductible and tax-exempt are wildly successful marketing strategies that direct billions of dollars into the coffers of insurance companies, state projects, and municipalities. Some investors want nothing to do with an investment unless it can create a tax dodge.

The smart wealthy make financial decisions based on the economic sense of the deal, not on the tax gimmicks involved. I'll bet some recent ex-CEOs who bought their accountants' secret tax shelters wish they could reverse the clock and pay their share of taxes, now that the IRS has labeled them abusive strategies. Tax gimmicks can restrict access to your money and apply severe penalties for early withdrawals. Don't let the tax tail wag the investment dog.

Dialing for Dollars

Boiler room operations—rented office rooms filled with paid phone operators—solicit consumers day and night. An illegitimate company targets an area, sets up its backroom shop with rented furniture and starts dialing for dollars.

Never give your Social Security number, credit card account number, or other personal private information over the phone. If the company is legitimate, it will send you literature so you can check it out through state agencies and other means.

Do not purchase securities, CDs, or insurance products from credit card offers, monthly statements, mail, TV, or radio solicitations. If someone notifies you that you have won a trip or any other type of prize, expect them to pay all related costs themselves. Reputable contests don't expect their winners to pay for shipping and other expenses.

The Laws of Investing

Law #1: You are a moving target. Financial companies spend billions of dollars to stalk you (this is called *prospecting*). You are statistically followed, tagged, and ticketed like some form of wildlife to be sold to someone's telephone, seminar, or direct mail list.

If you bought a new home, several insurance companies know because they buy mortgage lists. If you take out a personal loan, other vendors are notified. If you recently lost a spouse, every salesperson in town has read the newspaper obituary. Recently married? You have been erased off some lists and added to others. A new baby or a college graduate notice will bring out the car, yacht, insurance, and credit card mailings. Some retail cash registers will not open unless the customer provides their zip code or telephone number. These are your financial adversaries, not new friends.

Law #2: Where you are on the road to financial success is not as important as which direction you are moving. Time is money (or the opportunity cost of it). There will never be a better time, a cheaper time, or a more important time to start than today.

Law #3: The best defense is a good offense. It doesn't take a rocket scientist to control your financial destiny.

The inventor of financial planning was the ant who worked through the summer gathering up stores of food so he would be secure when winter arrived. The grasshopper, however, thought this type of goal-setting a complete waste of perfectly good recreational time. He spent his summer and fall eating, lounging on wild aster plants, and having tobacco spitting contests with his neighbors. He didn't notice the shortening days and the meadow plants losing their leaves and color as the fall nights became colder and colder.

When the first snow hit without warning, the grasshopper immediately jumped into action and scurried to the ant's home. He pleaded for shelter, but there was no response. Then he demanded refuge from the storm's onslaught and some of the bread he could smell baking in the ant's oven. Again he was ignored.

In desperation, he battered in the anthill's front entranceway taking his destiny into his own hands. But he was so fat from dinning on milkweed and grain pods all season that he could not slip down through the corridor. There he stuck, somewhere between salvation and starvation.

This prime example of poor planning, consuming everything today and saving nothing for tomorrow, is exactly the kind of tragedy that financial planning was designed to avoid.

Law #4: Learn to think like the rich. Middle-income Americans can develop "middle-class mentality" because they get so much advice from middle-class vested interests and well-meaning incompetents surrounding them. Start asking, what would Bill (Gates) do? How would Warren (Buffet) handle this issue? Maybe The Donald (Trump) has been in this fix before. To us, a dollar represents a cup of coffee, a pair of shoelaces or a lottery ticket. The wealthy view a dollar as the means to make more money. Wealthy folks don't have big mortgages, big ticket bills, and big dreams. They have money.

Law #5: Every potential sale is an adversarial event. Wall Street, they say, is a street with a river at one end and a graveyard at the other end. They forgot about the kindergarten in between: the sales force. The bank teller has a sales quota. Your insurance agent neighbor wants you to buy more expensive insurance. Even the muffler store owner wants you to take home the most expensive muffler in the place. Don't let personal relationships or friendly conversations interfere with your consumer activism.

Law #6: With accurate information, money will follow. Financial planning is not only for the rich. The less money you have to manage, the more important it is to use it wisely and get objective and competent advice. The best investment in the world is knowledge. Understand how capitalism works to gravitate money toward the wealthy. Money works its way back to the rich where it can live a long and useful life.

Law #7: It's what you make on your money *after* inflation that matters. Inflation will never go away. People worry about SARS, terrorism, lung cancer from second-hand smoke, high cholesterol, and nuclear radiation, while inflation's insidious erosion quietly eats away at financial futures, destroying comfortable retirements and college educations. Inflation isn't a concept; it's a continual loss of money year after year.

Law #8: Preserving your long-term purchasing power is more important than preserving your investment principal. If you hid all your money in a safe place in order to protect it against loss, in 12 years I *guarantee* you would have lost 50 percent, *half* of your worth, due to inflation. Folks aren't investing because they are daredevils. Their futures depend on higher returns than the increasing cost of living. If inflation averages 6 percent per year, you must yield 6 percent (after taxes) on your money just to stay in the same place you began at the beginning of the year. Fixed-income vehicles such as bank accounts, CDs, and insurance annuities will not make you rich.

Law #9: "Safe" is a four-letter word...and a big lie. There is no "safe" stock, no "safe" bond. All investments carry some type of risk. Banks pay as little as possible and fail to outpace inflation over time. Insurance companies can close their doors. The trick is to diversify enough to balance risk in your portfolio.

Law #10: Diversify, diversify, diversify. Most investors misunderstand what diversification really is. They are sold a few mutual funds, some individual stocks, an insurance annuity or two, and some bank deposits, then believe they are diversified. Not true. That's no more than buying a bunch of products sold by a bunch of salespeople.

Law #11: A paper loss is a real loss. If there is no such thing as a real loss until you sell, why is everyone so upset that their investment statements have been bleeding in the last three years? That is nonsense and a big myth perpetrated by Wall Streeters who don't want you suing them for two big lies: 1) "Brokers are experts who can predict the future"; and 2) "Don't sell it now—it will come back!" When you lose significant investment capital, it takes forever to rebuild your net worth. Significant investment losses are painful events to be avoided.

Law #12: There is no such thing as a free lunch. Salespeople make commissions immediately and from the top of your check, whether you see their money leave or not. No stranger is going to get you in on the ground floor of a blockbuster drug or a hot business opportunity or an insurance investment for free. Not even if you hold the contract for seven or 10 years. There is no safe 20-percent, 15-percent or even 10-percent return. Anyone who tells you there is will profit from your greed and naiveté.

Law #13: Investment performance is determined by p-r-o-f-i-t-s, not p-r-o-p-h-e-t-s. Who can predict a war, a famine, SARS, terrorism, or even global warming? Don't follow the crowd to the latest trend. Stick to prudent investing strategies, invest like the wealthy, and let them pull you along toward greater wealth over time. Small investors work primarily on greed and fear. Neither is a successful investment policy.

Law #14: It's not what they *say*, it's what you *sign*. When you receive an insurance or investment contract, read it carefully. Request specimen contracts *before* you purchase. Never take the sales pitch seriously. There are no fair or friendly contracts.

Law #15: It's probably not any different this time. All manias crash, and history repeats itself enough for us to realize that a fool and his money are soon parted. Don't attempt to match wits against tomorrow's markets via your monthly mutual fund magazine or quarterly newsletter as your financial weapon and investment guide.

Risky Business

Years ago, the state of Michigan upgraded its pheasant raise and release program. Managing pheasant farms had been grossly time-consuming because workers tended and fed the birds at numerous substations around the grasslands. It made sense (to those in charge) to cut down labor costs, optimize operations, and centralize work at one main location.

By the end of the third year, however, profits and results were down, not up. Bird deaths (mortality) and morbidity (sickness) increased. The problem? Before mechanization, the workers walked most of the land, tending to daily fencing and maintenance chores, supervising as they worked and walked. Once the efficiency program was in place, they had no method of detecting problems that were not in close range. Unchecked, such enemies as fox, bear, pests, and viruses were able to capture a stronghold on the flocks, weakening future strains as well.

The same thing happens when you let your money tend to itself. You may have put your financial life on autopilot because you have little time to actively manage it. If you have turned over the reins of decision-making to strangers in return for quarterly reports, organize your assets now and determine how well they are performing. To help, complete the "Portfolio Planning Worksheet" in the Appendix.

Diversification Is Better Than a Chicken

You've learned to pay yourself first, to use "OPM," and to read the fine print. But are you following the "chicken" theory of investing?

Let's assume you and I decided to start an enterprise, a poultry business. Chickens lay eggs, win prize money at county fairs, and make good broth and meat for the stew pot. We would be foolish if we pooled our life savings together and invested all in the grand champion county fair winner, one giant, fluffy white chicken, or even a large flock of the same type of poultry.

What do chickens have to do with investing? You don't have to be a chicken to recognize that egg. But you do to lay one! And you will lay a giant goose egg by putting all of your investment eggs into one basket, such as technology stocks or government bonds or bank CDs.

Diversification reduces risk to investment principal. How come the "experts" don't teach this theory? Because diversification isn't designed to help you "get rich quick" like money gurus advise. Diversification techniques will help you *not* to lose your savings.

To become a follower of diversification, you must be willing to give up some occasional lofty returns for consistent and steady progress. You need to avoid the "rabbit" investments and opt for the "turtles"—those all-weather, dull and stodgy investment portfolios that perform in many kinds of economic weather.

Real diversification goes beyond the idea of purchasing many things with your savings. *The individual assets that make up your investment portfolio must come from various types of securities.*

When one market or part of the economy sours (your chicken gets sick or, worse, dies), you are still in the investment business with the rest of your nest egg.

Investing Benefits Your Plan Should Offer

- **Simplicity.** It should be easy to understand and contain basic and simple investment vehicles. No fads, no new and innovative products, and no sophisticated strategies.

- **Easy management.** The plan should not have to be monitored or altered on a regular basis. Once the basic asset allocations are set, only major events such as enormous market swings, distressed economic conditions, or life-plan changes should cause your investment policy to significantly change. An annual tune-up (slight rebalancing) should be sufficient.

- **Total accessibility.** Every investment should be marketable in a crisis situation, and investment policies should not shrink dollars through large surrender charges when the money is recalled.

- **Window of observation.** You should have access to follow performance and check up on security holdings as often as desired.

- **Cost-effective expenses.** Investment choices should reduce or eliminate costly financial middlemen. Go directly to the investment vehicle whenever possible.

- **Flexibility to change.** Avoid investments that require years to develop positive returns, such as cash-value insurance policies, or charge high surrender fees, such as insurance annuities, in case you want to liquidate your investment pot early.

- **Tax advantages whenever prudent.** Control of your investment is more important than tax advantages. But whenever sensible, use tax shelters commonly available. In a 401(k), a 403(b) tax sheltered annuity, or an IRA, go directly to the investment vehicle instead of an overlapping insurance product that will charge extra for the insurance wrapping. Your returns may improve significantly the more you cut out middlemen.

- **Diversification principles.** No speculation, clairvoyance, or forecasting abilities should be necessary. If you use many kinds of securities for your investment nest egg, you won't worry about tomorrow's headlines.

- **Favorable risk-to-return ratio.** Establish an efficient portfolio, maximizing return, minimizing risks. You may never get paid more for putting extra risk on your principal.

- **Inflation protection.** Long-term money must constantly grow to outpace the ravages of inflation. Growth means stocks, and that means using mutual funds for lower volatility than by investing in individual stocks.

- **Few insurance products.** Investment and savings insurance policies and annuities are an expensive way to provide death benefits and investment performance. Term insurance can provide for your family's death benefit needs. Use the remainder of your money for your own benefit, not to fund large commissions for a vacation retirement home for an insurance agent.

- **Separate investment accounts.** Investments held in the general accounts of banks and insurance companies such as CDs and fixed insurance policies and annuities pose risks if the company should become insolvent or shut its doors. Mutual funds are diversified and owned by their shareholders, not by the mutual fund management company.

- **Quality investment vehicles.** Quality is important in everything you buy. All mutual funds are not created equal, and all insurance companies are not equally sound. Steer clear of new products that have not weathered the test of time.

- **Estate planning options.** Designating Will substitutes such as beneficiaries on every asset you can creates simple and effective estate planning. Chapter 15 will help you register your assets from IRA accounts and employer retirement plans to your home, cars, and life insurance. Taxable and general investments generally have different methods of directing assets to your heirs while avoiding the probate process.

Bulls (investors who believe that their favored markets are going up) make money, and so do the bears (those who fear that markets will fall) in bad times. But the piggies (those who invest first out of greed, then fear) can get slaughtered. If you remove all the animals from your investing equation, you will have a lot less manure to wade through.

CHAPTER 17

Investing Strategies: Short-Stop vs. Marathon Money

Genetic engineering, subatomic physics, quantum mechanics, investing for today's consumer. One of these doesn't have to be rocket science.

Devise one strategy for your short-term savings (sprint money) to guarantee the principal and another method for long-term funds (marathon money) to guarantee future purchasing power. Every household should establish a rainy-day fund for emergencies. A breadwinner could be terminated, medical emergencies occur, and many furnaces seem to be programmed to shut down in December. The car's water pump, the refrigerator, and your youngest son could simultaneously need repairs before next payday.

Short-term funds are savings you will likely need soon. This could include your rainy-day account, next year's Christmas gifts, a vacation, a new car, a romantic wedding and honeymoon, real estate taxes, college just over the horizon, or a new roof or house foundation. Short-term money strategies are for financial goals less than three years away.

The nature of the goal is not as important as the amount of time available before the funds are needed. Once you isolate short-term goals from long-term objectives, you will be better able to choose suitable investment vehicles.

In addition to your rainy-day fund, a healthy portion of cash can act as a cushion or shock absorber when other securities markets are on the decline or become volatile. The purpose of cash, whether for short-term or long-term goals, is safety, not yield.

Cash equivalents are short-term, interest-earning instruments with high liquidity. They are easily converted to cash with little or no risk to your principal. *Liquidity and marketability are not the same.* A *marketable* investment, such as a stock or a bond, can be quickly sold, at a profit or at a loss. But a *liquid* security implies that, in addition to gaining access to cash quickly, every dollar originally invested can be retrieved without loss of principal.

Stashing cash in your home, bank money market demand accounts, savings accounts, money market mutual funds, E or EE or HH U.S. savings bonds, and credit union share accounts are liquid accounts. *Your long-term funds will require different investment strategies in order to provide growth above the rate of inflation over time.* I recommend at least two sources of fast money for your personal and/or business activities.

Short-term bond mutual funds are *not* cash equivalents because they can lose principal when interest rates rise. Higher yields are not necessarily smarter banking. You need to understand how the manager is making the higher gains.

Certificates of Deposit

CDs are individual time deposit agreements made with your lender. You are usually paid higher returns the longer you allow a lending institution to keep your money.

Don't deposit all your funds with one institution, despite FDIC insurance. If FDIC reserves should become dangerously low, or if your lender shut its doors, cash transactions may be temporarily disrupted. The chances of two institutions in the same neighborhood going under at the same time are less.

CD deposits are issued with different maturities. Don't be lured into locking up long-term rates unless the yield is worth it. You could be locked in at lower interest rates when future rates have risen and banks are issuing higher yields than yours. Keep your cash as liquid as possible and use mutual funds to fight long-term inflation.

Credit Unions

Though credit unions are not backed directly by the federal government, they often have insurance of their own, such as NCUA, a federal agency for credit unions. Credit unions may offer better interest rates on their share-draft accounts and lower interest auto and personal loans. As part of your cash foundation, they can provide diversification and competitive rates of return. Members can benefit from loan sales.

Sweep Accounts

With a brokerage company, you can purchase an interest-bearing checking and savings account all in one. A *sweep account* offers a range of services bundled together: checking, investing, borrowing, and a short-term storage for funds. Excess (uncollected) funds are "swept" daily into short-term securities, similar to a money market mutual fund. This product is *not* backed by the FDIC or any other government agency, although they have been directing customers' savings into their own banks. You may pay additional internal charges and annual fees.

Be careful that opening a sweep account does not signal the nod to a stockbroker who may want your money in a different investment product.

Securities Investor Protection Corporation (SIPC) guarantees investor funds up to $500,000 total value ($100,000 in cash) if the brokerage should close its doors or suffer financial troubles. But this does not protect an investor from problems associated with an investment *inside* the money market mutual fund, such as an Enron default.

Brokerages and other large financial corporations may soon be getting their own banks. Be sure to differentiate between FDIC-insured accounts and a security.

Money Market Mutual Funds

A *money market mutual fund* is a large pool of investor money managed by an investment company. It seeks short-term interest and conservation of the investment principal. U.S. government money markets invest only in government treasuries, or U.S. agencies, or both. Others may invest in a combination of U.S. instruments and commercial paper with short maturities. Worldwide money market funds have currency risk and default risk due to the foreign securities inside.

Tax-exempt money markets are comprised of securities issued by tax-exempt entities. They offer tax-free income so they generate lower yields. Tax-exempts not insured or backed by insurance company policies, have the potential for default. Because the underlying money market mutual fund securities are short-term, their yields are relatively low.

Money market funds offer daily interest. Their yields vary and could be more or less when compared with bank savings accounts and FDIC short-term bank deposits. Not all money markets are created equal. You need to compare the safety of the underlying securities. Like all mutual funds, money markets are *not* guaranteed by the FDIC nor any agency of the government, even if they invest only in U.S. government-issued paper.

Copy Cat Bank Money Markets

Money market mutual funds originally generated so much appeal that banks started offering accounts bearing the same name to capture assets disappearing to mutual fund companies. A *bank money market demand account* has little in common with a money market mutual fund. When you purchase FDIC-insured bank products, you loan the institution your money. Mutual funds are owned by the shareholders (investors). Bank products are insured by the FDIC; mutual funds, even money market mutual funds, are not. *Read the prospectus and investment statement carefully before sending money to any mutual fund company.* (How to use a mutual fund prospectus is explained in Chapter 18.)

Savings Bonds

Sold by financial institutions at a discount to their face value, U.S. savings bonds have a double life: 1) the time it takes the bonds to double in value; and 2) the subsequent and final interest rate to their maturity date. The interest rates can be adjusted over time depending on the overall level of interest rates in the economy.

Recent savings bonds do not expire when they reach face value but continue to pay interest for up to 30 years. The interest can be tax-deferred until the bonds are redeemed. Then they are subject to federal income tax, but not to state and local income tax.

They are convenient to purchase; guarantee your principal; pay competitive, short-term yields; carry no up-front commission when bought; interest is exempt from state and local taxes; and bonds purchased for college by parents with incomes below certain limits are tax-free if used for qualifying educational expenses.

EE savings bonds can be exchanged for HH bonds with only the interest income taxed annually until redemption. If lost, stolen, or destroyed, they can be replaced easily. Savings bonds can be cashed in six months from date of purchase. As a cash substitute they can reduce risk in investment portfolios. A Savings Bond can be purchased for as little as $50.

Beware: Savings bonds attract inflation and are not generally recommended for long-term investing. Mutual funds are better inflation-fighters for long-term goals such as college or retirement. Bonds already purchased, however, as long as they are still earning competitive interest rates, can be considered part of your cash reserves.

Long-Term Marathon Money

In 1963, a pound of ground beef cost 33 cents. In 1974, one could purchase a full-sized car for $3,200. In 1980, healthcare was an item in the family budget, not a major purchase or worry.

Today, your next car could cost more than your first home. Inflation is in your refrigerator, lurking in your heating ducts, hiding in your car's gas tank, and cunningly waiting in your next real estate and income tax bills. Inflation is the deadliest money-killer over time.

The primary goal of long-term investing should be conservation of your purchasing power. The biggest mistake new retirees can make is to gather their assets around as if they had six months to live and invest primarily for safety and monthly income. Their nest egg will lag behind inflation, and their quality of life will shrink along with their money over time, all because they tried too hard to protect themselves against the one risk they could identify: the loss of investment principal.

How much risk to principal is enough to sustain growth and stay ahead of inflation? How can you identify and control risk? We know that diversification can help if you can learn how that concept works in your favor. The longer you invest significant principal in the stock markets, the more risky your position becomes. There is no correlation between how much risk you should take and your current age. There is no correlation between how much money you should invest in the stock markets and how long until you need your money (as long as you have a three-year time horizon before you believe you will need the funds). Taking more risk does not always equal greater profits over time. Tomorrow's stock markets couldn't care less how close to retirement you are or how devastating a loss of your student's college funds would be to their education future.

Some investors are terrified to venture outside FDIC-insured banks, Treasury Direct, or insurance companies for fear of any loss of principal. If you gave up investing altogether and decided to hide your money in your home so it would be totally safe, I guarantee you that at the current inflation rate (6 percent per year or more), you would lose 50 percent of your principal in the next 12 years. How? That's what happens to the real value of money over time due to the effects of inflation. Your dollars would shrink in half! Folks are not investing today for fun, because the last few years have been anything but! They have to combat inflation! I believe there is a prudent middle ground to strike a balance between conservation of principal and conservation of purchasing power.

The Long Run Is Really a Series of Short Steps

If I placed a narrow plank one foot above the floor, I could probably convince you to walk its length for a wager of $5. Would you walk that same thin plank perched 10 feet above the ground for $50? For 10 times the original $5 reward, would you take 10 times the additional risk? For $500, would you take your chances 100 feet up? I doubt it. When the risks are truly understood, the potential rewards of higher-risk investing don't look as appealing. Learn to invest for comfort, not for speed.

Focus on the prudent fundamentals of successful investing. You can fight inflation *and* remain risk-adverse through the diversification strategies in this book, the long-term natural upward bias of capitalism's equity markets, and time.

Less Pain, More Gain

High investment returns won't help much if you can't keep your profits during stock- or bond-market declines. Why are you rushing, trying to beat market benchmarks? Greater risk to principal exposes your money to greater potential losses, not necessarily greater returns, even over longer periods of time. *Let time and proper asset allocation create your wealth slowly but surely.*

The Right Way to Invest

We don't see things the way *they* are; we see them the way *we* are. The stock market has occasional upset stomachs, bonds can dance the Macarena when interest rates are on the rise or credit quality is in question, and international markets are unreliable. Where can you find solid ground when the landmarks keep moving?

1. Insist on excellent, long-term performance. Returns should not be measured by short-term market noise or past performance numbers (except when poor performance keeps repeating itself).

2. Have a stated objective. Don't change your investment policy every time market winds change direction. Maintain the discipline and confidence to stick to your plan.

3. Embrace a disciplined approach to investing. Invest regularly, not just when hot markets seduce you to jump in for some quick profits. Buy low and you stand a better chance of selling high later. Never invest out of greed or fear.

4. Know the difference between *risk* and *risky*. Though there are no safe harbors, no wealth without some risk, portfolio volatility can be managed and often controlled. Drive the investing speed limit through diversification and develop your wealth slowly but surely over time. Use the magic and miracle of compounded interest and the built-in wealth-building system of capitalism.

5. Always purchase quality products. Don't shop with a priority on price tags. The customer doesn't see all the charges anyway. You deserve the *best*, not the *cheapest* investment. Would you want your health to depend on the cheapest doctor in town? Maybe you don't want the cheapest money manager either.

6. Search for independent financial planning advice. Choose someone with more credentials than a license to sell products. Don't expect everyone in the financial industry to provide objective financial advice.

Don't Settle for Nothing

One of the drawbacks of conventional wisdom is the frequency with which it is just plain wrong. When comparing how well your investment portfolio is running the race against time and inflation, revisit your investment philosophy and avoid the following losing strategies:

The "Do Nothing" Theory

Perhaps you have made a lot of money in an aggressive mutual fund or high-flying stock over the last few years. You learned the hard way that it is volatile but you can't bring yourself to part with it because of taxes on the sale or the losses you want to regain before you sell. Maybe the security has gotten too large for your portfolio over the years. Perhaps you have decided to sell and accept some tax consequences in return for lower risk and a better night's sleep, but you haven't gotten around to reapportioning your money into a more diversified asset allocation. Remember: The longer you hold risky investments, the more potential for loss. Stock market risk increases over time and inflation is always working against you.

The "Pay Nothing" Theory

If you can't see the investment charges, internal fees, or other expenses, they must not exist, right? The financial industry has many subtle methods for securing distribution fees and other revenue-sharing profits without disclosing such charges and expenses to the customer. Get real! Would you invest some stranger's money for free?

If all mutual funds were identical, the cheapest one would obviously be the best choice. However, cheaper management fees don't necessarily convert into greater profits as we have seen with "cheap" index mutual funds during the last few years. Losing money year after year "cheaply" is a hollow victory. Maybe your investment policy should focus on value for your management dollar.

Are you feeding your children the cheapest food you can buy? Are you driving the cheapest car on the road? Have you chosen the cheapest physicians and sent your students to the cheapest colleges? Investors can misinterpret "cheap" when it comes to investing issues. Investors who would never rely on the cheapest doctor in town or feed their families only the cheapest food nevertheless can become so price conscious that they focus primarily on what they believe is cheap money management. Choose your investments as carefully as your friends, insisting on quality first at a fair price.

The "Know Nothing" Theory

Some investors are too busy earning money to spend time managing their financial lives. Is your investment portfolio stuck on autopilot?

If so, make a commitment to watch over your precious investment capital more consciously, to protect it from others, and to learn how the proper diversification can help reduce your risk to principal. Know all potential risks as well as the potential rewards from the full-page magazine advertisement. Collecting brand-name financial products in itself will not make you wealthy. Build your investment portfolio using all of the investment blocks (cash, stocks, bonds, and global) in moderation.

Relying on the advice of "money gurus," the media, financial publications, or using the "whatever-my-friends-and-neighbors-are-buying" method of investing is generally unproductive.

For goals less than three years away, limit your investing to the "safe" instruments we discussed. If your goal is longer than three years, fight the deadly effects of future inflation with conservative mutual funds.

CHAPTER 18

Mutual
Fund-amentals

"Do not gamble, take all of your savings and buy some stock and hold on to it till it goes up, then sell it. If it don't go up, don't buy it."

—Will Rogers

This book is all about getting rich, slowly but surely. Individual securities pose higher risks to principal than you may realize. From the world of more than 13,000 publicly owned stocks, what are your odds of picking a winner? Would you opt for an operation that had those odds of recovery? You need better odds of winning your money game, and that's the rationale behind the world of mutual funds.

A sturdy home can't be built with a few boards. You can't build a bulletproof, defensive investment portfolio with only a few securities. Learn how to diversify as though you were a millionaire, even though you don't have millions to invest!

Investing used to be simple. Your parents deposited their savings into a banking institution, a credit union, an insurance company, or they purchased U.S. savings bonds. They were savers, not investors. Consequently, financial institutions have grown richer at the expense of these savers who took risks they never understood, including the potential default of insurance companies and inflation.

The World of Mutual Funds

Today, any "little guy" can diversify like a millionaire, hire top money managers, have access to his assets at all times, choose how his funds are invested, and maintain the freedom and flexibility to change investment vehicles as his financial goals change. What are these popular investments, how do they work, and are they right for you?

Specifically, a mutual fund is a large pool of money from investors seeking similar investment objectives. For as little as $50 per month or for an initial investment of $1,000, investors can choose what types of securities to buy. Some mutual funds invest solely in U.S. government securities, while others may invest totally in stocks or even one type of stock market, such as technology. Most mutual funds invest in a combination of markets.

Investors pool their assets and hire professional money managers to choose the specific securities and manage the general business of each fund. There are thousands of mutual funds to choose from.

Shareholders sell their shares back to the fund, not to other investors like stocks and bonds. At all times, fund companies must be ready to redeem a shareholder's mutual fund shares for their current value. If your mutual fund has a good year, so do you. If your mutual fund has a losing year, you share those lumps as well.

The fund's investment policy and how it intends to meet those goals is described in the *prospectus*. Some funds have a lead manager while others hire a team. The manager is paid by the fund company whether you make money or not. Mutual funds have made it possible for ordinary folks to invest in the same instruments as the rich and famous.

A Mutual Understanding

After you deposit money into a bank, the bank owns the money. You are a customer of the banking institution. If the bank has a good year, the bank's owners (the shareholders) not the customers, receive the profits. When you purchase an insurance product and the company has a banner year, the stockholders get bigger profits, not you, the customer. But when you purchase a mutual fund, you are the shareholder. You own the mutual fund and the profits (and the losses as well), not the fund management company.

If you and I pooled our money together to purchase more securities than we could afford individually (*the fund*), we would share proportionally (depending on how much each of us invested) in all profits (*growth and income*), all *distributions*, all daily *expenses*, and any *losses* of investment capital. We could buy many types of securities and diversify our money. The value of the total investment pool would be its *total asset value*. The price per share of the fund would be its *net asset value*. The value of our account would be called our *account value*.

Every shareholder, no matter how much each had invested, would be equally entitled to the basic privileges of ownership. We would have the right to fire our money manager as well as vote on any proposed fundamental change of investment strategy. We would need similar investment philosophies and objectives to buy into the same investment pool. If you wanted to purchase gold or other precious metals, for example, while I was intent on buying only U.S. government bonds, our financial partnership would not work very well. *Therefore, shareholders in each mutual fund tend to share similar financial goals and objectives.*

You could choose to reinvest your distributions back into our fund and purchase additional new shares, while I could request the *dividends* or *capital gains* in cash and either spend the money or reinvest it into another investment.

Eventually, we might be investing alongside working folks, retirees, parents saving for college, high school and college graduates investing for the first time, and young married folks building a nest egg to buy a home.

Are Mutual Funds Safe?

We would need to understand that any type of investment carries risk of loss of principal as well as the hope of future profits. So, we would learn the inherent risks and limitations of the funds we choose. Various phases of the business cycle, the direction of interest rates, the general health of the economy, political forces, and international issues all affect the faces of investing. Hem lines, picket lines, gas lines, utility lines, and grocery lines affect our financial bottom line. Putting our investment eggs into many investment baskets would be vital to our future financial wealth. *The more we understand about risk and reward, the better our chances for success.*

The major advantage of purchasing mutual funds is to diversify your assets. The purpose of diversification is to reduce the risk to your investment capital. When folks caught the tech bug in 1999, they piled their money into lottery ticket stocks and mutual funds that contained mainly technology stocks and failed to diversify into different market sectors. Owning a bunch of technology companies will *increase* your risk, *not reduce* it. When that market crashed, their hard-earned profits (and principal) went south as well.

When folks lose lots of money in a mutual fund, it's generally because the securities inside their funds are similar and tend to decline at the same time. The tech wreck in 2000 was a horrific example of that. When one technology company got sick, they all caught the flu.

Remember the old camp song: "99 Bottles of Beer on the Wall?" If one of those bottles should happen to fall, 98 bottles are still on the wall. Mutual funds were created with a similar concept in mind. If a single company inside a diversified mutual fund portfolio defaults or otherwise disappears, you own other securities to balance out that risk. If you learn how to properly diversify, your portfolio should weather all kinds of stock market weather. Consider mutual funds as a method of prudently managing your money, not as a way to get rich quick.

Mutual funds are ideal underlying investments for a variety of tax-advantaged plans such as retirement IRAs, SEPs, SIMPLEs, KEOGHs, profit-sharing plans, and 401(k) retirement plans. They can also be utilized as custodial accounts for minors (UTMAs), for college fund savings and Coverdell savings accounts (formerly known as Education IRAs), and for nonprofit institution tax-deferred annuity 403(b)(7) programs. They are also ideal for long-term taxable accounts with no specific future investment goal in mind.

Mutual Benefits

As you become more familiar with this system of diversifying your investment assets, you will discover the many benefits mutual funds can offer the average financial consumer. Service and customer benefits include professional money management, economies of scale for cost efficiency, diversification of investment capital, a wide range of investment choices, and public newspaper/media reporting.

Direct wire transfers to and from your local savings institution or checking account and 24-hour telephone and Internet access to account information and pricing data make access and visibility to your money easy. Check-writing privileges, convenient transfers (exchanges) between funds in the same mutual fund family, monthly income checks automatically sent to your home or bank, and account linkups with the banking institution or the brokerage of your choice are easy to add to most accounts. Detailed and understandable account statements and timely earnings updates, prompt distribution of dividends, interest and capital gains, automatic free reinvesting and systematic withdrawal plans, and reduced sales charges for larger investors should be automatically offered.

They are ideal as the underlying investment for IRAs and other tax-sheltered retirement programs, tax-advantaged college savings programs such as custodial accounts and ESAs, automatic monthly investment programs, and payroll deduction plan options. Most mutual fund companies, upon request, will provide record-keeping and tax information statements for simplified tax preparation, and every investor, no matter how small, enjoys full investor privileges regardless of account value, optional Certificates of Ownership like those issued for stocks, and simple and convenient investing methods. Prompt telephone liquidation of account funds; a ready buyer when you want to sell your shares; joint, trust, and custodial ownership registrations; and reader-friendly periodic statements and reports complete the list of benefits.

You could soak in your tub, relax by the pool, or drive in your car, while receiving up-to-the-minute status reports on your investments. In today's fast-paced society, conveniences and services save time. But select conveniences only *after* you have chosen a high-quality mutual fund portfolio. Today's mutual funds are truly service-oriented.

31-Plus Flavors to Choose From

The last thing the world needs is another mutual fund. A better way to choose one, however, would be helpful. There are nearly as many categories of mutual funds as there are types of investors. They can be grouped according to their investment strategies and goals and the securities they purchase:

Higher Risk All-Stock Mutual Funds

* **Aggressive growth funds** seek maximum capital gains and invest in higher-risk companies that aim for higher returns than the stock market in general. (Not for investment wimps.)

* **Small company growth types** are comprised primarily of stocks of companies worth less than $500 million. (Here today, gone tomorrow types.)

* **Growth funds** mainly include medium-sized company stocks expected to grow faster than average. (Many of these were previously identified as the tech wreck of 2000.)

* **Midcap growth funds** usually focus on one sector: technology or other fast startup companies with a high attrition (death) rate.

* **Large capitalization funds** major in large "blue chip" stocks of major U.S. corporations that have consistently increased profits over the years and usually pay consistent dividends. (There is no such thing as a "safe" stock.)

* **Defensive stock funds** usually include utility and other companies that tend to hold up well in price during downturns in the economy until higher interest rates drive them down. (That theory didn't hold water—or money—during the latest bear stock market.)

* **International funds** specialize in stocks of companies outside the United States. Though only 65 percent of their assets must be invested abroad, they seek aggressive returns and may take large stock positions in one or two countries at a time. (You can reduce your risk to foreign economies and currency by purchasing funds that *don't* focus on single countries.)

* **Precious metals funds** buy stocks of gold, silver, or platinum mining companies and trade like stocks, not metals. (They don't have to hold metals as core investments.)

* **Asset allocation funds** may change investment mixes on a dime, moving between stocks, bonds, cash, and even gold. Their composition may change depending on the manager's outlook of market conditions. There's no telling what these funds may buy tomorrow.

* **Sector funds focus** on single industries or a certain market niche, attempting to enhance returns by leveraging profits through investing heavily into the same type of security. (Ouch! when that market tanks.)

- **Social awareness funds** invest in socially responsible companies and are generally invested in stocks. The thought of green money is attractive, but I doubt there is a company out there that doesn't put hamsters into experimental cages; pollute the environment; buy, sell, or make weapons; in a nonunion or sweat shop somewhere, in a naughty politically incorrect country.

A stock mutual fund is typically geared for long-term growth and higher risk. Conservation of principal and current income are generally not investment objectives. Your return is primarily dependent on appreciation (or growth) if the stock prices go up. Current income is rarely an objective. Most investors I know have had all the risk in the last three years they care to take. I recommend that you find a more conservative menu than funds totally invested in stocks with similar characteristics.

Medium-Risk Stock Mutual Funds

- **Balanced funds** generally have several objectives, such as growth without undue risk, conservation of investment principal, or paying out current income. They aim to achieve multiple goals through common and preferred stocks, bonds, and some cash, typically 60 percent stocks and 35 percent bonds.
- **Growth and income funds** are made up of high dividend, mature stock companies, some technology or higher-risk upstarts, a few bonds, and some cash.
- **Equity income funds** invest primarily in stocks with high dividend payouts for current income. They claim to be less risky than other types of growth stocks. Equity income funds generally contain stocks from many industries, a few U.S. bonds, corporate bonds, and cash equivalents.
- **Global stock funds** tend to diversify among more countries than international types, betting less on the fortunes of a single foreign economic or currency market. They are generally under less pressure to produce stellar short-term returns and often don't spend fund assets to hedge currencies because they own so many within the pool. Portfolios vary a lot. (Global funds, like international or foreign funds, can purchase domestic American securities as well.)

High-Risk Bond Funds

- **High-yield (junk) corporate funds** tend to invest in lower-quality credit corporations.
- **High-yield (junk) municipal funds** hold lower-rated municipal bonds issued by cities, states, counties, and revenue or public projects with impaired credit ratings.

- **International bond funds** are portfolios of foreign debt that carry economic and currency risk of the country where they are issued.

- **National municipal bond funds** (tax-free munis) contain long-term, tax-exempt bonds of states, revenue projects, hospitals, nursing homes, schools, highways and other public projects. Though income is not federally taxed, these funds are vulnerable to interest-rate hikes and defaults, many riding on healthcare costs and public sentiment.

- **State municipal bond funds** (double tax-free munis) are issued solely by public projects within your own state of residence. Often tax-exempt from both federal and state income taxes, they intensify risk to principal because they are not geographically diversified. If state budgets contract or industry leaves, municipal revenue can dry up fast and they could default.

- **Mortgage-backed securities funds** contain complicated mortgage obligations packaged by brokerages or quasi-government agencies, but may also invest in complex derivatives that fluctuate wildly when interest rates move quickly. They have both prepayment risk and interest-rate risk. They are more risky than they look when interest rates become volatile, especially during times of rising interest rates.

- **Target funds** buy groups of bonds that tend to mature together. They may hold corporate or government, municipal or zero coupon obligations. Prices fluctuate wildly with interest rates, and the longer maturities are more sensitive to interest-rate risk (loss of principal when interest rates rise). Managers may promise to redeem both principal and interest if you hold the fund to the maturity of the portfolio.

Medium-Risk Bond Funds

- **Ginnie Mae funds** (GNMA) seek high levels of income by investing in mortgage securities backed by the government. They are safe from default but not from loss of principal when interest rates rise. They self-liquidate during falling interest rates (prepayment risk) as folks trade in their existing mortgages for lower rates. As interest rates rise, they lose principal, similar to bonds, to preserve the income they generate. Generally sold for income, they may sacrifice principal to produce higher income at difficult times. (In other words, the dependable monthly income check may be a partial return of your principal to supplement the lack of yield on the mortgages.)

- **Income funds** seek a high level of current income for shareholders by investing in high-yielding stocks or high-yield bonds, or both. They may seek income at the expense of their investment principal if interest rates rise, or may invest in lower quality issues that pay higher dividends or interest rates.

- **High-grade corporate bond funds** are higher-quality private corporation debt, which tend to lose less principal than government bonds during periods of rising interest because their yields are higher. Unlike U.S. bonds, however, they can default.

- **Triple bond funds** tend to diversify among various sectors of the bond markets. These may include long-term U.S. government bonds and mortgages, high-yield (junk) bonds with higher ratings, and international bonds. Because the bonds are not all vulnerable to the same type of bond risk, one portion may zig when another is zagging. They are more diversified than a bond fund that holds just one variety of IOU.

- **High grade tax-exempts** hold higher-quality municipal debt that may be insured (this costs the fund more to buy the insurance against default) and hold up better against default, but suffer more in rising interest rate markets.

- **U.S. government bond funds** are protected from default but not from loss of principal when interest rates rise. That is the curse of owning bonds. Depending on the length of time to maturity, these bonds can suffer as much as a 10-percent loss of principal when the prevailing interest rate rises 1 percent.

Lower-Risk Bonds Funds

- **Short-term U.S. government bonds** and mortgages and agency notes have little or no default risk and less interest-rate risk due to their short-term duration.

- **Short-term taxable bond funds** have two- to five-year corporate debt obligations, which makes them less vulnerable to rising interest rates.

- **Short-term tax-exempt funds** contain shorter maturity municipal bonds that, due to shorter durations, lose less principal when interest rates are on the climb. In addition, they may be less likely to default because time is one of the greater risks on IOU promises.

- **Principal-protected funds** promise the return of your principal if you hold their shares for a certain number of years. They may employ complicated investment techniques (perhaps shorting stock markets or purchasing options). Complex strategies have a way of unwinding at the most inconvenient times.

A bond fund invests primarily for current income and pays a monthly income distribution called a *dividend*. The potential risk and returns can vary greatly depending on the type of bonds within the fund's portfolio and the direction of interest rates in the economy. Generally, the lower the *yield* (the interest rate that the bonds are paying), the more principal they lose when interest rates rise. The higher the yield, the less interest-rate risk exists but the more *default* risk enters the risk picture. Bonds tend to have less long-term potential for growth than stocks. They can be used primarily to mix and match when building a balanced and diversified portfolio of mutual funds.

How Risky Is a Bond Fund?

When interest rates rise, most bond prices go down. *Bond maturity* is the average time to maturity of the bonds inside the mutual fund wrapper. But to understand how much bond prices may move up and down, *bond duration* is a better measure to determine how much interest-rate risk you may be buying. The longer the bond time to maturity and the lower the yield (interest rate), the more the bond will lose in price when interest rates are on the climb. *Bond duration* assumes that a bond has a shelf life that may not coincide with its maturity date. For example, a 30-year GNMA may have a reduced investing life of less than two years when interest rates decline as they have in the recent past.

You can find the duration of a bond fund in its prospectus. The lower the number, the less the fund's net asset value (your principal) is expected to fall when the interest rate rises. A duration of, say 2.5, indicates that the net asset value (NAV) should fall approximately 2.5 percent when interest rates rise by a full 1 percent. A duration of 9 means that the price of the fund may fall by as much as 9 percent on an interest-rate hike of the same 1 percent. Long-term U.S. government bonds suffer the steepest price declines when interest rates rise significantly. There is no such thing as a safe bond. (You can add that wisdom to the list you have started that states there is no such thing as a safe stock.)

Even low-duration (short shelf life) bond funds are not substitutes for guaranteed investing. Stick to money market funds and bank deposits for short-term cash equivalents, even if today's rates are not too great.

Understanding how the "experts" view risks versus rewards can help you become better acquainted with the challenges investment advisors face when managing your money.

Money Market Funds

Money market mutual funds generally hold short-term securities that tend to make the investments safer for short-term investing purposes. They are managed to maintain a steady $1 per share principal and pay high income. Investors often substitute them for "cash-in-the-bank" purposes. They generally come with check-writing privileges. Following are various types of money market mutual funds.

- *Treasury only* money markets invest only in U.S. Treasury issues, but may have derivatives inside to boost yields. Check the underlying prospectus for a definition of how risky the securities are. They also pay less than other money markets.

- *U.S. government agency* funds are not all U.S. T-bills (Treasury bills) as some securities are issued by federal agencies or even quasi-government agencies, which most folks equate as belonging to the U.S. government, such as Freddie Mac and Fannie Mae, but are not. They can contain volatile derivatives in their mix. They pay slightly higher rates of income.

- *Taxable money market funds* usually invest in IOUs (commercial paper) issued by private corporations whose securities are backed only by the creditworthiness of the company issuing the short-term debt. They pay a little more than the U.S. government agency funds.

- *Tax-exempt money market funds* use short-term municipal IOUs and may even employ foreign debt instruments to generate higher yields. These can carry currency and global risks as well as suffer the vagaries of the municipal bond market. They are sold for their tax-exempt federal income, and occasionally for some state and local tax relief. But they can default, especially during times of economic upheaval.

Money market funds are designed to provide income and stability of principal. Although no money market fund is insured or guaranteed by the U.S. government, risk of loss of principal is minimal in most of them.

Because money markets are short-term securities, you earn less interest income than on other fixed income investments such as long-term bond funds. Money market mutual funds are often temporary comfort stops for funds looking for a more permanent home.

Clean Money

Socially responsible investing is popular today. To date, such funds have not performed in line with their peers, partly because funding for such altruistic projects is languishing, and partly because of the nature of the companies inside the funds. In many cases, they are not traditional money makers like industrials, pharmaceuticals, and other heavy hitters that socially aware investors attempt to avoid.

Being socially responsible seems to be in the eye of the money manager. One fund may invest in a company that sells guns, but is kind to its employees. Another avoids companies with sweatshop labor practices, but ignores the fact that its products are putting Americans out of work with their foreign competition.

Who is the mutual fund primarily socially responsible to? I believe you should find the best performers and send some of your profits to those organizations that are "dear to your heart."

It's getting harder to find companies who don't put hamsters into cages; pollute the environment; pose health hazards; produce, sell, or transfer weapons; or produce politically incorrect products in politically incorrect countries. How they actually produce their earnings may be quite different from their annual corporate mission statement and what you were told by the sales force.

Going Global

We can buy T-shirts at coffee shops, coffee at bookstores, books at the drugstore, drugs at the grocery store, and groceries at the gas station. Then there are the superstores where under the same roof you can buy water skis, bagels, farm tractors, antiques, PVC piping, rare books, prescriptions, jeans, jewelry, piano music, and various types of livestock. And get delivery through a drive-in window. I remember when all Mr. Whipple had to worry about was who was secretly squeezing the Charmin in the store aisles.

Today, there are nearly 40 countries that recognize the concept of private ownership and capitalism. Diversifying into many parts of our planet and through different types of companies may help reduce any negative impact from economic, political, or military strife in one part of the world at any time, including here at home.

International funds must invest 65 percent of their total assets in foreign issues. In addition, they tend to take large positions in emerging markets for potential stellar returns.

Global funds tend to spread their investing bets among many foreign sectors (and the United States), instead of bunching investments in only a few locales or countries. Therefore, you may reduce the risk of owning foreign securities by searching for funds that invest in as many as 30 countries (and their underlying currencies).

A *global* fund may benefit your portfolio more than it can hurt your total return due to the negative correlation it has with domestic stocks and bonds. An *international* or *foreign* fund, on the other hand, because it focuses on a few countries or types of securities, offers less of a soft landing when instability or crisis affects those foreign markets.

Decoding the Prospectus

There may be stricter labeling laws on a $2 carton of cottage cheese than on a $2 billion dollar mutual fund. A mutual fund prospectus is your written contract with the mutual fund company. It outlines the investment objective(s) of the fund, the methods management intends to use to achieve its goals and the special strategies, techniques, and hedging options that might be used. The prospectus can give you a general idea of how much risk the fund will tolerate, although in the past a few have utilized riskier strategies than they voluntarily disclosed to shareholders.

In the prospectus, you will find that most costs are listed along with the various pricing methods as well as how to buy and sell shares, a brief synopsis about the fund managers and outside directors, and other helpful pieces of information. The trick is to decipher the code in which the prospectus is written.

A typical prospectus might sound like this:

> XYZ Company Agreement provides that the compensation of the Advisor will be reduced by the sum of its parts and divided by the number 18 (because that's his lucky number) plus the straight line depreciation of the office furniture, assuming the reinvestment of all dividends and capital gains, and unless changed by a majority vote of the shareholders, upon the receipt of all proxies (and if you don't send them in the first time we will spend more of your money to send them out to you again). In accordance with the investment objective and policies of the Advisor to provide current income and growth of the brand new shrubbery at the lobby entrance, there can be no assurance that XYZ will achieve its original investment objectives (whatever they were—as defined in subsection 4-f-A2).

An exaggeration? Well yes, but not much of one! Is it any wonder that consumers rely on newspapers and magazines to tell them what funds to invest in? Who wouldn't feel intimidated by such gobbledygook?

Most mutual funds offer toll-free telephone numbers. Call information or check the Internet for a complete listing. The Investment Company Institute in Washington, D.C., the fund industry's trade association, can connect you with individual fund families and can send their own generic publications to learn from.

Request the Statement of Additional Information that will tell you more about the fund's holdings. In it you will find what percentage of the fund is being invested into stocks, bonds, or cash, what the top-10 securities holdings are, what percentage of the assets are invested in certain industry categories, and how much the CEO and the Board of Directors (who are supposed to be working for you, not for their own pocketbooks) made last year.

The Securities and Exchange Commission (SEC) has its own disclaimer on the front cover of the prospectus, which states that it will not approve or recommend any securities or guarantee the truth of any prospectus statements even though it regulates mutual funds or authorized the fund when it was first organized. That is not heartening. This hint tells you just how far away the SEC may be if your investment stalls and you are left with one oar for a leaky investment boat. It's up to you to "approve" or "disapprove" of a particular fund. And you do that by learning to read under the labels. When folks lose lots of money in a mutual fund, it's generally because the securities inside are similar and can decline at the same time. By looking at recent holdings, you can see how many industries are represented, how balanced the fund seems to be regarding stocks, bonds, and cash, and whether it satisfies your investment goals and objectives. Until you are familiar with the underpinnings of a mutual fund, you are *not* ready to invest in it. Stay awake—if you snooze, you could lose.

Forget all the past performance figures because they're not going to be repeated—not the good ones, and hopefully, not the bad numbers either. Pursuing past performance as a guide toward future returns was the most dangerous mistake investors made during the last three years. Because they had no other knowledgeable method of determining how to gauge the value of a fund, they picked up the Sunday newspaper or a money magazine and looked at the history, as if they were picking a horse based on his previous win history! Different securities react differently during different market periods. Therefore, you will get different returns from the same fund than were heralded in the historical charts.

The prospectus should highlight the kinds of risks inherent in its securities, limitations, and special concerns. Also included is information on how to buy and sell shares, multiple price structures (if available) and technical data about the fund's past history. Try to separate extraneous information from what you should know: how much risk is inherent in this investment and how it should handle future negative market factors.

The prospectus defines the rights of each shareholder, whether he or she has a $25-per-month account or $1,000,000 invested. Shareholders vote on major business matters and choose the investment advisors' contracts approximately every three years.

Retirement accounts such as IRAs often require a small annual trustee fee to the fund to report your progress to the IRS. Funds have different policy positions and occasional fire sales on management fees. But these are minor compared to finding permanent high-quality investments to create your wealth.

Upon your request, the mutual fund will redeem shares at the next pricing per share, usually at the close of that business day, called *"forward pricing."* Everyone receives the same price per share, whether redeeming $100 or $1,000,000.

A signature guarantee may be needed to request a change of account registration, a large liquidation *(redemption)* from your account, funds from a retirement account, or a check payable to anyone (or any address) other than you. Take the appropriate forms to a U.S. registered securities brokerage, U.S. commercial bank or trust company, a savings association, credit union, national securities exchange, or clearing agency where an officer can vouch for your signature.

In this case, size matters. Two billion dollars to $10 billion in invested assets is a comfortable broad range. Any bigger and the money manager has little control over individual investment calls, and a few great picks don't make a big difference in the fund's return. Too much smaller, and one clinker can kill the fund's performance.

As we are attempting to avoid the riskiest mutual fund selections, I advise that you ditch the all-stock funds, most all-bond funds, the special types of focus or sector funds, gimmicky funds that supposedly work best under uncertain markets or bear stock markets. This elimination narrows down the list significantly.

You might pick out a couple of nicely balanced funds, a global fund, a short-term U.S. government bond fund, perhaps a bit of a triple bond fund, and go home to take a nap until your money compounds nicely over time.

How Do I Get Rich?

Not all funds earn returns in the same manner. Mutual funds can distribute *dividends* and *interest* periodically, distribute *capital gains* from the securities sold at a profit inside the fund portfolio, and the *share price* can rise over time. The investment policy is key. If you are uncomfortable with terms such as "junk," "speculative," or "lower quality," cross those selections off your research list. If the investment policy states that it seeks better-than-average stock returns (beating the stock market), it will employ riskier investment methods to strive for high returns, use lots of stocks, and increase your risk to the stock market foibles. Nix those, too.

If the prospectus states that the fund intends to stay fully invested in stocks or bonds at all times, don't expect your manager to run for the hills to preserve principal in the middle of a stock market meltdown. *Most balanced funds have the right to move all to cash during bad markets if they choose.*

If the fund emphasizes current income, it won't tear up the track with opportunities for growth. If the fund states that it is not interested in current income or conservation of principal and contains mostly stocks, your risk of loss of principal will also rise. If the goal is to reach for very high income, the manager may be buying higher-risk securities to create those higher yields. Make sure to read carefully! Eventually, the words will sound more like the English language you and I learned in high school.

Stocks go up and down whenever they want to. Bonds move up and down in opposition to interest rates and against credit quality rating changes on the companies. Because no fund can be all things to all people, it stands to reason that you may want conservative middle-of-the-road types that are looking for a bit of income, conservation of principal, and some growth. That's a winner for the "get rich slow" investment policy. Don't use high-risk funds to get even with your recent market losses thinking that you can replace the money you have lost. You will just load up your portfolio with more risk. Investing only in bonds will not completely protect your principal because even U.S. government bonds go down in price when interest rates in the economy start to rise. In fact, U.S. bonds tend to suffer the most.

All investments contain some type of risk, even those "safe" ones we gravitate to in times of fear. If you try too hard to protect your principal, you will succumb to the ravages of inflation and lose money over time. If you take too much stock market risk, you will lose big time as well. Risk is everywhere; the trick is to learn how to manage it. We do that by putting our investment eggs into many different types of investment baskets. The secret word is "diversification."

Bearing Up In Bear Markets

Big investors run *to* stocks (domestic and foreign) out of greed and run *from* stocks to U.S. bonds out of fear. Their big bets with large money makes tomorrow's markets. Our money tags along.

If you structure your portfolio for comfort, buying all four basic investing blocks at the same time—stocks, bonds, cash, and global—mixed together in your individual mutual funds, your financial ship will not run aground and should weather the stormy stock market rain or shine.

What's the Sticker Price?

Mutual funds have management fees, brokerage fees, custodian fees, transfer fees, 12b-1 distribution fees, shareholder servicing fees, accounting fees, administrative fees, legal and audit fees, reporting fees, daily cost-of-doing-business fees, insurance fees, and printing and postage fees, interest expense for funds that borrow on margin, or revenue sharing fees for fund distribution that are not listed in your program (the prospectus).

Most of the fund's sticker price is listed, although there are some charges that may not show up in a prospectus. This price structure section discusses whether an investor will pay up-front charges for A shares (a front load) with discounts for larger purchases; declining surrender charges with no up-front sales charge for B shares, but higher internal expenses (12b-1 fees); or no upfront charges and permanent higher internal annual expenses with a smaller surrender charge for early exits from the mutual fund family.

Just because you can't see the charges doesn't mean the fund isn't paying distribution fees from other sources or higher brokerage costs (sometimes to its own affiliated companies), paying out transaction fees to distributors or "soft dollar arrangements" not disclosed in the prospectus. It is highly unlikely that you or I will ever know all the hanky panky that goes on in the mutual fund or brokerage industry. Therefore, look for *reasonable* expenses, an *appropriate method* to purchase your shares, and the *best value* for your money. *Do you understand how you are paying for your fund?* There is no such thing as a free mutual fund or insurance annuity, even if you hold the contract for seven years. The cheapest mutual fund is not necessarily the best all-weather performer. Be price-smart, not price-driven.

Who Is My Superstar?

Most studies have shown that the market makes the money, while the fund manager provides the human element and a steady hand. Much of the investment return seems to come from outside forces and market momentums. A good stock-picker manager can bring home a whole ham while others simply bring home the bacon. But even great managers go through bad patches when their style of investing shifts out of favor.

When technology was raging, all tech funds were doing well. The market sector that's favored will determine how easily your manager can make the returns you are paying for. The fund's superstar may not be actively managing your money. Some managers are hands-on, while others prepare for TV appearances and spend time in administrative or training duties. They may not be slaving over a hot desk to make your financial dinner. Because you are not an insider in the industry, you will rarely know the difference. Therefore, buy funds that don't need to be hooked up to ICBM missile systems ready for lifeoff. Less experienced staff could be directing basic buying decisions.

You couldn't single-handedly cater 500 Thanksgiving meals in your dining room. Likewise, no one human can manage billions of dollars. Funds advertise their managers to bring in business. By branding with a certain money manager, the fund hopes the public becomes groupies and loyal investors.

A major landmark in the debate over who makes the money, the market or the manager, occurred with a 1986 study by Brinson, Hood, and Beebower. The study over a 10-year period (1974 through 1983) sought to explain how much the money manager contributed to annual return figures of pension funds. As much as 92 to 94 percent of investment returns may be more the result of the right asset allocation or being at the right place at the right time, rather than the superior security selection ability of the investment advisor. To put it another way, when they're hot, you're in the money. When they're not, you lose.

If you look at historic fund results, most annual winners come from the same asset selection category. One year, international funds are golden, while the next year, the U.S. stock market may move ahead. Then it's gold in January and anything but gold in December. Healthcare issues may be killed in March and financials may take a hike in July.

You can avoid the thrill of victory followed by the agony of defeat by avoiding sector bets, mutual funds that do not diversify among many industries, and different market sectors. Look for true diversification instead of a miracle money manager who can't predict the future any better than you.

Going Once, Going Twice, Sold Out!

Occasionally a high-powered mutual fund will advertise that it's closing so investors can flock to it before the deadline. Its performance may later deteriorate because of the high volume of money already invested (that's why they are closing to new money) and due to new last-minute money coming in. They often have a special investment style driven by market momentum but that could increase risk when that market fades. Our objective is to get rich slowly, not to get through the door just before it closes.

Don't Live In the Past

Consumers are often so confused by how to choose mutual funds that they succumb to letting the "pros" do it for them. Everyone can give you past performances. The trick is to tell you how the funds will perform in the future. All that ratings or stars or grades do is to rate the past. They cannot predict tomorrow's returns or the markets that will dictate those future performance numbers. While one magazine shows you returns from that date into the past, another may run numbers from other time periods. A third source may reduce its data to a list of grades that it feels you can rely on for risk and return judgments. This is all pish-posh! If this method could be relied upon, the world's best money managers would simply subscribe to their favorite money magazines and choose their underlying investments based on grades or stars or number ratings and golf the other 29 days each month. There's a lot more to predicting the future of the financial world than a journalism graduate with an upbeat writing style can possible know.

The financial media makes their money in the *publishing* business, not the *investing* business. When you buy their editions, advertisers spend money for full-page ads. Their agenda here should be obvious. Who holds them responsible when you depend on them and they guess wrong? The fund rating industry wants you to believe they can extrapolate the future onto a single page for your convenience and determine the direction of future events that haven't happened yet!

Past performance is no guarantee of future results and is a lousy method of picking your serious retirement nest egg investment portfolio! Repeat that sentence until you believe it. You don't drive your car looking in the rear view mirror. You don't live your future exactly like you did in the past. And nothing in the past will give you a clue to tomorrow's financial headlines! Look beyond simplistic columns of past returns and concentrate on building a mutual fund portfolio using investment fundamentals and scouring the Additional Statement of Investments to see where your money will be invested.

What Are Rights of Accumulation?

Some funds offer price discounts *(breakpoint purchases)* for volume purchases of *share-priced* mutual funds. For example, you might pay less per share if you invested more than $50,000 than if you had invested only $10,000. As your contributions and earnings grow to, say $50,000, through *Rights of Accumulation*, you may pay less per share on future purchases of a specific fund or on any fund managed by the same mutual fund family. Volume discounts can become greater as more money is invested at higher levels. See the mutual fund prospectus for details on fund pricing options.

What Is a Letter of Intent?

A *Letter of Intent* may reduce your price per share if you are planning to invest a certain sum of money over a certain period of time, say the next 13 months. By signing a future commitment called a Letter of Intent to invest a certain amount, you can pay the reduced price from the beginning. If you fail to reach the investment goal within the 13-month period, your price per share will be adjusted to reflect the amount of actual contributions during that time. In the meantime, a part of your investment is held in escrow so it cannot be liquidated until your goal is reached.

Flip to the Index

Many stock, bond, or foreign mutual funds aim to beat a bellwether index for their peers. Because so many managed funds have under-performed the various market averages in recent years, index funds have become popular. The theory has been: Why buy a manager when you can make just as much, maybe more, and pay less without one? Why not buy the market average? Index mutual fund portfolios mirror a specific security market and aim to replicate their related benchmark's performance without much managing of assets. Because there is little management responsibility, index funds cost less than their managed fund peers.

Try to remember why you are buying mutual funds in the first place. You hate risk! What increases risk? Lack of diversification. By definition, index funds lack diversification, and therefore, increase risk. They contain similar types of securities that tend to move up and down at the same time. This is *not* how a conservative mutual fund should perform in a down market.

Because indexing was cheaper, it became a clever sales strategy when the benchmark stock markets were moving up famously. But in the last three years, if you had indexed the most popular stock index, the S&P 500, you would have lost principal big time. Balanced mutual funds can be helpful during times of turmoil and uncertainty, especially when the indexes are losing their financial shirts because the money manager can't get out of the market. He has to go down with the ship.

Indexing is a little like taking a plane ride without a pilot. The "pilot on board" ticket costs more and may not be necessary when instruments can handle the aircraft. However, when turbulence erupts, every passenger wants an experienced pilot in the cockpit. Recent stock market declines have pummeled stock indexes and, hopefully, emphasized the inherent risks of indexing. Because an index fund represents only one type of investment market, there is no diversification or soft landing should that market suddenly decline.

Buying different indexes in an effort to diversify may not generate the same bottom-line effect that diversified funds would produce. *Indexes can't become defensive or go all to cash during a crisis.* You need a money manager and diversification *within* your mutual funds as well as diversifying *among* several funds.

When the next bear market occurs, and small investors see how quickly prices can decline, they may exit these funds wholesale. Remaining shareholders will note even further market declines if managers are forced to redeem stocks because they don't have cash or bonds on board because they are not allowed to diversify.

Cruising the Barbary Coast without a captain, boarding the Space Shuttle without a ground crew, or driving around town in the back seat of your car with your cruise control in place aren't worth the risk when your Titanic hits an iceberg. Markets are fickle, react quickly, and don't care how close you are to retirement. I recommend diversified managed mutual funds. Purchase managed mutual funds and let the manager create your wealth slowly but surely.

Rating Fund Risk by Beta

Beta is a theory that attempts to quantify a fund's sensitivity to risk by comparing it to certain market benchmarks such as the S&P 500. A fund with a beta of 1.00 is supposed to closely track the movement up or down of that part of the stock market. A fund with a beta of 1.50 is expected to perform 50 percent better than its index in "up" markets and 50 percent worse in "down" markets.

The benchmark for equity (stock) mutual funds is the S&P 500 Stock Index. For fixed income (bond) funds, the bellwether is the Lehman Brothers Aggregate Index. The EAFE, Europe Australasia, Far East Index compares international funds with their peers.

Historical returns, however, have shown that the further up or down from 1.00 a fund's beta measures (say 1.5 or 0.5), the less correlation there is between its performance and its benchmark return, and the more meaningless the exercise becomes. Therefore, forget this as a dependable tool for measuring fund risk.

Alpha Isn't Much Better

Alpha supposedly measures the difference between a fund's actual returns and its expected performance, given a certain level of risk (which was extrapolated from beta). In plain terms, it is supposed to measure a money manager against others in the same fund category. The higher the percentage above 1.00, the better the manager. Supposedly. A positive alpha figure indicates the fund has performed better than the norm. In contrast, a negative alpha indicates a fund has under-performed, given the expectations established by the fund's risk level (beta). That's a no-brainer. Just by looking at the numbers from 2002, we can figure that much out. How dependable is this theory? No more dependable than the beta theory. Everything still hinges on past performance. Stick to learning investment fundamentals and leave the theories to the Ph.D.s who get prizes for such theses.

Are You Ready to Rock?

After reading the prospectus and before sending any money, track the progress of your picks for several weeks to see how they move up and down. Here are some key points you should have learned from the prospectus:

- The date of the prospectus.
- Minimum dollar amount.
- Basic investment policy.
- Competitive benchmarks.
- Fundamental objectives.
- Basic strategies.
- Statement of Additional Informormation
- Statement of Investments.
- Special techniques.
- The management team.
- General risk level.
- Special risks involved.
- Total fees.
- Percent Portfolio turnover.
- Name of Transfer agent.
- Shareholder rights.
- Services.
- Reporting methods.
- Distribution methods.
- Tax information.
- How to buy shares.
- Alternative share pricing.
- How to redeem shares.

Most newspapers publish a "Mutual Fund" section page. Find the alphabetical listing of the parent group or mutual fund family that manages the specific fund you wish to research and track. You may see an abbreviated name title (for example, "Gwth" for growth fund, "EqInc" for equity income, or "G & I" for growth and income, and so on).

There may be other symbols beside your fund:

- **(r)** indicates that a redemption fee might apply when you liquidate your shares. This redemption charge may decline over time or remain fixed over the life of your investment.
- **(p)** indicates periodic distribution expenses may be charged after the original sale. They might be as small as 0.20 percent, as large as 2 percent. They may be called 12b-1 charges.
- **(x)** means that the fund has just distributed a dividend and is currently trading at a price without the dollar amount of the dividend just credited to its shareholders.
- **(e)** signifies that the fund has just distributed a capital gain to shareholders, and the price is shown without the capital gain included.
- **(t)** means the fund has both 12b-1 plan and back-load redemption fees.
- **(NA)** means that the price is not available that day because of incomplete information provided by the fund or the information service before the publisher deadline.
- **(y-t-d)** means the percent of positive return or loss from January 1 of the current year. This could be a positive or negative number.

- **(1-yr)**, **(3-yr)**, **(5-yr)** are past performance percentages from the current date, not from the beginning of the year or from inception. If there are no past performance numbers, the fund may be new.
- **(f)** signifies that only the previous day's quotation is available.
- **(k)** discloses that the figure has been recalculated by another rating firm.
- **(nl)** stands for no-load, which does *not* always mean no charges. No-load funds may have internal front or back-loaded charges or revenue-sharing agreements with their distributors.

With newspaper reports (or the Internet) you should be able to track:

- The investment objective based on stated goals in the prospectus.
- The net asset value (NAV), the per-share value, based on closing quotes from the fund.
- The offer price (Public Offering Price—POP), the NAV plus any sales commissions.
- The NAV change from the previous reporting period, usually the previous business day.
- Occasionally you may be able to learn the total year-to-date return.
- Some publications may also show the performance calculations during certain periods such as a 1-year, 3-year, or 5-year return from the current date.
- The maximum initial sales commission based on information in the prospectus.
- The grade the news media has given the fund based on its standing against other fund performances during the same period.
- The highest and lowest price during the latest 52-week period. This has little bearing because many funds distribute much of their profits to shareholders during the year and those distributions have reduced the subsequent price of the fund.

The most important column is the day-to-day change, up or down from the day before. If you create a chart recording each of your potential fund combinations on a daily basis, after several weeks you should be able to see if your hypothetical investment portfolio has enough diversification to hold together as markets fluctuate. If most of your numbers move up and down at the same time, you are duplicating the same types of securities baskets. Review once more the seven key securities markets we have discussed and reallocate your portfolio. It is normal for each fund to move up and down on a daily basis like your blood pressure moves, like your checkbook moves, and like your heart rate moves. Daily fluctuations should not vary too much.

How a fund reacts during crisis says a lot about how it may perform under normal conditions. Heavily diversified funds tough it out better in stormy economic weather, and are likely to perform well during the sunny periods.

Your fund manager will send account statements every time some financial activity occurs—for example, when a dividend or capital gain has been credited to your account. An end-of-the-year statement will provide an easy-to-read picture of your entire year's activity.

Some funds also provide the cost basis of shares you have redeemed through the year, to make your accountant happy.

When Should I Buy?

To get the most shares for your money and avoid immediate taxes on your account, be mindful of the date you purchase your shares. You are better off buying *well before* or on the day *after* a fund's *distribution date* of the dividend or capital gain, which generally occurs quarterly, sometimes only annually. Such payment, on the *ex-dividend date*, reduces the net asset value of the fund's shares by the amount of the distribution because the fund is actually distributing part of itself, and the selling price of shares drops by a similar amount. By buying in *after* the dividend is declared, you avoid paying taxes on that particular payout.

Call the fund's customer service department for the next ex-dividend date. On the day after a fund goes ex-dividend, an "x" appears beside the fund's net asset value in the newspaper.

Why Does My Mutual Fund Price Go Down?

Mutual fund prices move up and down on a daily basis because fund prices are calculated after the close of each business day and the value of the securities in the fund becomes worth more or less than the day before. However, when *distributions* such as dividends and capital gains are made available to the shareholders, the price of the mutual fund (market forces excluded) should decrease by a similar amount because the fund is actually divesting itself of a part of its whole. Dividends, capital gains, and other distributions are *not technically profits*. They are pieces of the fund total spun off to shareholders due to the legal requirements of the tax-free structure of mutual funds in general. Many investors mistake distributions for profits. You have neither gained nor lost value on your mutual fund when the price changes due solely to a dividend or capital gain distribution. You gain or lose money due to market fluctuations over time, which distributions tend to reflect.

How Much Am I Making?

You can calculate exactly how much your fund account is worth on a daily basis by multiplying the total number of shares you own by the latest net asset value (NAV) reported in the newspaper or on the Internet.

In order to see what profits your fund has made over a full year, add the value of all distributions throughout the year made to you to the latest account value (the current net asset value multiplied by the number of shares you hold) and subtract from your beginning value. Don't forget to add in the amount of any liquidations (called *redemptions*) you may have taken during the year. The difference is your profit or loss.

I Didn't Sell, So Why Do I Have To Pay Taxes?

You can elect to have all distributions paid to you in cash when they are distributed or have them reinvested by purchasing additional shares. You may want to reinvest all distributions even if you need income, because the mutual fund company can arrange for a certain amount of money to be sent to you or your bank on a regular basis.

Unless you have a tax-advantaged wrapping over your mutual fund such as an IRA, SEP, SIMPLE, KEOGH, 401(k), 403(b), or other tax-deferred registration, you will pay taxes on all distributions, whether your profits are reinvested or taken in cash and sent to you. This may seem unfair because you have not really taken receipt of the money and are reinvesting it back into your fund. However, the fund must distribute most of its underlying profits to shareholders annually in order to maintain legal standing. Therefore, someone must pay the taxes—and you have been chosen. There may, indeed, be double taxation afoot because the underlying companies' dividends are first taxed to the company, then taxed again when you receive them. In 2003, Congress has softened the tax bite of dividends and capital gains and may offer more financial support later. Complain to your Congressperson how difficult "getting rich slow" is becoming to get your vote tabulated now.

Can you avoid paying current taxes by exchanging from one fund to another in the same mutual fund family? Unfortunately, no. *Any exchange*, even if considered a *like* exchange, is considered by the IRS as a *taxable sale* and a *new purchase*. There may be a profit, a loss, or perhaps no taxable results. But your tax advisor must know an exchange has taken place to determine whether taxes are due on the transaction.

To minimize tax consequences, you can sell the shares you paid the most for first— the *specific shares* method. You must inform your mutual fund *before* you sell or you will have sold those shares you *purchased first* (called *FIFO*: first in, first out), the general method of selling securities.

Keep purchase and redemption records in case the IRS questions you later. Keep in mind that if you sell only higher-cost shares as you liquidate your funds over time, you will be left with only lower-cost shares and may incur even greater taxes in the future. You may want, instead, to sell a combination of more expensive shares and lower-cost ones at the same time to even out your current tax liability. Your tax advisor can help.

Confessions of an Investment Chicken

Any daredevil investor will tell you that over the long term, mutual funds that put you through the rockiest ups and downs reward you with fatter returns than turtle-like funds that crawl along, slowly but surely. That was the prevailing theory prior to the tech wreck.

From the time you were a child, you have been taught to avoid risks whenever possible. "Don't play in the street." "Don't talk to strangers." "Buckle your seatbelt." Those who cared for you warned against risks lurking in the shadows.

Who cares that over the last 30 years, stocks performed better than any other one class of investments? Who cares that a certain mutual fund has been able to beat its benchmark over the last 12 years that could still indicate negative performances? Who cares whether you could have paid less and bought index funds that still lost your money? You care about your bottom line. Anyone who tells you a little red ink shouldn't bother you is not looking at his or her own red-ink monthly statements. The two biggest lies of the financial industry are: "You need higher risk to get higher returns," and "Don't sell now or you'll lose money. It will come back!"

Some mutual funds had you convinced that all you had to do to make money was to show up with your check. Their ads were seductive: "If you had invested $10,000 in our Sure Fire mutual fund, today you would be worth $50 gazillion and your friends would be paying *you* for advice." The illustrative graphs and bar charts were even more appealing. By compressing all those hiccups and down years, marketing departments produced graphs that looked like the back side of Mount Everest—straight up. Only in small print came the following disclosure: "Past performance is no guarantee of future results." And they meant it.

Diversification 'R Us

Get Rich Slow is not just the name of this book. It represents developing a different attitude about managing your money. Crashing through red traffic lights is certainly not safe driving, and ignoring financial warning lights and the unforgiving laws of the investment world is downright dangerous to your financial health. Today's hot investment may quickly cool tomorrow. It's not that shooting stars are bad, they just burn out quickly.

Every investment portfolio should have a healthy portion of cash or cash substitutes such as bank deposits, credit union accounts, money market mutual fund savings, or even previously purchased U.S. savings bonds. On that foundation you will add your combination of different mutual funds using all seven of the financial building blocks: *cash*; *bonds*; *global stocks and bonds*; *domestic stocks*, including the Dow Jones, the S&P 500 group, the NASDAQ or tech sector; and the remainder of the group that I call the "etc. guys."

No market is rational. The domestic cash, stock, bond, international, and currency market figures result daily from the two most critical motives of large investors: greed and fear.

Risk cannot be totally eliminated. But through a system of mutual fund investing, you can diversify like a millionaire, cut out financial middlemen for a greater share of the profits, become your own money manager to a greater extent, and take better control of your own financial destiny.

How to Buy the Wrong Fund

More people choose a dog over any other pet. More people choose blue over any other color. More sports fans choose football than any other televised sport. More small investors are in the wrong investment at the wrong time, therefore, buying high then selling low.

Mutual funds total more than $7 trillion. More than 50 percent of all households own shares in at least one fund. Mutual fund companies rival commercial banks and insurance companies in financial power.

Mutual fund investing is not about tracking down the hottest fund of the moment. It's about settling in with funds that could serve you for years to come. Wealth doesn't happen overnight. It accumulates over time.

Here are 22 ways to purchase the *wrong* mutual fund:

1. **Grab last year's best performer.** Last year's winner could be this year's dog. Or vice versa.
2. **Select the most popular mutual fund category.** The crowd is an idiot. Don't become their king.
3. **Choose the mutual fund with the highest year-to-date (current) return.** This isn't a horse race, it is a marathon. Different horses run best through different market conditions. If you are truly diversified, not all of your investments will go up at the same time. Look for consistency and stability.
4. **Use long-term past performance as a reliable predictor of future results.**
5. **Become seduced by sector (single industry) funds**. That's di-*worse*-ification, not diversification. You are buying *more risk*, not less.
6. **Concentrate on funds that invest only in stocks or only in bonds.** Not enough diversification.
7. **Buy funds that invest in hard assets such as real estate and precious metals.** Stick to the basic building blocks: cash, stocks, bonds, and global securities.
8. **Choose funds for income when you really need growth.** No matter what age, even if retired, always invest for some growth.

9. **Scramble for higher yields as smarter banking.** Higher returns generally indicate greater risk.

10. **Purchase a new fund.** Would you bet part of your retirement on a horse that had never run a race?

11. **Use mutual funds as short-term trading vehicles.** Switching generally increases volatility to your portfolio. You hired a money manager. Let him or her manage.

12. **Choose funds that use market-timing strategies.** Same problem. Market timing is dangerous.

13. **Follow newsletter or TV money gurus.** If they are smart enough to foretell the future, why are they selling advice to you, when they could be busy buying stocks for their own accounts?

14. **Purchase on recommendations from consumer publications.** You're not buying a toaster. You can't foretell future winners by looking backwards at historical data. Some things improve with age. Mutual fund track records don't.

15. **Buy on the advice of friends, colleagues, coworkers or relatives.** Well-meaning incompetents can do as much financial damage as any vested interest. Get a competent and useful financial education instead.

16. **Believe that "no load" always means "no charges."**

17. **Buy the cheapest mutual funds.** You deserve the best—good value for every consumer dollar spent.

18. **Buy without reading—and understanding—the prospectus and the Additional Statement of Investments.**

19. **Believe the biggest funds must be the best.** This is simply another version of following the crowd.

20. **Investing solely within the same family of funds**—unless you can find quality in each of your selections.

21. **Staying with a losing fund because you paid a ton of money.** Sucker!

22. **Trying to make money when you should be trying not to lose it.** Capitalism is a rigged business system, remember? The big guys will pull you along.

How Many Funds Do I Need?

The answer depends on how much money you invest. If you have only a few thousand dollars, two funds with different investment objectives can give you all four investment building blocks at the same time: stocks, bonds, cash, and global. With a much larger sum, a well-diversified portfolio might contain five to six funds with different objectives. Beyond that point, diversification benefits may be minimal and your return may suffer due to duplications of the same underlying securities. You can only diversify so much.

Dollar-Cost-Averaging:
You Don't Have To Be a Fat Cat To Invest

Discipline: What was your parents' approach? "Do it because I said so?" "If Joey jumped off the bridge, would you jump off after him?" "It's about time you grew up." "We're doing this for your own good." Discipline, when it comes to investing, can be good for you. Knowing when to buy low and sell high is impossible, even for the experts. But an old investing strategy—dollar-cost-averaging—may help increase your profits over the long run.

Dollar-cost-averaging, in simple terms, is putting a regular systematic investment plan into action. By contributing the same amount of money on a regular basis into a mutual fund (no matter what price per share), you automatically limit your purchases when prices are higher and purchase more shares when prices per share are lower. Over time, this may yield a comfortable nest egg for your long-term financial goals. For example:

Amount	%	# of Years	Accumulation Value per Pay Return
$50	10	10	$10,328
$50	10	15	$20,896
$50	10	20	$38,285
$50	10	25	$68,695
$50	10	30	$113,966

This automatic investment plan accomplishes several major goals:

- You pay yourself first.
- You develop a habit of disciplined long-term investing.
- If you don't see the money, you will be less apt to spend it.
- You get used to various market ups and downs.
- You provide a relatively painless method to invest for your future.

It is not really known whether dollar-cost-averaging helps to lower the cost of your shares over the long-term. But it is certain that a disciplined "pay yourself first" investing program accumulates wealth over time. The point is, there is never a bad time to make a good investment. You send your check (or automatic deposit draft) whether you feel like it or not, rain or shine, whether you need new tires for the car or you want a nicer living room couch. Every week or every month, your systematic savings plan kicks into action.

Value Averaging

This new investing strategy of *value averaging* takes the dollar-cost-averaging averaging concept one step further by focusing on the value of your investment rather than the cost. Instead of investing a set amount of, say, $100 each month, you set an investment objective of increasing the value of your portfolio by $100 per month. At the end of each given time period, depending on the current value of your portfolio, you either invest or divest whatever amount is needed to bring the value of your portfolio to the desired level.

If your stocks have *decreased* in value, you put in more than the $100 to replace the lost value. If they have *increased* in value, you put in less than the usual amount, perhaps even sell shares. By reducing your investment and taking profits off the table when stock prices are high, you may achieve an even lower average cost per share than with dollar-cost-averaging. However, you may also accumulate less overall money in your account because you are not consistently adding as much as possible to fund your portfolio on a regular basis. You also attract short-term capital gains taxes like mad when certain markets are rapidly rising.

Honestly, I cannot see the benefit and common sense of this strategy. I didn't even want to bring this strategy to your attention because I think you could end up with a lot less money in the end. Stick to dollar-cost-averaging as your regular investing plan.

ETFs—Big Things Can Come In Small Packages

What are Exchange Traded Funds (ETFs)? In short, they are similar to index mutual funds, but are packaged and then traded more like individual stocks. As their name implies, Exchange Traded Funds represent a basket of securities traded on an exchange. As with all investment products, Exchange Traded Funds have advantages and disadvantages.

Like a traditional mutual fund, an index ETF pools the assets of its investors and uses public indexes to invest the money to meet clearly identified objectives, such as current income or capital appreciation. Unlike a mutual fund, however, an index ETF is created when an institutional investor deposits securities into the fund in return for creation units. The investor receives a fixed amount of shares, which move up and down in price, depending on their value to other investors who purchase and sell the shares. ETFs can be bought and sold throughout the trading day in contrast to most mutual funds that offer forward pricing, the share price after markets close at the end of the next business session.

Traders can employ such profit strategies as shorting (selling securities they don't own if they believe the markets will fall) or buying (going long) ETFs on margin. Low annual expenses rival even the cheapest mutual funds. If held in a taxable account, they are tax-efficient because little trading is done inside the ETF.

Disadvantages include paying commissions like on stock. Trading ETFs will cost you. Only institutions and the wealthy can deal directly with the ETF companies. Therefore, you must buy them from a broker. Small investors may realize better pricing with mutual funds. Active traders will pay commissions on each trade, while exchanging funds inside a specific mutual fund family will generally escape further commissions on your investment capital.

Unlike mutual funds, ETFs don't necessarily trade at the net asset values of their underlying holdings, meaning that an ETF could potentially trade above or below the value of the securities inside the portfolio. They tend to trade like stocks, which can increase their volatility, a risk that mutual funds are designed to reduce. Finally, there is slippage, a bid-ask spread, meaning that you might buy the ETF for retail then sell it for a wholesale price, the difference being a markup that goes to the ETF distributor.

These products have not withstood longevity studies of time. It's hard to predict how they will react during negative market implications. Because they trade like stocks, they could be just as volatile.

Taxing Matters

Some "experts" recommend that you buy tax-managed mutual funds (which allow the accounting department instead of the money manager to make major buying and selling decisions) or keep tax-efficient investments such as individual stocks and stock mutual funds outside of tax shelters, placing your bonds and other lower-yielding investments inside your IRA, 401(k), and other tax-deferred retirement accounts.

Both pieces of advice are suspect. Plenty of accountants have been on the front pages of the newspaper in the last few years. You are paying a money manager, not a backroom accounting department, to get you to retirement as comfortable as possible. Accountants don't have the same skills as professional money managers and should not be determining when and what to buy or sell.

As for putting all your growth-oriented investments in a taxable position so the IRS can whale the devil out of your higher returns over time, I suggest you hide your strongest weapons against inflation inside retirement or other tax-deferred registrations and let the tax beast get paid from those investments that don't make very much profit. Otherwise, the *lower return issues* get the *best tax advantage*, while the growth investments (stocks and stock mutual funds), get pummeled when you sell or when the mutual fund sells and issues those big capital gains taxes at year-end. It's amazing what a 500-word newspaper column journalist can think up.

The Rap on Wrap Accounts

Brokerages want their share of money management fees. For an annual fee you can hire your own private money manager. This product has snob appeal. What great cocktail conversation! However, you pay extra for the right to name drop. Performance results vary but generally are no better than regular managed mutual funds.

Brokerage fees can be exorbitant, considering both the broker and the money manager get a piece of your commission. You are paying commissions to two financial intermediaries. Mutual funds are more visible, more regulated, often cheaper, and you can monitor their daily progress in the daily papers.

Discretionary account agreements with brokers who can buy and sell without your approval can be dangerous. The free rein can cause *churning*, excessive buying and selling to generate commissions for the broker and for the brokerage, and large portfolio turnover, which can result in larger tax bills. Market timing is a fruitless passion, so stick with mutual funds that can cost you less, provide top-notch professional money management, offer 24-hour services, and lots of additional benefits to boot.

Don't be a commission to some stranger. You are blood, sweat, tears, lots of sweat equity, and special dreams and goals for you and your family. Find someone to fuss over you for your intrinsic value, not for your investment account. Don't give up your role as money manager and decision-maker.

Final Points to Remember

- Rating agencies and the media are not psychic hotlines. They record only the past.
- Past performance records are often a rotten guide to future results.
- You are purchasing pieces of businesses, not lottery tickets.
- Even poor-quality funds may briefly rank as top performers.
- Higher risk often means the potential for greater loss of principal.
- There is no substitute for doing your own homework.
- There is no such thing as a free investment.
- Names can be misleading. Mutual funds may carry more risk than you think.
- Markets make much of the profits; the manager can add value.
- Markets have no memory and don't care how precious your funds may be.
- Greed exacts a price, given enough victims and enough time.
- The longer you remain in the stock markets, the riskier your position becomes. Risk increases over time.
- It generally is not any different this time. Higher yields may mean greater risks to investment principal.

- Total return includes both a *yield on* your money and the *return of* your principal.
- Risk reduction and management are often least appreciated until *after* you lose money.
- No one knows the financial future.

The 5 Best Investments
for Getting Rich,
Slowly But Surely

1. Pay off your credit card debt. I can promise you a safe, guaranteed double-digit return on your money if you will stop living life on the installment plan. If necessary, put your credit cards away to provide a "cooling off" period, or use "plastic surgery"—cut them up.

2. Pay yourself first. Develop a "rainy-day" emergency fund through payroll deduction or an automatic bank draft. If you don't see and handle that money, you will be less tempted to spend it.

3. Complete and follow a financial roadmap. A budget is your first step toward financial independence. A budget doesn't *take* time; it *saves* time. It doesn't prevent you from having what you desire; it makes your financial dreams possible.

4. Learn to live *beneath* your financial means. Stop transferring your wealth. The most dangerous status game you can play is purchasing a home you can't really afford just to impress a lot of people you don't really like anyway.

5. Give your children *who* you are, not *what* you have. Stop buying your kids. Instead, build around them a useful structure of integrity, common sense, intelligence, and caring and teach them the meaning of those honorable four-letter words—"Hard Work."

Appendix

Worksheets begin on page 228.

Current Status Financial Goals and Objectives

Name _____ Date _____

CURRENT STATUS

Statement of Financial Position _____

Debt Management _____

Emergency Fund: Liquidity _____

Active Financial Goal _____

     Short-Term _____

     Long-Term _____

ASSET ALLOCATION

     CHANGE _____

_____

_____

RISK MANAGEMENT

Homeowner Insurance _____

Auto Insurance _____

Liability Insurance (umbrella) _____

Life Insurance _____

Business Liability _____

Disability _____

Health _____

Nursing Home Care _____

Fire Proof Box / Safe Deposit Box _____

ESTATE PLANNING

Living Will _____

Medical Power of Attorney _____

Financial Durable Power of Attorney _____

Current Will _____

Trusts _____

Special Considerations _____

Deed Ownership _____

Monthly Budget and Expense Sheet

If any of the expenses below are based on weekly outgo, multiply by 4.3 weeks in each month for accurate monthly figures.

NET TAKE-HOME INCOME _____

– TOTAL EXPENSES _____

= REMAINING MONEY $ _____

Monthly Cash Flow Statement

Mortgage/Rent	$	Health Insurance	$
PMI Insurance		Medicare B	
Property Taxes/Condo Fees		Long-term care Insurance	
Water		Medigap Insurance	
Electricity		Cable TV	
Heat		Dining Out	
Telephone		Entertainment	
Property insurance		Vacation	
Auto Insurance		Groceries	
Liability Insurance		Clothing	
Garbage Collection		Support (child, depend.)	
Home Maintenance		School Tuition/Supplies/Classes	
Dept. Store Accounts		Contributions/Charity	
Credit Card Accounts		Organization/Union Dues	
Bank Loans		Subscriptions	
Other Time Payments		Income/Self-employed Taxes	
Car Payments		Household Items	
Gasoline/Diesel		Landscaping	
Car Maintenance		Pets	
Commuting/Parking		Miscellaneous	
Holidays/Gifts		Childcare	
Medical/Dental		Allowances	
Life Insurance (spouse/child)		Personal care	
Disability Insurance		Dry-cleaning	

TOTAL EXPENSES $

LUMP SUM OBLIGATIONS		REGULAR SAVINGS & INVESTMENT PLANS	
Mortgage Balance	$	Employer	$
Home Equity Loan Balance		Savings/Credit Union Accounts	
Consumer Loan(s)		Checking Accounts	
Major Debts (Car Loan, etc.)		College Plans	
Credit Card Balances		Savings Bonds	
Education/Student Loan(s)		IRAs/SEPs/KEOGH	
Personal Loan(s)		Taxable Investment Plans	
Other		Other	
TOTAL DEBT	$	**TOTAL INVESTMENTS**	$

What Are You Worth?

LIQUID ASSETS	OWNER	DATE:
Cash/Liquid Money:		$
Checking Accounts:		$
Credit Union:		$
Savings Accounts:		$
Savings Bonds:		$
Money Market Funds:		$
Life Insurance Cash Value:		$
Total Liquid Assets (a):		$

PERSONAL PORTFOLIO ASSETS	OWNER	
Certificates of Deposit:		$
Stocks:		$
Bonds:		$
Mutual Funds:		$
Insurance Annuities:		$
Personal Loans Owed to You:		$

RETIREMENT PLANS	OWNER	
Vested Company Pension/Income		$
IRAs/SEPs/KEOGHs:		$
401k, TDA (403b), Thrift Savings Plans:		$
Other (example—company stock):		$
Total Investment Assets (b):		$

REAL AND PERSONAL ASSETS	OWNER	
Vacation Home or Land †		$
Rental Property:		$
Business Assets:		$
Investment Collectibles:		$
Total Illiquid Investment Assets (a):		$
TOTAL ASSETS (a + b + c):		$

† (Personal home not included)

LIABILITIES	OWNER	
Personal Residence Mortgage:		$
Home Equity Loan:		$
Rental Property Mortgage:		$
Vacation Home Mortgage:		$
Credit Card Balances:		$
Car Loans:		$
Time Payments/Personal Loans:		$
Education Loans:		$
Life Insurance Loans:		$
Other Outstanding Debts:		$
Total Liabilities:		$

YOUR NET WORTH

Total Assets (from previous page):		$
Minus Total Liabilities (from above box):		−$
Your Personal Net Worth:		$

ADDITIONAL LIVING ASSETS*	OWNER	
*Fair Market Value of Personal Home:		$
*Current Value of Auto(s):		$
*Market Price of Personal Belongings:		$
*Jewelry/Furs/Art/Antiques		$
*Other		$
*Other		$
*Other		$

FINAL TOTAL	$

*Do not include these assets in earlier net worth calculations unless you plan to sell a bedroom, couch, or car to pay for healthcare & three meals a day!

College Savings and Investing Plans

529 Plans

- Funds grow tax-free until withdrawn; there is no cap on withdrawals.
- Tax-free withdrawals if used for qualified higher education expenses; may be subject to state taxes.
- Expenses include tuition, books, supplies, equipment, and more—not car, travel, or clothing.
- Funds can be invested in a combination of equities, fixed income, and cash or asset models.
- Contributions can be made to both a 529 Plan and a Coverdell savings plan in the same year.
- Adults can contribute to their own account for future education.
- No income limit restrictions for contributor/the owner does not have to be related to beneficiary.
- Assets are treated as the account owner's for financial aid formulas.
- Lump sum gifts more than $11,000 removed from owner's estate after five years; before then, prorated at death.
- Account value may reduce financial aid dollar for dollar.
- Withdrawing funds voids other tax credits/can roll an UTMA into a 529 Plan.
- Account owner can choose from other states' plans, but not every state allows out-of-state contributions.
- Some states offer tax deductions for state residents if invested in their own state program.
- Parents' assets are assessed at 5.6 percent, students' assets counted at 35 percent for financial aid formulas.
- Prior withdrawals are penalized at 50 percent as student income for financial aid.
- Assets remain under the control of the owner/funds can be use for most post-secondary education.
- The minor beneficiary does not gain control of funds at age of majority.
- Once-a-year rollovers to another state's 529 Plan are now permitted.
- To avoid 10-percent penalty if original beneficiary doesn't go to school choose a new beneficiary in the same family.
- The new beneficiary can be another family member (including cousins).
- The maximum gift transfer exclusion per year is $11,000 per beneficiary.
- Owner can gift up to $55,000 in one year ($110,000 per couple) per beneficiary without gift tax consequences.
- Total contributions depend on in-state five years' cost for undergraduate and 2 years' cost for graduate education at highest cost facility.

- 529s are subject to expiration after 2010 when earnings will be taxed at beneficiary's rate if not reenacted.
- There is a 10-percent penalty plus taxes due on earnings for nonqualified withdrawals.
- No penalty on withdrawals due to death or disability or scholarship that replaces the purpose of funds.
- 529 Program will likely change in the future.
- States must direct the investment options—participants cannot direct investments.
- Individual stocks, bonds, or mutual funds not allowed—state plans are managed by investment companies.

Education IRAs/Coverdell Education Savings Accounts

- Trust or custodial account for qualified education expenses/program does not expire after year 2010.
- Contributions are not tax-deductible.
- Can contribute to a 529 savings plan also.
- Contributions can be made until April 15 of following tax year for previous year.
- Withdrawals are federally tax-free to pay eligible education expenses.
- Nonqualified withdrawals are taxed at owner's rate plus 10-percent penalty unless death or disability of beneficiary.
- Value of the account is removed from the owner's taxable estate.
- Includes elementary and secondary public or private schools.
- $2,000 contribution limit per year per beneficiary—no maximum limit on total contributions.
- Upper income limits of contributor is $110,000 (single) and $220,000 (married filing jointly).
- No state tax deduction available.
- Owner makes the investment decisions—can use mutual funds, stocks, or bonds.
- Funds are considered child's assets for financial aid treatment/can eliminate other financial aid.
- Mandatory withdrawals with tax and 10-percent penalty from account when beneficiary is age 30 within 30 days.
- Funds can be rolled over to another family beneficiary under age 30 to avoid tax and penalty.
- Funds that match scholarship or other aid can be withdrawn for the same amount without penalty.
- Age limit for beneficiary contributions to age 18.

UGMA/UTMA

- $750 of profits per year are deducted off minor's tax return if no other income.
- Next $750 earnings per child per year are taxed at child's rate until age 14; remainder taxed at parents' rate.
- At minor's age 14, remainder of earnings taxed at minor's tax rate.
- Funds can be withdrawn at any time for anything for the child other than basic needs.
- Custodian controls the account until minor's age of majority—age 21 in Ohio.
- Funds can be spent down for child's needs if not attending college before age 21.
- Child is taxed at withdrawal time—minor usually in lower tax bracket—currently 5 percent capital gains.
- Custodian can change investments anytime/can roll over a UTMA into a 529 Plan.
- Can name a contingent/secondary custodian.
- Old broad trust so chance of fewer law changes in the future.
- Money is shifted into the child's name as irrevocable gift.
- Funds can be invested in most mutual funds, banks, and other investment vehicles.
- Minor beneficiary on the account cannot be changed.
- No state tax deduction for contributions.
- Value of the account can be included in custodian's estate.
- Assets are considered the child's for financial aid.

Tax Credits

- Can't use Hope or Lifetime Credit together with 529 funds or Coverdell IRA in the same year.
- Hope Scholarship Credit reduces taxes by $1,500 per year per student for first two years—income limits apply.
- Lifetime Learning Credit is $1,000 for juniors and seniors, graduate students and workers—same income limits apply.
- Both credits phased out for taxpayers above $51,000 (single) and $103,000 (married filing jointly).
- Both credits must be deducted from expenses before 529 Plan funds are free withdrawals.
- Up to $3,000 tax deduction if not qualified for Hope or Lifetime Credits due to income limits.
- Up to $3,000 annual tax deduction available up to certain income limits—may expire in 2006.
- Student interest tax deductible up to $2,500 up to certain parents' income limits.

Borrowing From a 401(k) or Tax-Sheltered Annuity [403(b)]

- No special tax benefits.
- Loan amount is not subject to tax unless owner defaults on loan payments.
- Value of the account is included in owner's taxable estate.
- Maximum amount of loan is the lesser of $50,000 or half of vested amount of account.
- Can be used for any education expense the investing company plan allows.
- Loan must be repaid within five years.
- No tax credits allowed.
- No income restriction limit for borrower.
- Funds are not considered in the expected family contribution (EFC) formula.

Series EE and I Savings Bonds

- Earnings are federal income tax-deferred.
- Earnings are state and local income tax exempt.
- Earnings fully or partially excludable from federal taxes—income limitations to qualify.
- Redemptions are tax-free only if used for qualified higher education expenses.
- Value of the account is included in the bond owner's taxable estate.
- Up to $15,000 per year, $30,000 per couple can be invested.
- Qualified expenses included tuition and fees only.
- Included as parents' assets for financial aid if for a student, as students' assets if for oneself.
- Guaranteed returns.
- Can reduce other tax credits.
- Can be redeemed after six months with a three-month penalty if redeemed within five years of issue.

Traditional and Roth IRAS

- Owner can contribute up to $3,000—$3,500 per person for tax year 2004.
- No penalty for early withdrawal if used for higher education expenses—taxes are not waived.
- Not considered in the expected family contribution calculation.
- Owner makes the investment decisions.
- Roth IRA has income restrictions on contributions—$95,000 to $110,000 (single), $150,000 to $160,000 (married filing jointly).
- Roth IRA earnings are taxed for college but not the annual contribution amount.
- Traditional IRA has no income limitations on contributions.

Taxable Mutual Fund Investing

- No tax is paid on net asset value growth until funds are sold.
- Favorable capital gains tax treatment on sale of shares if held for more than one year—maximum 15 percent.
- Special capital gains tax rate available on funds held for more than one year—currently as low as 5 percent.
- Appreciated securities can be gifted to minor, then sold in a lower tax bracket—as low as 5 percent.
- Gifting removes funds from owner's taxable estate.
- Fund shares can be sold by several different accounting methods.
- Owner controls the funds until they are liquidated or gifted.
- Value of the account is included in the owner's taxable estate until gifted.
- No maximum limitation on total investments.
- Funds can be withdrawn for any purposes.
- Funds are considered part of parents' assets for financial aid formulas.
- Owner makes all the investment decisions.
- Can qualify for other tax credits.

Direct Funding to College or Institution

- Adult owns the funds until gifting time in case owner needs the money.
- Owner can invest any way they want and can liquidate any security they choose.
- No gift exclusion limit of $11,000 on the amount of money that can be gifted directly to the institution.
- Funds invested for growth can receive favorable tax-deferral until sale of securities.
- Owner can get favorable capital gains tax rates when time to sell.
- Just-in-time delivery of funds for education in case laws change on other programs.
- No restrictions on type of investing while adult is the owner.
- Adult owner may get tax credits available under the law at time of gifting.
- Because no money is pre-funded, not important if above programs change over time.

Home Equity Loans/Equity Lines of Credit

- Subject to financial condition of borrower at the time funds are needed.
- Puts home at risk for default if lender demands full payment.
- Puts home at risk if borrower defaults on loan payments.
- Borrower is increasing major debt when funding for retirement should be major goal.
- Greater potential for downsizing after age 50—borrower could lose paycheck to repay loan.

- Loans are usually structured for 10 years, which lengthens amount of total interest paid over time.
- Loan interest is itemized deduction on tax return and eliminates the standard deduction credit.

Insurance Annuities

- There is a 10-percent penalty for withdrawals from the contract before age 59.
- Heavy surrender charges for many years if more than 10 percent is withdrawn per year.
- High fees and internal charges eat away at annual returns.
- Not appropriate for relatively short-term funding purposes.
- 100 percent of withdrawals are taxed at ordinary income rates until all earnings are withdrawn from contract.
- Cannot use tax-favored capital gains tax rates.

Prepaid Tuition Trust Plans

- Payments purchase credits which supposedly guarantee future tuition costs.
- Payments not easily refunded back before college age.
- If a child is not college-bound, funds may be restricted until age 18.
- There is no control over how money is invested.
- There is no visibility to how funds are growing inside the plan.
- There is an inflation risk of returns not matching future tuition increases.
- Funds are taxed at child's rate, funds may be included under child's assets for financial aid.
- Withdrawals may eliminate other financial aid dollars.
- Biggest risk is trusting others to guarantee your student's education.

Independent 529 Plans

- Certificates bought today are cashed in tax-free for future tuition expenses.
- For students who expect to attend private colleges.
- If child doesn't attend, refunds make -2-percent to +2-percent interest—owner must wait 36 months to redeem a certificate.
- No control over investment vehicle; big risk of trusting others to guarantee student's education.

Do You Know Where Your Documents Are?

Name _____ Date Organized _____

- ❑ Original BIRTH CERTIFICATES (if married, for both spouses, children, other dependents); BAPTISMAL CERTIFICATE(s); CITIZENSHIP/ADOPTION/GUARDIANSHIP/CUSTODY PAPERS

- ❑ Original SOCIAL SECURITY CARD(s); PASSPORTS

- ❑ MILITARY RECORDS and DISCHARGE PAPERS; EDUCATION DEGREES

- ❑ LEGAL MARRIAGE LICENSE (not church religious certificates); MARRIAGE CERTIFICATE(s)

- ❑ DIVORCE DECREE or LEGAL SEPARATION DOCUMENT; DEATH CERTIFICATE of SPOUSE (if widowed)

- ❑ PROPERTY DEED (not Title Insurance Contract); TITLES of OWNERSHIP to REAL ESTATE in other states; RENTAL CONTRACTS

- ❑ MORTGAGE NOTE; SATISFACTION OF MORTGAGE; TITLE INSURANCE; REAL ESTATE PURCHASE CONTRACT; REFINANCING AGREEMENT(s); AUTO LOANS; PERSONAL DEBT OBLIGATIONS

- ❑ RECEIPTS for REAL ESTATE IMPROVEMENTS, BUYING and SELLING COSTS

- ❑ FEDERAL and STATE TAX RETURNS and SUPPORTING DOCUMENTATION (for the last 6 years); ESTATE/GIFT TAX RETURNS

- ❑ HOME and AUTO INSURANCE (declarations *and* underlying contracts); AUTOMOBILE TITLES; LEASING AGREEMENTS; BOAT/RV OWNERSHIP TITLES and REGISTRATIONS

- ❑ LIFE INSURANCE and ANNUITY CONTRACTS; all current beneficiary designations (include benefits through employer)

- ❑ RIGHTS of INTERMENT for cemetery plot; PRE-PAID FUNERAL CONTRACT; BURIAL INSTRUCTIONS

- ❑ EMPLOYER PENSION, RETIREMENT, HEALTH, DISABILITY, and other benefits; EMPLOYEE HANDBOOK; EMPLOYMENT CONTRACTS; PARTNERSHIP AGREEMENTS

- ❑ MEDICAL HISTORY of family members; current PRESCRIPTION(s); special MEDICAL INSTRUCTIONS

- ❑ EMERGENCY TELEPHONE NUMBERS (police, fire, hospital); CREDIT CARD NUMBER(s) and their 1-800 TELEPHONE NUMBERS; DRIVER'S LICENSE(s)

- ❑ PERSONAL and SUPPLEMENTAL HEALTH, DISABILITY, and OTHER INSURANCE POLICIES

- ❑ INSURANCE /SURVIVOR BENEFITS and SERVICES (through professional/ consumer associations, societies, credit cards); PROFESSIONAL & FRATERNAL MEMBERSHIPS; PROFESSIONAL LIABILITY CONTRACT (if applicable)

- ❑ BACK-UP DISKS for business files and records; location of SAFE DEPOSIT BOX (keys, passwords, or security measures); home/business SAFE LOCATION and COMBINATION

- ❑ Location of NEGOTIABLE SECURITIES (stock/bond/mutual fund certificates; savings bonds)

- ❑ Name and location of BANKS, CREDIT UNIONS, MUTUAL FUNDS, other INVESTMENT HOLDINGS

- ❑ SAVINGS and CHECKING ACCOUNT STATEMENTS and PASSBOOKS; IRA, KEOGH, SEP, 401(K), 403b, PROFIT-SHARING RECORDS; CANCELED CHECKS; CERTIFICATES OF DEPOSIT; current and past INVESTMENT STATEMENTS; BROKERAGE RECORDS; STOCK OPTION PLANS

- ❑ Originals and copies of WILLS; POWERS OF ATTORNEY; LIVING WILLS; TRUSTS; PROMISSORY NOTES; LOAN AGREEMENTS; other legal and estate documents; list of SPECIAL BEQUESTS

- ❑ NAMES, ADDRESSES, TELEPHONE NUMBERS of FAMILY, PHYSICIANS, CLERGY, PERSONAL/BUSINESS ATTORNEY(s), ACCOUNTANT, STOCKBROKER, FINANCIAL PLANNER, INVESTMENT ADVISOR, EMPLOYER BENEFITS CONTACT PERSON, INSURANCE AGENTS, other professionals

- ❑ Jewelry and antique APPRAISALS and CERTIFICATES of Authenticity; INVENTORY of household goods and furnishings (photos or video tapes); GUARANTEES, OWNER'S MANUALS, WARRANTIES and RECEIPTS for PRODUCTS PURCHASED

Credit Card Management Strategy

Name of Company	Balance of Payoff	APR*	Minimum Monthly Payment
Total	$	%	$

*Annual percentage rates—They are deceptive because they lead you to believe that the interest is not compounded, while the monthly interest is compounded each and every month throughout the year on an unpaid credit balance. You will pay almost 2 percent more interest per year to the average cost of credit card borrowing in addition to the stated interest rate if you pay your credit card debts over long installments.

Credit Card Register

Card Issuer	Expiration Date	Balance Owed	Credit Limit	Card Number	Phone If Lost
1.					
2.					
3.					
4.					
5.					
6.					
7.					
8.					
9.					
10.					

Other Important Information

Driver's License #_____ Spouse _____

Social Security # _____ Spouse _____

Passport #_____ Spouse _____

_____

_____

_____

_____

_____

Total Compensation Benefits Checklist

		Yes	No
1. Group basic term life insurance amount	$_____	_____	_____
2. Optional term or other life insurance amount	$_____	_____	_____
3. Deferred compensation amount	$_____	_____	_____
4. Retirement health/dental plan amount	$_____	_____	_____
5. Flexible spending account (cafeteria plan) amount	$_____	_____	_____
6. Retirement insurance plan amount	$_____	_____	_____
7. Basic pension amount	$_____	_____	_____
Employer match	_____%	_____	_____
8. Supplementary retirement savings	$_____	_____	_____
Employer match	_____%	_____	_____
Lump sum retirement option			
(Such as 401(k), ESOP, 403(b), TSA)			
9. Thrift savings plan/profit sharing	$_____	_____	_____
Employer match	_____%	_____	_____
10. Spouse/dependent plan: type	$_____	_____	_____
11. Special benefits	$_____	_____	_____

Retirement Benefits

Type of pension benefit	Amount $	Lump sum $	Monthly benefit $	At age	Eligible for IRA rollover?	
					Yes	No
Basic pension	_____	_____	_____	_____	____	____
401(k)	_____	_____	_____	_____	____	____
Profit sharing	_____	_____	_____	_____	____	____
Tax-sheltered annuity (TSA, 403(b),TDA)	_____	_____	_____	_____	____	____
Thrift-savings/ supplemental	_____	_____	_____	_____	____	____
ESOP/stock plan	_____	_____	_____	_____	____	____
Previous employer plan	_____	_____	_____	_____	____	____
Deferred compensation	_____	_____	_____	_____	____	____
Employer match (if separate)	_____	_____	_____	_____	____	____
Social Security	_____	_____	_____	_____	____	____
Other pension benefits	_____	_____	_____	_____	____	____
IRA accounts	_____	_____	_____	_____	____	____
Investments	_____	_____	_____	_____	____	____
Other	_____	_____	_____	_____	____	____
Retirement life insurance	_____ (level)	_____ (decreasing to)	_____	_____	____	____

Portfolio Planning Worksheet

Short-Term Goals Investment Objective: _____

Long-Term Goals Investment Objective: _____

I. Cash and Cash Equivalents/Savings, Checking, Credit Unions, Money Market Funds

Where Deposited	Owner	$ Value	Current % Rate	Maturity Date
	SUBTOTAL			

II. Bank CDs (Regular and IRAs), Treasury Bills, Savings Bonds

Fund or Security	Owner	$ Value	Current % Rate	Maturity Date
	SUBTOTAL			

III. Company/Employee Investments (401ks, 403bs/TSAs, SEPs, KEOGHs, Stock Plans)

Name of Investment	Owner	$ Value	$ Amount of Contribution	Frequency
Vested Pension/Income Check				
	SUBTOTAL			

Notes: _____

_____

_____

Supplementary Portfolio Planning Worksheet

IV. Insurance Policies/Cash Values

Name of Company	Owner	Cash Value $	Dividends $	Loan $	Death Benefit $

SUBTOTAL

V. List of Securities (Stocks, Bonds, Mutual Funds, Annuities, Other)

Name of Security	Owner	IRA? Y	N	$ Value	Maturity Date	Restrictions

SUBTOTAL

TOTAL

Notes: _____

_____

_____

2003–2004 IRA Distribution Rules
Uniform Table

Age	Distribution Period (in Years)	Age	Distribution Period (in Years)
70	27.4	93	9.6
71	26.5	94	9.1
72	25.6	95	8.6
73	24.7	96	8.1
74	23.8	97	7.6
75	22.9	98	7.1
76	22.0	99	6.7
77	21.2	100	6.3
78	20.3	101	5.9
79	19.5	102	5.5
80	18.7	103	5.2
81	17.9	104	4.9
82	17.1	105	4.5
83	16.3	106	4.2
84	15.5	107	3.9
85	14.8	108	3.7
86	14.1	109	3.4
87	13.4	110	3.1
88	12.7	111	2.9
89	12.0	112	2.6
90	11.4	113	2.4
91	10.8	114	2.1
92	10.2	115+	1.9

Index

C

G

H

I

N

O

S

T

U

V

W

Y

About the Author

Tama is a syndicated radio talk show host in Cleveland, Ohio, a Certified Financial Planner, Certified Employee Benefit Specialist, Certified Fund Specialist, Chartered Mutual Fund Counselor, Accredited Asset Management Specialist, a frequent contributor to national financial media such as *The Wall Street Journal*, CNBC, and CNN, publisher of a financial newsletter, and a national seminar speaker. Her financial planning practice includes a broad base of clients, and she teaches community education classes on personal finance and investing.

What separates Tama from other money personalities? She writes in down-to-earth language and makes money matters interesting and insightful.

Whether your financial goals include avoiding common investing mistakes, buying your next home, stomping out credit card debt, finding the right mutual funds, or "covering your assets" with the right kinds of insurance, Tama will guide you to wise financial choices.

You will learn controversial personal finance truths may *not* be in your best interest, such as why retirement plans [401(k)s, for example,], why your home could be your *worst* investment, how some no-load mutual funds can cost you *more*, and why your guaranteed pension may *not* be so guaranteed. *Get Rich Slow* was written for the novice as well as the investment sophisticate.

More useful reference books to improve your skills and knowledge.

How to Protect and Manage Your 401(k)
by Elizabeth Opalka, CPA, Esq.
ISBN: 1-56414-660-X
6 x 9, 192pp.

Make Your Paycheck Last
by Jason R. Rich
ISBN: 1-56414-706-1
5.25 x 8.25, 128pp.

The 5 Minute Investor
by Michael Craig
ISBN: 1-56414-627-8
5.25 x 8.25, 256pp.

What's Your Investing IQ?
by Carrie L. Coghill
ISBN: 1-56414-632-4
5.25 x 8.25, 256pp.

Comfort Zone Investing
by Gillette Edmunds
ISBN: 1-56414-591-3
6 x 9, 224pp.

Identity Theft
by Robert Hammond
ISBN: 1-56414-636-7
5.25 x 8.25, 224pp.